DEAD
OPPOSITION

Tiffany L. Gobble

ELECTIO PUBLISHING
first century principles.
a twenty-first century approach.

Deadly Opposition

By Tiffany L. Gobble

Copyright 2018 by Tiffany L. Gobble. All rights reserved.

Cover Design by eLectio Publishing.

ISBN-13: 978-1-63213-498-1

Published by eLectio Publishing, LLC

Little Elm, Texas

http://www.eLectioPublishing.com

5 4 3 2 1 eLP 22 21 20 19 18

The eLectio Publishing creative team is comprised of: Kaitlyn Hallmark, Emily Certain, Lori Draft, Court Dudek, Jim Eccles, Sheldon James, and Christine LePorte.

Publisher's Note

The publisher does not have any control over and does not assume any responsibility for author or third-party websites or their content.

ACKNOWLEDGMENTS

All glory is given to Jesus, the Author and Finisher of all things! He's blessed me with the gift of writing and I'm honored and humbled that He chose me to be His vessel! His love for us is unmeasured!

My sweet husband Dave, you encouraged me, read my novel in its infancy, and even edited the first draft, which should get you an award. Your words of wisdom and reassurance when I thought this wouldn't happen carried me through more than you know. Thank you for believing in me when I didn't. I love you to the moon!

Momma bear, You're my hero. You've been there for me no matter what. All the hours we've spent talking about audiobooks led to this! Thank you for all the time you invested in me and my novel! I'm so thankful that you're not only my mother, but my best friend! I love you!

Dad, you've been such an encourager through the years I've written, edited, and slogged through this ordeal. You always had a way of making me think of things in a positive manner, which helped in darker times. Thank you for being my cheerleader and my dad! I love you!

Koinonia ladies, oh, how blessed I am to have you in my life! Many of you read and critiqued this novel, and the help was invaluable. Each of you has encouraged me, prayed for me, and loved me throughout this entire process! I'm forever grateful for the sunshine you bring to my life! Love you all to pieces.

Christopher Dixon, Jesse Greever, and the staff at Electio Publishing, thank you for taking a chance on me, a first-time author. I'm eternally grateful for your investment in my career, and the encouragement provided along the way.

There are dozens of unnamed individuals who poured into me, helped with this novel, and offered advice over the years. You know who you are. I'm blessed to have you in my life, and although I can't name each person, individually, my love and care for you is no less! Thank you for contributing to my confidence, this novel, and ultimately, my life. Love you!

PROLOGUE

SARAH BLACKWELL'S EYES DARTED around the family room so quickly that her mind struggled to process what had happened. From her seat on the sofa, she saw blood. So much blood on the floor. She blinked, trying to focus on her husband's lifeless body. A pool of blood, black as tar, pooled under his head. The high-pitched ringing in Sarah's ears persisted from the thunderous crack of the gunshot, which had sliced through the normalcy of the evening.

Her husband Paul had just stepped out of the room to turn off the bath water when the chain of events began. Sarah hadn't given much thought to her final seconds. If she had, this wouldn't have been in the realm of possibilities.

Lord, what's happening? Sarah asked, seconds before a tall, bulky man stepped over her husband, facing her and her daughter, Faith.

Sarah studied the man. He appeared to panic before leveling the gun with her head. He wore dark clothing. A black bandanna was tied around his face, revealing only his eyes. She held the man's gaze, deep and intense. She knew the end of her life was imminent. She turned from the man to her daughter, who trembled beside her.

Sarah moved forward on the couch and angled her body to shield Faith.

"You don't have to do this," Sarah said, "You can have anything you want. My purse is on the counter by the phone. Take everything. We have a-a safe upstairs." Her voice shook.

He didn't speak. He shook his head and fired another shot. Sarah knew he'd killed Faith. Now, Sarah wanted to die.

Thirty seconds, she thought, *that's all it took to ruin her life.*

When she looked up at the man, he trained the gun on her. Her last thought before she encountered darkness was about her nanny. *I hope Cassie is already gone.*

A third blast, and the Blackwell family was dead.

CHAPTER 1

ON THE LAST OF SEVEN MILES, Roxanne Hollis forced her legs to move as she fought the demons that were impossible to elude. Her bright red hair bounced with each step. The fierce spring Texas sun reflected off her aviator sunglasses, and a steady stream of perspiration dripped from her nose. Homes lined the streets on each side. The bur oak's arching arms shaded the sidewalk, a respite for what would become a sunburn for Roxy. The memories played like a movie in her mind. She tried to stop the visions but couldn't.

While running, with her mind free to roam, Roxy confronted Texas's execution chamber. The pungent smell of antiseptic and death. Bright fluorescent lighting that made the walls appear to glow. An excessively-waxed floor resembling the reflection of placid water. Raleigh outstretched atop snowy sheets, tan restraints around his wrists and ankles in the middle of the room. Starched prison garb clung to his fit frame, and his eyes were like the emerald city of Oz. Bile climbed the back of Roxy's throat. He was innocent, Roxy believed, but remained powerless to halt the injustice. Deep within, she screamed at the medical personnel behind the wall whose hands grasped syringes, waiting to inject the fatal three-drug cocktail into his veins.

Raleigh had been convicted of murdering his on-again-off-again girlfriend, Keren Hope. During the investigation, Roxy had uncovered unknown DNA on the murder weapon. In addition, Raleigh's mother was his alibi. Roxy fumed over the judge's admission: "His mother's alibi doesn't make an iota of difference because any mother would lie to protect her offspring." The unknown DNA—well, that too was deemed insignificant. The police ran the DNA profile through CODIS, the national database, which also included Raleigh's profile and every felon in the state. Although the DNA resulted in "no hits," the judge dismissed the merits of the claim altogether.

Before the flood of familiar emotions, Roxy's phone buzzed. Refusing to stop running, she sprinted the last hundred yards. She paced in the front yard of her stone-faced Victorian and checked her phone. A message from Sam Rollins stared back at her.

"My office nine a.m.? A new case to discuss."

Roxy felt something akin to panic at the thought of taking another case. For the last year, her life had been reclusive at best. She had sulked and grieved the loss of Raleigh in private. Before she could talk herself out of the meeting, she sent back "Sure."

Roxy walked in her front door, and the familiar aroma of home hit her nostrils. Her body relaxed in the sanctuary of her own space. She went to the kitchen, fetched a bottle of water from the fridge, and headed down the ivory-painted hallway toward her bedroom. Just before the threshold, she looked at the closed door across the hall and turned around.

Roxy twisted the knob, pushed the door open, and rested her shoulder on the doorframe. *If these walls could talk,* she thought.

Stepping into the room, Roxy ran her fingers across the top of her mahogany desk. She moved down the wall and faced the success of her career, which hung in colorful picture frames. Relief and joy painted the faces of three men and one woman on the days of their release. Roxy stood next to each client, her triumph evident and frozen in time. Even as her achievement was apparent, there was a photo missing, and the reminder was like a punch to the gut. Ahead of the torrent of grief, she left the room, and closed the door.

Roxy showered, dressed, and ate breakfast before leaving to meet Sam.

Roxy opened the glass doors of the law firm. The modern building was a breath of fresh air with its floor-to-ceiling glass walls, pine hardwood floors, and the elegant Rollins and Carmichael lettering etched in glass behind the reception desk.

"Hello, Roxy," the receptionist said. "Sam's waiting for you in conference room one."

"Thanks," Roxy said.

"Roxy," Sam said, his voice deep and his arms open.

Roxy fell into his hug. "Good to see you. I like the colors you're sporting today."

Sam smoothed his tan suit jacket and loosened his neon-green tie. "Thanks."

Sam had never planned this endeavor, but when a smaller law firm contacted him for financial support on a wrongful conviction case, Sam jumped at the opportunity. After that, he and his partner, Seth Carmichael, decided to try cases on their own and brought Roxy to their team.

Sam pulled out a chair for Roxy. She sat and waited, her heartbeat thudding in her ears.

"It's a triple homicide, Rox. I know we've never tried a case this big before, but Seth and I think it's a good one."

"Let's hear some facts," Roxy said.

"Paul, Sarah, and Faith Blackwell were shot execution style in their home on February 9, 2001. Our client is Cassandra Lovejoy, the family's live-in nanny."

Sam patted the file. "If we take the case, this is her last shot. We have nine months until her execution."

Roxy rocked her knee under the table. "How certain are you she's innocent?"

"Enough that she deserves a fresh set of eyes."

Sam's voice perked up. "Let me answer your other questions; Cassandra was a Christian before this happened, but now she isn't sure what she believes. Except that she's flat-out mad at God. You have all our resources available for the investigation. Seth and I will formulate the legalities after your analysis. We have fourteen boxes of case files ready for you to take home, should you accept."

Roxy stared at Sam, flicking the fingernail of her right index finger. "You get so fired up, don't you?"

"These cases provide a nice intermission from the circadian drudgery of mergers and acquisitions, banking and structured finance, high profile clients, and securities," Sam said, "We enjoy the change of pace."

Before rising to her feet, Sam put his hand on Roxy's shoulder. "It's time to get back to work. It's been a year. I know you feel like you can't, but you can. You're an extraordinary investigator, and our clients need you."

Roxy bit her bottom lip, offered a perfunctory nod, hugged Sam, and left.

Roxy felt like her car was closing in on her. *Another case—I don't think I'm ready.*

Rather than going home, Roxy knew where to go. She fed her car fuel, reached I-45 south, and headed to Corsicana.

As the highway passed by in front of her, the sun shining above, Roxy's memory flashed to the stale-aired visitation room on death row. Raleigh wore fresh prison garb, the black "DR" on his back less significant on this occasion. A prison chaplain stood at his side. Rebecca and Roxy stood outside the bullet-proof partition.

"Mr. Jacobson, do you accept Jesus Christ as your Savior?" The chaplain asked.

Raleigh lifted his head toward heaven before lowering his gaze and locking eyes with his mother. "Yes, I do. Now, Momma, do you?"

Rebecca, her complexion glowing and a single tear snaking down her right cheek, said, "Absolutely."

In unison, Roxy and the chaplain took small bowls of water, and poured the liquid on their foreheads. Loud enough for both to hear, Roxy said, "We baptize you in the name of the Father, the Son, and the Holy Spirit."

Roxy shook the memory off. "Welcome to Corsicana" came into view, and she prepared herself for the emotional blow of visiting Rebecca. It wasn't the company that pained her but the reminder that Raleigh should be there. Roxy pulled onto the long driveway moments later, and, true to character, Rebecca met Roxy at her car with open arms.

"Honey, what do I owe this unexpected visit?" Rebecca asked, wrapping Roxy in an embrace, her ample chest making it impossible to get too close.

"I needed some sweet tea and a good rocking."

Roxy and Rebecca walked arm-in-arm to the sprawling front porch.

"You sit, and I'll go get the tea," Rebecca said.

Roxy sat in an old-fashion rocking chair.

Rebecca returned to the porch, two large glasses of tea in hand, and sat down.

"Sweetheart, what's wrong?"

"Sam asked me to take another case this morning," Roxy said.

Rebecca nodded. "Well, it's about time you get back to saving lives."

"I don't think I can do it. I mean, it's clear I'm not as skilled as I thought."

Rebecca sat knee-to-knee with Roxy. "You're doing God's work, and for reasons we still don't understand, Raleigh's death is part of His plan. You're gifted at what you do, and your work isn't finished."

"But—" Roxy said.

"Take your time to consult God, and He'll tell you what to do. You don't need me to advise you one way or another. Don't you give up. You hear me? You've worked too hard for too long."

As Rebecca's words sunk in, Roxy covered her face and allowed the grief to seep out. Everything Rebecca said was true—and yet, somehow, hard to believe.

"I don't know what I'd do without you. Thank you. I needed this more than you know."

Rebecca touched Roxy's knee. "What better way to put the pieces back together than by battling for someone's freedom? Perhaps that's where your redemption will come from."

When Roxy reached her car, Rebecca said, "Remember, seek *veritas*."

Roxy nodded and heard Raleigh's voice echo in her memory. *Veritas: the truth. Seek the truth.*

***

Dusk fell outside Roxy's office window, and her insides mirrored the coming darkness. She pulled an oversized pillow to her chest, situating herself on the soft rug of her prayer corner. With her face to the floor, "Thy Will Be Done" by Hillary Scott floated off her tongue, albeit terribly, and tears splashed the carpet beneath her.

"I know You see me," Roxy prayed. "I know You hear me, Lord. Your plans are for me; goodness You have in store, so Thy will be done."

Roxy unfolded herself, reached for her Bible, and began walking her fingers through the truth of God's word. She was drawn to Romans 5:3-4: "And not only that, but we also rejoice in our afflictions, because we know that affliction produces endurance, endurance produces proven character, and proven character produces hope."

When she read those words, Roxy said, "Well, Lord, I should be Hercules at this point."

When Roxy's vision began to blur, she sat her Bible down and crossed the hall to her bedroom. She crawled in bed and prayed in earnest that she'd have a peaceful night's rest without visions of Raleigh's final moments. Three words sounded off like a gong in her mind: *continue your work.*

Her answer became clear.

In the morning, I'll start the investigation, Roxy thought, before her eyelids cut off her vision.

CHAPTER 2

ROXY PICKED UP THE BANKER'S boxes from Sam, agreeing to process the information and meet with him afterward. In her office, Roxy looked around and felt a surge of excitement. For the next two weeks, she stayed home and digested every sheet of paper within the boxes.

The smell of old paper hung thickly around Roxy. Dust sprinkled the air in rays of sunlight peeking through the blinds. Sitting in the middle of her office, she organized the documents in chronological order, the stacks of paper rising above her head. She filled notebooks with copious notes, and a picture took shape in her mind's eye.

Roxy stood and paced the room, a portion of the trial transcript in her hand and a pen tucked behind her ear. Roxy read the opening statements of each side multiple times to deduce the theory of the state's case and how the defense defended Cassandra.

"Ladies and gentlemen of the jury, this case is simple." Roxy stopped, crossed the room to her computer, and searched for a picture of the prosecutor. Not that it mattered, but she liked to imagine the scene in her mind, and the appearance of the DA helped.

His name was Jack Panshin. *A smug, pocket protector-looking nerd,* Roxy thought when she saw his picture.

She paced again, cradling the paper. "The Blackwell family was well-liked in their community. Not a single person spoke an ill word about them. Their nanny, Cassandra Lovejoy, was another matter entirely. The state will show that the defendant's childhood was a stark difference from that of Faith Blackwell, the seven-year-old victim in this case. The defendant's mother was a drug-addict, and child protective services tested multiple men to establish paternity of the child. She lived in many foster homes. When she couldn't hack it in a traditional home, Cassandra ended her time in state's custody, residing in the closest thing to jail for a minor without being incarcerated. She was troubled, to say the least. Then, she lands a nice-paying job with the Blackwells and, a year later, moves in with them. After another five years of employment, Cassandra's had enough. She can't stand to watch Faith live such a perfect life. You might say her jealous rage could stew no longer. Cassandra shoots Paul Blackwell as he was leaving the room. She then stepped over him and turned the gun on Sarah and Faith. Blood splatter suggests that the defendant shot Faith first and ended with Sarah. The state will illustrate Cassandra's history of violence. In addition, we will show that the timeline makes it virtually impossible for anyone else to have committed this crime."

Roxy rolled her eyes. *They should call court drama class.*

Roxy found the defense opening and continued pacing. "Jury members, the state would have you believe this case is simple, but it's more complex than it seems. My client had a horrific childhood. She was sexually abused. Physically abused. Emotionally abused. Every form of mistreatment you can think of, my client endured as a young child. What the state doesn't want to tell you is that, through therapy and mentorship, Cassandra had a radical change at the age of seventeen. So much so that her mentor, who will testify on her behalf, allowed Cassandra to live with her after her eighteenth birthday. I'm sure at least one of you did something when you were younger that you wish you hadn't. My client is in the same boat.

Despite her many imperfections, she had no reason to kill the Blackwell's, and we will prove that to you."

Roxy flipped the page to continue reading, but that was the end of his opening. *Well, that was a baseline opening,* Roxy thought. She knew Cassandra's attorney, who she had no problem picturing as she read his joke of an opening.

Roxy sat down the transcripts and fingered a family photo of the Blackwell's, studying each face.

"Who murdered you?" She asked.

Taking to her whiteboard to condense the case, holding a red dry-erase marker, she wrote out the victims' names and known details: Paul, thirty-four, Sarah, thirty-three, and Faith, seven. Occupations— Paul was head of the IT department at VX Oil, and Sarah was an independent interior designer. Faith was in second grade at a private Christian school. The police found no known enemies, which Roxy noted, writing, "NKE."

Stowing away that stack, Roxy fetched the interviews and coughed as new dust stirred.

In blue, Roxy drew the Blackwells' street, noting the neighbors interviewed by the police, although they provided little information. The Blackwells lived at 206 Pear Tree Street, which Roxy put a star above, indicating the scene of the crime. Roxy drew another stick house for the Overlys at 204 Pear Tree. Their interview amounted to no more than a blip on the page. Beth Overly acknowledged seeing Cassie outside the home. After drawing another pitiful illustration of a house, Roxy wrote, "Websters 208." They heard Cassie screaming, but nothing more.

Roxy found the enlarged satellite image of the neighborhood, spread it out on her desk, and noted the house that backed up to the Blackwells, 203 Peachtree, and drew it in on her whiteboard. Flipping through the pages she had, she couldn't locate any additional interviews from the neighborhood. She also noted that the neighborhood was gated. Residents had a sticker on the upper right-hand corner of the windshield, which granted them unhindered entry to the neighborhood.

Not only did the police not canvas any further than that, but they didn't get the security camera footage from the guard shack in time, Roxy huffed.

In green, Roxy wrote Cassie's name, circled it, and drew lines to list important information. She wrote, "state's custody until eighteen," "didn't play well with others," "met Jesus at seventeen," "made more enemies than friends," "nanny to twin boys before the Blackwells," "college graduate," "absent father, mother dead," "Treehouse and Four Corners shelters," and "lived with her mentor before the Blackwells."

Roxy shook her head. *She didn't have an easy life, that's for sure.*

In purple, Roxy wrote the timeline for the evening—murders occurred on February 9, 2001. Medical examiner suggested the murders happened between six and seven p.m. Sunset at 6:07 p.m. Cassie arrived at the grocery store at six thirty and left at six fifty, empty-handed because she left her wallet at home. Security footage from the store nailed down the times. Store was roughly ten to fifteen minutes away. 911 call at 7:06.

In orange, Roxy jotted down, "Keller PD–Detective Dale Kenton." She also wrote, "An apparent superstar, some say legendary." He solved more homicides than anyone else, which stroked his ego. After a few keystrokes, Roxy learned that detective Kenton goes by Sheriff Kenton these days.

Roxy laughed and thought, *Right—yet he didn't do the basic steps of an investigation.*

Picking up the prosecution file, Roxy chose the brown marker. She listed those who had testified for the state: Holly Franklin, roommate at Treehouse Shelter. Amanda Hilltop, fought with Cassandra at Treehouse. Hamilton Baker, staff at Treehouse. Detective Kenton. Medical examiner.

In black, Roxy wrote out the defense witnesses. Suzanna Parker, Cassandra's case worker. Sandy Holmes, psychiatrist at Four Corners, and Patricia Miller, Cassandra's mentor at Four Corners.

Scooping up the last file, she grabbed the hot pink marker.

As with most unstable cases, a jailhouse snitch named Jackie Sparse testified against Cassandra. Although jurors believe these witnesses, they lack credibility and almost always receive leniency or a plea deal for their "cooperation." Jackie and Cassandra shared a cell for three weeks. After the twenty-one days, Jackie claimed Cassandra admitted to the murders. Without question, the state needed more evidence because the case against Cassandra was weak. Jackie joined the fight, saving the day for the prosecution but tightening the hypothetical noose around Cassandra's neck.

Finally, in black she wrote out the physical evidence, which was scant at best. Three-shell casings, a black bandanna found in the backyard, Cassandra's fingerprints on the back-door handle, and that's it. The bandanna had never been tested for DNA. Cassandra wore bandannas when she cleaned and cooked. The state argued that the fact that she didn't have one on suggested that the bandanna found in the yard was hers. No blood-stained clothing that belonged to Cassandra. No murder weapon. No blood-riddled footprints. The state's entire case was circumstantial, but the jury bought it, hook, line, and sinker.

***

"Well, I have it all in my head, but I need some resources, and I need to know if we can test the bandanna," Roxy said.

Roxy sat in front of Sam's desk at the law firm in a high-backed, brown chair.

"I filed the request already. We should hear back soon, and once we do, I'll have you go to the Keller PD and pick up the evidence box. Does this mean you're in?"

"Yeah, it does. I'm going to visit Cassandra tomorrow."

"That's great. I'll tell Seth."

Roxy pushed her hair behind her ear. "What if we lose again?"

"Don't go there. We'll do the best we can. Now we know we're not invisible in this fight. Don't think that way. Pray and be prepared to fight," Sam said.

Roxy nodded, still unsure whether she could live through another loss but knowing she needed to try.

Before Roxy left, Sam said, "This business isn't for the weak heart, remember? You're a warrior. Act like it."

"I remember. Thanks, Sam."

***

The pungent and musty air assaulted Roxy with one step inside the Mountain View women's death row. Roxy signed in, went through the many intrusive security measures, and sat at a table in the visiting room. A few minutes later, the doors at the other end of the room opened. Cassandra walked in, dragging shackles at her feet, clanging in cadence with her handcuffed hands.

Reaching the table, the stocky guard asked, "Miss, would you like me to leave her shackled and cuffed for your meeting?"

"Release her hands, please," Roxy said.

Roxy noticed that the young, healthy-looking woman in her pictures appeared defeated and resigned to her fate. Cassandra's once promise-filled eyes were dull, her formerly well-groomed hair was unkempt, and her previously perfect physique was all but gone.

Once the guard sat at the other end of the room, Roxy introduced herself, offering her hand, and Cassandra wearily accepted.

Cassandra said, "Who are you? I mean, I heard you say you're Roxanne, but who are you?"

"I'm a private investigator hired by Sam Rollins and Seth Carmichael, the attorneys you met several weeks ago," Roxy explained. "I'll be investigating your case."

Cassandra nodded. "I'm not sure what I can tell you, but I'll do my best. I didn't kill the Blackwells."

"If that's the truth, I'll prove it, Cassandra," Roxy said.

"Please, call me Cassie. Cassandra's too formal."

Roxy obliged. "Cassie, as hard as it is, I need you to go back to February 9, 2001, and tell me everything."

Cassie took a few beats to compose herself.

"Faith and I dressed for the day. We ate breakfast and read. I took her to school at eight thirty. After dropping her off, I had Bible study with Patricia, picked up dry cleaning, and went back home. I cleaned the bathrooms, washed the bedding, and cleaned the floors. After making the beds again, I ate lunch, emptied the dishwasher, and planned the evening meal."

Cassie ran her hand through her hair before she continued, the pain visible on her face.

"I picked up Faith from school at two, and we grabbed a smoothie before ballet. She practiced from three to four. I made asparagus, mashed potatoes, and lamb chops for dinner with a double-mousse chocolate cake for dessert. After supper, I cleaned the kitchen, made Faith's lunch for the next day, and changed into comfy clothes. I left after telling Faith good night, knowing she'd be asleep when I returned."

Cassie's emotion took over after several long moments of silence.

"If I'd known I wouldn't see her again, I would've told her so many things."

Cassie sat back, rubbed her eyes, and sucked in deep breaths. Roxy bit back the urge to break the silence and just observed her.

Roxy heard Seth's teaching in her head. "Never, and I mean never, interrupt a witness during their story. Let the interview flow. Don't comfort them. Don't redirect them. Let them talk."

Cassie's word shook Roxy out of the memory.

"When I left, Paul and Sarah were spending their evening with Faith. They kept the same schedule of Bible time, bath, and putting Faith to bed at seven thirty." Cassie stopped and bit her bottom lip.

"I left the house at six fifteen p.m., give or take a few minutes. From what the police said, I arrived at the store at six thirty. I made it through about the first five aisles, but when I went for my phone, I realized my wallet wasn't in my purse. I left my cart by the front door. I searched my car, and when I didn't find it, I drove back home."

Cassie's breathing became rhythmic, and her words spilled out through clenched lips.

"I went through the backdoor because that was the quickest way to my room. Before I made it to my bedroom, I heard the bathwater running, but no talking or laughing, which wasn't normal. I abandoned my path and went to the bathroom. It was a matter of steps before I walked into the saturated carpet."

Cassie shook her head.

"I turned the water off and started yelling. I ran downstairs, and when I turned the corner toward the family room, I saw Paul in the entryway. He was face down in a pool of blood. Without moving another step, I peeked into the family room and saw Sarah and Faith slumped over on the couch." Cassie put her hand over her mout., "Faith still had her Bible open in her lap."

Tears snaked tiny rivers down Cassie's cheeks.

"I screamed and ran outside. I called 911 from inside my car. When the police arrived, they put me in the back of a squad car, not under arrest or anything, but because I couldn't control myself. One of the officers took me to the station and asked me about the evening. I told him everything I just told you, and they let me go. I had to call Patricia to come get me, and I stayed with her. I mean, I couldn't go home. The next day, the police picked me up and took me back to the station. This time another detective interviewed me. He acted real macho like."

Roxy replied, "Detective Dale Kenton?"

Cassie nodded. "Yeah, that's him. He was Mr. Nice Guy at first, asking me if I was all right and if there was anything I needed. That ended fast. I didn't realize he thought I killed them until he started yelling at me. I was at the station all day. I thought he was going to arrest me, but he let me go."

Roxy sat her pen down and even though she knew the answer, she asked, "When did they arrest you?"

Cassie's eyes hardened.

"February 20. Guess I was fortunate to attend the funerals, even though I hid myself because of the media. I sat in the back of the church with a black veil over my face. After the burials, I went back to the cemetery with Patricia and cried for hours. I remember staring at the piles of dirt and feeling my heart break. I couldn't wrap my brain around them being dead. They were the closest thing to a family I've ever had. Why did God allow this to happen when He knows I didn't kill them?"

Roxy said, "Cassie, you know He doesn't work like that."

Cassie rolled her eyes. "Our relationship is professional. We'll work my case together, but this—" she motioned circles above her head "—isn't something I'll discuss with you. I have enough people trying to convince me all of this is part of God's master plan, but that's bull."

Roxy knew not to push.

"I know that was hard, but thank you. I needed to hear the story firsthand. Just so you know, I visit my clients a lot, especially when I find something or need your help. Your assistance is vital. I know our relationship will take time to build, but the sooner you trust me, the better."

Cassandra nodded her head in acknowledgment but offered no further words.

The dig is in, Roxy thought when Cassie folded her arms.

The fresh air hit Roxy with a gust of wind when she left the prison. On the drive home, she replayed the interview and Cassie's visible changes at various points in the narrative. The pain in her eyes was undeniable. Roxy felt a kinship of sorts in her pain. She knew what that felt like.

Roxy headed straight to the firm when she made it back to town. Entering the conference room, she saw Sam and Seth studying something on the table.

"Roxy, I'm glad you came by," Seth said.

"We need to talk," Sam said, hugging her and pulling out a chair.

"They claim they can't find the evidence in Keller," Sam said, matter-of-factly.

"What? You're joking, right? Do they not know they're required by law to keep evidence in death penalty cases?" Roxy asked.

"They agreed to allow you and Seth access to their evidence room Friday morning," Sam stated.

"Perfect. I love doing their jobs for them," Roxy said.

Seth nudged her. "Come on, Roxy; it'll be like old times. We'll make it fun!"

"Can't wait!" Roxy exclaimed.

Before leaving, Sam said, "Don't forget about brunch."

Roxy had eaten brunch with Sam and his wife, Heather, every Saturday for the last five years. She enjoyed the fellowship, especially since she lost her mother in a car wreck at the hands of her father when she was sixteen, but that was another story, entirely.

At home, Roxy fixed dinner and sauntered to her office for computer work. She needed to analyze the chain of custody documents for the evidence. With a fresh notebook opened, she noted the evidence piece-by-piece and who last signed for it, which she discovered was Sheriff Kenton. He'd be responsible for answering to its location if she and Seth couldn't find it, which, she mused, would be an entertaining conversation.

CHAPTER 3

THE SKY WAS A MYRIAD of pinks and oranges Friday morning during Roxy's run. She cleaned up and changed into her "working outfit," which meant knee-high boots, jeans, and a t-shirt. She put rubber gloves and face shields in her purse, just in case. Much to her dismay, a sense of excitement for the day surged.

Her memory flashed to Sam, poking her side. "You should consider Seth. You're not getting any younger you know," he said, with an added wink.

Here's the thing about Seth—he definitely fit in the "tall, dark, and handsome" category. His frame was a muscled six-four, hair dark-brown, his caramel complexion smooth, with blue eyes that could make a girl weak in the knees. At thirty-three, Roxy never thought about settling down. She was in the prime of her career. Seth would understand that, but the idea still seemed preposterous.

The doorbell made her jump.

"Are you ready to get dirty?" Seth asked, after Roxy opened the door.

"I'm hoping they have a clean and organized space for us to dig through, but I brought latex gloves, facemasks, and protein bars, just in case," Roxy answered with a big smile. "You know me; I'm always prepared for the worst."

Sheriff Kenton surprised them in the parking lot at the Keller Police Department. The man was built like a brick house and didn't miss a meal, or a snack, by the looks of his frame. His thinning dark hair jumbled below the brim of his hat. He glared at Roxy with dull brown eyes.

"What're you two looking for?" Sheriff Kenton asked.

Seth spoke before Roxy could formulate words.

"Well, Sheriff, we didn't expect you to join us in our efforts today. We're looking for the evidence from the 2001 Blackwell case, but I'm certain you already knew that."

"If you think you're going to question my ethics by attempting to overturn a rock-solid case, be my guest, but don't expect us to go out of our way to aid in your efforts."

Roxy couldn't hold her tongue. "Let's not go overboard here, Sheriff. You're on the defensive a bit prematurely, don't you think?"

Walking away from them, he responded, "Good luck in your investigation; you'll need it."

Seth looked at Roxy. "Small town syndrome? You know he's offended that we're even attempting to find the evidence."

Roxy rolled her eyes. "I knew he'd get his feelings hurt, but I never thought it'd be so soon."

Once they gained access to the "evidence room," which was the department's basement, Roxy glanced at Seth, pulling out her gloves and masks. "Aren't you glad I brought these?"

The low-lit room was dingy, cluttered, and, much to Roxy's dread, a wreck. At least an inch of dust covered every bit of the one thousand-square foot space.

Seth laughed and touched the ceiling without effort.

"Thank goodness I'm not claustrophobic."

After donning their gloves and facemasks, they starting working from opposite ends of the room. Nothing was arranged by date or even crime—homicides were alongside drug charges. Roxy saw a 1990 case on top of a 2006 box.

Two hours later, the pair had barely searched through twenty-five percent of the room.

Roxy stopped, retrieved a protein bar, and sat on the floor.

"This is like searching for the proverbial needle in a haystack."

Seth joined her on the ground. "I once went on a search for evidence in a basement twice this size and even less organized, if you can believe that, and I didn't have help. It took me a week, but I found the boxes I needed."

Roxy gaped at him. "You can't be serious. I don't know if the Sheriff will allow us to come back tomorrow."

Five hours later, after trudging through almost the entire basement, Seth yelled, "I found it!"

Roxy abandoned her pile and ran to him. Working together, they removed the pile of boxes, loose papers, and binders on top and freed the mangled box.

Roxy and Seth changed into a clean pair of gloves and opened the box. Roxy grabbed the evidence list and started naming off what should be there, while Seth took inventory.

Everything listed on Roxy's evidence log was accounted for and, surprisingly, in good condition. The most crucial piece of evidence, the bandanna, was stored and sealed according to Texas law. Since they couldn't confiscate the evidence without a court order, they photographed and documented each piece and placed the box on a shelf close to the door.

After signing out with the clerk, Seth alerted her to the location of the box.

With glasses halfway down her nose, the clerk said, "Thanks. I'll be sure and tell the Sheriff."

When the outdoor air entered her lungs, Roxy said "He isn't going to make this easy on us. I bet he throws a hitch in everything we try to do."

Seth agreed, saying, "Probably, but we have the law on our side, regardless. You wanna grab dinner before we head back?"

Roxy paused to calm the sudden frantic pace of her heart. "Sure."

I wonder if Sam said something to him. I mean, we've always been friends, but I've never gone to dinner with him, Roxy pondered.

She could feel her pulse quicken when they pulled into the parking lot of a fifties-style diner.

"Is this all right? Do you even like diner food?" Seth inquired.

"Yeah, this'll be fine."

After settling on the bright-red vinyl of the booth cushion, Roxy watched Seth flip through the menu, and before she could divert her attention elsewhere, he caught her.

"What is it, Rox?"

Did he just call me Rox? She thought. "Nothing. I was lost in thought."

"Are you sure? Because it seemed like you were staring at me and not lost in some far-off place," Seth said, a mischievous look in his eyes.

Shaking her head, she picked up her menu to redirect the topic. "What are you going to eat?"

"A juicy burger with the works, you?"

She glanced up from her menu. "That sounds good. I'll second your order."

"Remember when you didn't know the basic steps of an investigation?" Seth asked. "Now you're obsessed with your work, and one of the best investigators in the business."

Roxy laughed. "Well, yeah, I was fresh out of college and didn't know what I wanted to do with myself. And what do you mean obsessed?"

"Your master bedroom is your office. I'd call that obsessed."

"I call that dedicated, not obsessed. Besides, I spend more time in there than I do my bedroom anyway."

On their way back to Dallas, Roxy wrestled with the implications of what had transpired. She had left with Seth this morning on a business adventure and ended the day with dinner and side-cramping laughter. She had briefly dated in college but wasn't the type to pine over a man. She felt that aspect of her life falling away.

What's happening to me? Roxy pondered.

CHAPTER 4

SETH ENTERED HIS CONDOMINIUM building and ran up the stairs to his second-story corner flat. His living room had one wall of windows with a sizable balcony. Two tan-leather chairs and a matching couch fit comfortably in his living room, over a large-white area rug that covered light-hardwood floors.

He felt an adrenaline high from finding the box of evidence, but more so from his time with Roxy. From the moment he met her, he'd been crazy about her but had never acted on his feelings. He wasn't even a believer then, but over their first few years of friendship, she'd witnessed to him and helped him mature in his faith after he had accepted Christ. That alone was enough to make him fall for her, but the more time they spent together, albeit only for work, the more the depth of her as a person made him fall for her.

Tonight, he felt like he made progress.

Sam's face entered his mind. "Seth, go for it! Ask her out, and see what happens."

The problem was his past, which mirrored a four-year-old's finger painting, and even though God's grace wiped his slate clean, the staggering truth remained: Roxy was pure, and he wasn't.

For almost eight years, Seth had matured in his faith, ceased his reckless behavior, and hardly dated. Every time he took a woman out, he wished she was Roxy and couldn't bear doing that to someone. So, that resulted in no second dates and only three first dates, because, in his heart, nobody held a candle to Roxy.

Closing his eyes, he prayed for the prospect of earning Roxy's love. He pleaded, "Lord, if it's Your will that I'd have the honor of guarding and tending to Roxy's heart, I'll take Your lead and love her like You love us."

***

Roxy opened her eyes the next morning and saw Seth's face in her mind. Luckily, she had brunch with Sam and Heather in a few hours, which provided an opportunity to hash her jumbled thoughts out in confidence and receive sound advice.

With her feet in rhythmic step, earbuds snug in her ears, she listened to the beginning of Cassie's interrogation. After her encounter with the Sheriff, she found it easier to picture him sitting across from Cassie.

"So, let me get this straight, you found them dead, right? I mean, that's what you're telling me," Detective Kenton said.

"That's the truth. You're not insinuating that I had something to do with this, are you?" Cassie fired back.

"Funny you should say that because nobody else fits the evidence but you, so, yep, that's exactly what I'm betting on. You shot them, went to the grocery store to establish an alibi, and called 911 to cover your tracks, but you screwed the pooch in leaving something behind," Detective Kenton declared.

There was a pause in his words almost as if he expected Cassie to admit something. When she said nothing, he carried on. "You left your bandanna in the backyard. Whether you were coming or going when it fell off, I'm not sure, but we found it near the backdoor."

Cassie lashed out. "I don't wear solid bandannas, and I already told you that. You'll see when you search my room. All of mine have the classic white and black designs on them."

***

Roxy drove across town to Sam's house for brunch. When his house came into view, she noticed Seth's car in the driveway. A rush of exhilaration hit her at seeing Seth again, as well as dread when she realized she couldn't talk to Sam as she had planned. Walking around the lightly-colored brick home to the back gate, Roxy heard Seth's laughter before entering the yard and a smile broke out across her face.

"Hey, there she is," Seth said, heading over to her. "I hope you don't mind if I join you for brunch. Sam invited me."

Glancing at Sam and seeing the expression on his face, Roxy said, "Of course not. You're family."

Heather ambled out the sliding glass door, carrying plates of vegetables and fruit. "Roxy, it's so good to see you."

Roxy adored Heather and her bigger-than-life personality. "Adding Seth to the mix is wonderful, don't you think?" Heather asked, winking at Sam.

"It sure is, if he doesn't break the cardinal no shop-talk rule," Roxy said and chuckled.

Seth gasped in mock offense. "I wouldn't dare talk about work at a non-work gathering."

Sitting at the table, Roxy's mouth watered as she eyed the grilled chicken, homemade potato salad, deviled eggs, and baked beans on her plate.

After Sam blessed the food, he said, "So, I hear you had a good diner-style burger last night."

Roxy dropped her fork as her head shot up. "Well, we were pretty hungry after digging in that dungeon of a basement all day."

Seth chimed in sarcastically. "And the burgers were amazing."

In her mind, Roxy turned over what that meant. Seth had talked to Sam about her before she arrived.

Did that mean it was a date? She thought, retrieving her fork.

Sam said, "Well, I'm glad you two spent some time together outside of work. You might like each other."

"Okay, Sam. They're adults and can figure out their love life without you playing cupid," Heather interjected.

Roxy felt the lobster-red of embarrassment creep up her neck before shading her face.

"Don't blush, Rox. It was nothing, right?" Seth said, with a pat on her arm.

There he went calling me Rox, again, she thought, but admitted she liked the sound of it on his lips.

After the meal, Roxy went inside and helped Heather clean up.

"He means no harm, you know," Heather said. "He just wants what's best for you both."

"I know he does. I wanted to talk to him about dinner anyways, but Seth beat me to it."

"Well, it's about time he followed through. He's been crazy about you for years," Heather said, offering the tidbit.

The expression on Roxy's face told Heather she'd messed up.

"Oh, no, here I go running my big mouth, again. Please keep that to yourself. I figured last night was a clue."

Heather put a soapy hand over her mouth. "Oh, shoot. I'm going to stop talking now."

Roxy stood there in disbelief. Her mind ran wild with questions.

Did she say what I thought she said?

Years? How many years?

Why hasn't anyone told me, and why hasn't Seth done something about it?

Her thoughts raced like hummingbird wings as she watched Seth and Sam throwing a Frisbee in the backyard. Like a movie playing in her mind, the memories of Seth's overwhelming attentiveness toward her when she found out that they had lost Raleigh's case assailed her.

She sat at her computer that fateful Tuesday morning, awaiting the release of the opinions. This was a groundhog ritual of sorts, while working a case. The higher courts published their rulings on certain days, and this opinion came on Tuesdays. So, every Tuesday, she was glued to her desk with the site opened, compulsively reloading the page until the newest list appeared.

When Raleigh's name flashed on the screen, her body began to shake, making clicking the link difficult for her trembling hand. When her eyes scrolled through the form to the section she needed to see, she felt lightheaded.

Conviction Affirmed.

She lost. Raleigh would be executed in a matter of days. Her vision blurred as the world began to spin, and sobs escaped her throat uncontrollably. Several minutes later, Seth flew into her house and hurried down the hall.

"Roxy, Roxy. Come here," Seth called to her.

He pulled Roxy from the chair to his lap on the floor. Seth caressed her hair, whispering encouragement in her ear. He stayed glued to her the entire day, even insisting on driving Roxy to see Raleigh's family.

Turning onto the driveway, Roxy saw Rebecca and Cliff, rocking on the porch with a pile of Kleenex. Roxy leapt from the car. Before she got too far, Seth put his arm around her, finishing the walk with her.

"I'm so sorry, Rebecca. I failed him. I failed you," Roxy cried out.

"Don't you dare. You fought the good fight. You tried your hardest, and you're not to blame here," Rebecca said, holding Roxy's face in her hands. Behind her, she felt the slightest touch of Seth's hand on the small of her back.

He was always there. Why had she never noticed before? She'd accepted that their friendship was strong. He was one of her dearest confidants, her teammate in the fight for justice, her protector in times of pain, and her partner in times of persecution, but a significant other?

Shaking the memories off, Roxy finished cleaning the kitchen.

"Are you sure you don't need help with anything else?" Roxy asked Heather.

"Nope. That was the last of the dishes. I'll get the rest. Thanks for your help."

Sam and Seth walked in as Roxy was gathering her things to leave.

"Are you leaving, sweetheart?" Sam asked, extending his arms for a hug.

"Yeah. Thanks for lunch," Roxy said, returning Sam's hug.

Before she could reach out to Seth, he said, "Can I walk you to your car?"

"Of course," Roxy answered.

"See you two at church in the morning," Sam yelled.

Roxy heard her footsteps and her heart thudding in her ears as they walked.

"So, I was wondering if you'd like to go play mini golf or take a walk around the park with me?" Seth asked, after they reached the driveway.

When Roxy reached her car, she fought the urge to say no. "I'd love to beat you at mini golf."

"Is that a fact?" Seth said, "Well, you're on. I can follow you home, and you can ride with me."

***

Before she opened the back door to go inside, Heather said, "I have a confession to make."

Sam whirled around. "You didn't tell her?"

"I'm sorry. She was looking out the window, watching Seth throw the Frisbee. She told me she wanted to talk to you about their dinner last night."

Sam shook his head. "Well, cat's out of the bag now. I talked to him this morning about his feelings of inferiority. He's done right by himself and his future bride, even if it's not Roxy. I just hope he has the courage to come clean with her."

***

Roxy clutched her steering wheel, navigating to her house with Seth behind her.

This must be a date, right? Heather said Seth has liked me for years. I wonder what's changed. Why is he just now acting on his feelings? Roxy wondered in her silent car.

"Are you sure you can handle this?" Roxy asked sarcastically when she climbed in his car.

"Handle what? Seeing your face when you lose?" He belted out a laugh. "Oh, I'm more than ready."

"I never knew you were so competitive," Roxy noted. "I guess since we worked together, and you were the one mentoring me, there was never a reason for this to come up, but I like it."

"There's a lot you don't know about me," Seth said, "but I'm hoping to change that."

Roxy kept quiet. She liked the thought of knowing him more. She had spent time with him when they first met, witnessing to him, and bringing him to church with her, but she had focused on his salvation. When he brought her in to work with him and Sam, they remained colleagues and teammates on several cases. They also attended the same church, but nothing more.

***

On the last bank shot, Roxy swung the club, "Oh, oh, yes!" Roxy said, after the ball landed in the cup. "Sorry, but I think I won." She beamed up at him.

Seth shook his head. "All right, I think you're right. I was distracted, so, that wasn't my best game."

"I'd say that, too."

They returned the balls and clubs. Before they reached Seth's car, he sucked in a breath. "Roxy, may I take you to dinner this evening? We won't go to another diner, I promise. I'd like to go somewhere nice, maybe the Rooftop Terrace?"

Her heart started the loud thudding again. "I'd like that," Roxy answered.

"Really?" Seth questioned, "Because if you have other plans—"

"I did, but I think the case can wait another day."

"Well, okay, then, it's a date," Seth said, fumbling over the word.

"It's a date," Roxy agreed, blushing.

Pulling up to Roxy's house, Seth parked, ran around, opened the door for her, and walked her to her door.

"I'll pick you up at six p.m."

"I'll be ready," Roxy said, stepping into her home.

"Okay, I'll see you then," Seth said, almost skipping back to his car.

Several minutes later, Roxy still had her back against the door, unable to move or process a formulated thought. She had a date with Seth Carmichael, an actual date, at a very nice restaurant. That called for a dress. Roxy looked at the clock and realized she had less than two hours. She ran to the bathroom, turned on the shower, hopped in, washed up, and shaved. When she got out, she went into her office and sat in her prayer corner.

"Father, I don't know how to do this. If Seth is who You've picked for me, help me to know." Roxy prayed, a smile lifting the corners of her mouth.

She stood in her closet, flipping through her dresses. "No — definitely not—aha!"

She found her floor-length blue dress. Not too fancy, but nice enough for the Rooftop Terrace. She dried her hair, pinned it up out of her face, applied a little eye makeup, and slipped into her dress and shoes. She grabbed her purse and paced in her entryway, attempting to quiet her insides.

***

Seth elected for casual slacks and a blue button-down shirt. With his palms drenched in sweat, he had difficulties even tucking in his shirt.

"I can't pick her up with sweaty palms. Come on, man, get control of yourself," he muttered to himself.

He called Sam before leaving. "I asked her out and she accepted. We're going to dinner."

"I'm proud of you, Seth, but I need to tell you something. Heather let it slip when she and Roxy were cleaning the kitchen."

"So, she knows? What did she tell her? Everything, or just that I have feelings for her?" Seth asked, the panic evident in his voice.

"Well, she told her you've liked her for years and that it's about time you came clean."

Seth combed his fingers through his hair. "What do I do now? I can't believe this. I have to pick her up in twenty minutes, and I feel like I'm about to throw up."

Sam chuckled. "Calm down. Just go with it. There's no need to panic. She's interested, or you wouldn't be picking her up."

"What if she's doing this to let me down gently?"

Another chuckled slipped from Sam's throat. "Can you see her doing that? Don't get me wrong, she's a thoughtful woman and all, but I don't think she'd waste her time."

"You're right."

Seth hung up the phone and left. His emotions ran the gamut. High and low. Excited yet terrified all the same.

Seth rang Roxy's doorbell with a shaky hand. When she answered, his breath hiccupped at the sight of her. The royal-blue dress hugged her fit frame like a leather glove on a familiar hand.

"You're beautiful," Seth said, opening his car door for her.

"You don't look so bad yourself," Roxy answered, eyeing his crisp blue shirt.

They sat at a corner candlelit table with polar-white, shimmering stars overhead. Seth looked up from his menu and caught Roxy's gaze.

"You're staring at me again," Seth said.

"You caught me. I can't help it," Roxy admitted.

Seth looked shocked at her admission. *That was unexpected.*

"What're you going to order? I'm thinking a filet mignon with mashed potatoes and mixed vegetables." Seth asked.

"That sounds delicious, but I'll skip the potatoes and double the vegetables."

After the waitress brought their food, conversation ebbed and flowed.

"Is there any reason they'd say no?" Roxy asked.

"Well, the Sheriff can make a fuss over the suggestion, but often, the judge will sign the order," Seth explained.

"Did you get the feeling Sheriff Kenton knows something he doesn't want us to find? I mean, by the way he pounced on us so fast the other day?"

"You know, I wondered why he was even there."

"Well, I'm going to find whatever he's hiding."

"I know you will."

After the waitress took their plates, Seth perked up when the tune of the perfect song graced his ears. *Thank you, Lord.*

He swallowed hard. "Will you dance with me?"

In answer, Roxy stood and brushed her dress off.

Seth rose, led her to the middle of the room, took her in his arms, and swayed to the music.

"Is it true?" Roxy asked, almost in a whisper.

He stiffened before putting his finger under her chin, turning her head to look up at him. "As true as God's word."

After letting that out, Seth felt like the weight of the world had left his heart, and he was free to act. He held her tight and danced through four more songs.

Seth put his head on the top of Roxy's hair and breathed deeply, catching the smell of her shampoo. She smelled so good. The scent caused his insides to do flips. "What is that smell," he said, his nose still to her head.

"Lavender-vanilla."

"You smell amazing," Seth said, pulling her tighter.

Roxy giggled.

***

On Roxy's front porch, Seth said, "Thank you for coming with me."

"I had a nice time."

With his heart thudding in his ears, he said, "I'd like to kiss you."

She smiled. "Are you asking?"

He nodded.

Roxy mirrored the nod. Seth bent down, and when their lips met, his insides became a warm, mushy mess. The kiss lingered and grew deeper.

Roxy pulled away, breathless.

She tucked a strand of hair behind her ear. "I'll see you at church in the morning."

The smile on Seth's face stretched so wide that his jaw ached. The night with her was magical, and something he'd wanted for years, but he had never imagined it would be like tonight.

CHAPTER 5

ROXY FELT A CHILL IN THE AIR before walking into the church lobby. She spotted Seth, Sam, and Heather in their usual spot.

Roxy caught Seth's eye, and he hurried to greet her.

"Good morning, beautiful," Seth said, hugging her and placing a soft kiss on her cheek.

"Good morning, Seth. I love the blue," she said, pointing at his shirt.

"I wore it for you," he answered, winking, before they assumed their seats.

After worship, Roxy opened her Bible and held her pen ready to take notes during the sermon. When the pastor began to preach, Roxy stilled.

"We're not meant to be alone. God created us to be in community and to join into marriage with the one God chose for us." The pastor continued. "In Genesis two, we read that man had no helper as his complement. Then God created woman: 'This one, at last, is bone of my bone and flesh of my flesh; this one will be called woman for she was taken from the man.'"

Roxy felt Seth squirm in his seat as her mind reeled with what the pastor said. She recalled her prayer to make it known to her if He chose Seth. Roxy felt like standing up to alert the congregation. "Everyone can go home now; this one's for me."

As Roxy's thoughts raced, Seth's hand reached for hers. She felt a tingle ride up her spine, as if his touch sent electricity coursing through her. She rolled her hand over, interlocked her fingers with his, and glanced at him. Before Roxy could turn over a steady stream of thoughts in her mind, the sermon ended, and the pastor led them in prayer.

"Father, You're the giver of joy and love. You also made us emotional beings to remain in community through life because our journey is better together. Father, I ask that You touch the hearts of Your saints, soften the hardened spirits, strengthen the couples, forge new relationships, and allow anyone with doubts to obtain resolve."

Roxy shot her eyes up, staring at the pastor.

What did he just say? Allow any doubts to be resolved? Father, what are You doing? Roxy asked.

She needed time in her prayer corner to talk this out. Nothing else would settle this dilemma. Didn't she ask God to let her know if this was right? The pastor just preached a message to her and prayed that doubts be resolved.

Come on, Roxy, she thought, *what more do you need?*

When the service ended, Seth turned to her. "Come to lunch with me."

Roxy noticed his urgency. "Okay, sure. I'd like to change first. Pick me up in twenty?"

"Okay."

***

While they ate, Seth made the decision to tell her afterward. He'd ask her to take a walk around the lake. He wanted privacy to bare his soul.

"So, after this, do you want to drive to the lake and talk?" Seth asked.

"The weather's perfect," Roxy answered.

After they both merely moved the food around on their plates, Seth said, "We should go."

In the car, Roxy looked over at Seth. "Are you alright?"

"I'll explain everything at the lake, I promise."

Seth parked and fetched a blanket from his trunk.

"Let's sit down for a few minutes under the tree over here," Seth said, motioning to a meadow covered with plush grass. Roxy followed his lead and sat across from him on the blanket, long tree branches overhead providing shade and a cool breeze.

"There are some things I need to tell you," Seth said, fidgeting with his hands.

"You're making me nervous."

"In all the years I've known you, so many changes have happened. You opened my heart to Christ, and I'll forever be indebted to you for that. I began to seek the Lord, asking Him to restore things in me that were lost and to change aspects of myself that needed adjustment. Throughout it all, you remained, encouraging me, guiding me to scriptures, and answering questions I had."

Seth looked up from his lap toward her and took a deep breath.

"When we watched the first client walk out of prison and the overwhelming joy lit your face, that started something up in me. The expression you had is a memory I can still conjure up. You see, you're the most loyal and honest woman I know. You carry yourself in a way most women only wish they could. You're confident but in a modest way. You know what you want, and you work as hard as you can until you reach your goal. Even when defeat is screaming in your face, you press on without blinking. I've watched and admired you from afar, never believing I was good enough for you. I didn't feel like I could be the man you deserve."

Seth cradled Roxy's hands. "I know what Heather told you, but that's not everything. The truth is that I fell in love with you somewhere along the way. At church this morning, I couldn't believe what our pastor preached on after the last two days. I've prayed the last eight years, begging God to make me pure again, so I could be that man for you. Sam encouraged me that God can, and will, do that for me, and I believe He has."

"Stop. You're wrong," Roxy said.

"What do you mean? Wrong about what?"

"I've never told anyone this before." Roxy's voice shook. "I'm not pure. When I was seventeen, I was raped."

Seth felt like he'd been sucker punched, and questions roared in his mind, but he sat, motionless.

"After my mom died and my dad went to prison, I hopped from house-to-house with people I thought were my family. Nobody cared what I did or where I was. It was June eighteenth, and I was hanging out with some friends, in a field of all places. This guy came out of nowhere, put something that felt like a knife to my back and whispered in my ear to walk backward. All my friends were drunk or high, so nobody paid attention. He took me behind a hay bale and—"

Tears flooded down her cheeks. "I tried to stop him, but he was too strong, and I couldn't get away. I remember laying there thinking this was what my life would always be. First my mom and then my virginity, stolen from me, and I was powerless to stop it."

Seth watched her wipe her cheeks with the back of her hand, rage permeating in his gut like a ravaged animal stalking its prey.

He felt the tremor in her hands. "Although I had every excuse to throw my life away and make reckless decisions, I made the opposite choice. This was a turning point for me. I'd finished high school the month before and considered community colleges in Dallas. I did odd jobs around town, saved enough money for a bus ticket, and never looked back. I decided that nobody would take another thing from me without a fight. During my first few months of college, someone invited me to students' night at church. That evening, not only did I find Jesus, but the trajectory of my life shifted. I realized my worth wasn't determined by anyone in this world. It took me a long time to become the woman you just described, but after Jesus eradicated the hypothetical veil and restored my heart, my life made sense."

Before she could get another word out, Seth grabbed her face and pressed his lips to hers. Her mouth opened, he followed, and their tongues mingled. The kiss was long and passionate, giving him goosebumps.

"Thank you for telling me. I'm honored you trust me enough to divulge such a painful experience."

"The truth is I'm afraid of you. I've never been in love before, and I don't know if I can allow myself that privilege because of my work."

"I know how you are when it comes to cases, and I won't interfere. Just trust me, and let's see where this goes."

Roxy smiled, holding his gaze. "I trust you."

"I think I should pray before we take this a step further," Seth said, smiling and grabbing Roxy's hands.

CHAPTER 6

ROXY WATCHED THE SUN RISE during her morning run, longer than normal because of the interrogation playing in her ears. She felt righteous anger when investigators lied and used all manner of trickery to trap suspects into thinking they had to admit to crimes, whether they were guilty or not. She thought it was constitutionally offensive. The Supreme Court deemed the practice legal, but she always found the so-called art deplorable. Maybe with almost four-hundred exonerations in America, there'd be new considerations for tightening the reins.

After cleaning up and eating, Roxy went through the files she needed for the day. When she walked out the door, Seth came to mind for the first time, and although it was just after nine a.m., she felt guilty and second-guessed her ability to balance her professional and personal life. Closing her car door, she decided to call Seth on her way to interview Patricia Miller. After inputting the address in her phone's GPS, she put in her earphones and called Seth.

"I was just thinking about you," Seth said, in place of the customary hello.

"I'm on my way to meet with Patricia. Have we received the order to test the bandanna yet?" Roxy asked, mentally kicking herself.

"Uh, no, not yet, but we don't expect to hear anything until later in the week," Seth answered, a small amount of tension in his voice.

Breaking through the quiet, Seth inquired, "Do you have time for lunch today?"

"Probably not. I have a packed day. In fact, my week's full of field work, but I'm sure I'll end up at the office," Roxy responded. She could sense the disappointment through the connection and hated to admit that she felt it, too.

"Well, all right then. Keep in touch."

How will I manage this? Roxy thought, ending the call.

Roxy had felt things over the weekend that she'd never experienced before, but an active case took precedence over her personal life, right? People balanced relationships with their careers all the time. Sam and Heather did it; surely she and Seth could, too. Establishing the way to accomplish such a task remained the kink in her chain.

Patricia's garden was full of a rainbow's pallet of colors in flowers. The wraparound porch mirrored the cover of Home and Country magazine with hanging pots of bright-green potato vines and red periwinkles. Each column had vining plants wrapping from top to bottom. Two cherrywood porch swings hung on each end with blue cushions.

Roxy rang the bell and waited. Ms. Miller answered with an enormous grin on her face, blue coke-bottle glasses in front of kind, brown eyes. "Miss Hollis, I'm so glad you came over. We can sit out here or in the sunroom, wherever you would be more comfortable."

Roxy grinned, taking Ms. Miller's hand and squeezing more than shaking. "Thank you for having me. It's nice to put a face to your name. We can sit on the porch. It's beautiful out."

Ms. Miller grabbed a wicker chair and pulled it toward the swing closest to the door, offering it to Roxy. "Would you like something to drink, some lemonade or water perhaps?" She offered.

"Water sounds great. Thank you."

While Ms. Miller grabbed drinks, Roxy sat down, pulling out her legal pad and pen before putting her bag under the swing.

"Miss Miller," Roxy began.

"Please, call me Patricia." Patricia instructed.

Nodding, Roxy continued. "Patricia, before we get started, I want you to know that, although we plan to investigate Cassie's case thoroughly, there's no guarantee of the outcome. My team and I dedicate our efforts and resources to each case selected, but we prefer to be upfront."

"I believe God sent you just in time. You'll find the truth," Patricia said.

Roxy nodded. "Okay. Now that we've handled the preliminary matters, I read through your statements to the police and your trial testimony. I'd like to ask you about the days following the murders. I understand that Cassie stayed with you after the police questioned her that first evening and up until her arrest, is that correct?" Roxy asked.

"Yes, ma'am, that's right. After her first meeting with those detectives, Cassie called me from the station to pick her up. I've never seen her so broken up, not even when I first met her. She was like a shell without her insides and, frankly, her day-to-day was more robotic than living. She cried for hours at a time and, at night, woke up screaming with nightmares."

Patricia shook her head. "She'd sit at the kitchen table, staring at the wall without saying a word, often breaking out into gut-wrenching sobs. After the second meeting with the police, she came home angry and remained that way until they arrested her eleven-days later."

Roxy could tell that, the more she discussed those long-ago days, the harder the memories were for her to get through.

Patricia put a hand over her mouth. "The day of the funeral, she threw up several times before we left."

She lowered her hand. "She insisted on sitting in the back to hide from those camera-holding snakes. They were like vultures, always following her around, waiting outside my house, day and night trying to question her. It was awful. She barely ate anything unless I made her, and by then, she ate more to appease me than for her own necessity. She went inward—it's hard to explain because you don't really know her—but she reverted to her younger self, closed off from everyone around her."

Her eyes pooled with tears. "She had transformed from this broken little girl into a victorious woman of God. I watched her blossom. I witnessed Christ change her. I don't know if you've ever seen that, but it's a remarkable thing."

When Patricia said those words, Seth's face entered her mind, and Roxy nodded, signaling that she'd indeed seen such a conversion. She remembered Seth as the partying-womanizer he'd once been, to the man of God he was now.

Patricia's words tore her from her thoughts.

"You should see her journals. I still have them. Part of the Four Corners program required the residents to journal daily, as a therapeutic measure. Her early entries are disturbing. They portray her sense of low self-worth, the intense pain she endured, and her internal woes."

Light returned to Patricia's eyes.

"But then, almost as if the wool had been pulled from her eyes, she began to see her significance, her beauty, and her place in Christ. She discovered how everything that happened to her could bring glory to God through her life. At the end of her time at Four Corners, she gave a remarkable speech at her graduation; her testimony would bring you to tears. She wrote the speech in one of her last entries. You can take them with you and give them back to me after you've read them. I already asked Cassie, and she agreed but requested that you keep them to yourself."

"I'd love to read them. I'm surprised they weren't used against her in court," Roxy said.

"She left them here, and the police didn't search my house when they arrested her. I wasn't going to offer anything to them."

Patricia's demeanor changed. "I need to say something to you," Patricia said, leaning in toward Roxy. "There's nothing in the world that could make me believe Cassie is capable of murder. The things she went through before I got to her were enough to take down the strongest man, and now this." She shook her head. "She's turned her back on God because she can't understand why she's going through so much after surviving such discord. I've tried to minister to her, but she shuts me down."

Patricia put her head down, and Roxy saw tears splashing her knees. Her body quaked with emotion.

When she lifted her face to Roxy, a blotchy mess revealed her dismay. "I have cancer. I don't know how much longer I have, and I can't die without knowing I'll see her again. She doesn't know I'm sick, and I won't tell her because that'll just give her another reason to be mad at God. I know you're a woman of faith, and I researched your victories, not only in the courtroom, but also for the kingdom."

The impact of Patricia's confession stunned Roxy. Fiddling with her fingers, the words poured out like an opened dam.

"I lost the last case I worked. I—I'm still confident in his innocence, but I lost, and it's important for you to know that. The only bright spot was his relationship with Jesus."

Roxy's eyes landed in her lap.

"The truth is I didn't know if I wanted another case, but after praying and remembering his final words to me, I took this case. I cannot promise I'll win on either assignment, but you have my word that I'll contribute every bit of myself to the case and to Cassie's salvation."

When Roxy reached her car, she plopped into the driver seat and hung her head. The conversation weighed heavily on her heart. She took some deep breaths and tucked Cassie's journals in her back seat.

CHAPTER 7

SANDY HOLMES LIVED IN an old town that shoehorned many historical sites. Roxy found her home without issue. Although not as well kept at Patricia's, it was an adorable cottage-style home. Walking to the front door, she was startled when it opened abruptly to reveal Sandy standing there.

"Hello, Miss Hollis," Sandy said shakily. "Please, come in."

"Thank you, Miss Holmes, for meeting with me today," Roxy said, following her inside and closing the door.

"Well, it's about time someone took a second look at that poor girl's case," Sandy said, leading Roxy into her small, cozy living room. Roxy sat on a brown leather ottoman close to Sandy's recliner.

Before Roxy could get a question out of her mouth, Sandy spoke, negating preamble.

"Many years ago, I would've said Cassandra possessed the culpability to kill that family, but something happened to her. It's still difficult for me to explain, this "made new" business," she said, "but there was a variance within her. Previous patients attempted to fake their evolvement with me, but I'm quite perceptive. Call it intuition or what have you, but I knew dishonesty when I saw it. With Cassandra, there was nothing artificial about her transformation. I'm just not sure what caused the elaborate about-face. I know some people claim God had something to do with it, but that's for others to believe."

Roxy perked up. Denying God was as old as time, but Roxy still struggled with how Sandy, in her profession, could see so much evidence, yet still deny the existence of God.

"Perhaps it was the medication and therapy regimens she engaged in for the many months she spent within the program. This poor soul came to us damaged, shattered really. I still remember our first session; she turned her back to me and remained like that the entire hour. The next two sessions were the same. The fourth session she spent insulting me with a very colorful vernacular. Sometime after that, she began to open, almost like a blooming lily, one petal at a time."

Sandy stopped, got up, and left the room without a word. Coming back in, Roxy noticed her holding a binder with Cassie's name on the spine.

No way I could be this lucky twice, right? First Cassie's journals and now her psychiatry profile and notes.

"For some reason," Sandy began, "I kept her files. Maybe it was the trial and the awful things the police said she did, or perchance it was destiny, but I kept them. I made notes at every session, during and after, to mark the patient's progress. I cannot let you take them, but I'd be happy to go over the important parts with you."

Roxy could barely stay in her seat with the excitement coursing through her veins. She stared at the binder like a kid waiting to open the largest present under the tree on Christmas morning.

Sandy looked up. "Ah, here's a session with a breakthrough," she said, tapping the paper with a shaky finger. "She described her first encounter of sexual abuse by one of her foster fathers. She was ten years old when he took advantage of her, late in the night. She said he'd come to her room and pull her to bathroom and have his way.

She was graphic in her description of what he did to her over the six months she resided with the family, before she told her caseworker about the intrusion of her innocence. Her caseworker reported the incident, and he went to prison."

Sandy shook her head.

"After Cassie came to trust me, we worked through much of her pain. She endured not only sexual assaults but also physical abuse at other foster homes. She recalled one family who withheld food from her for days at a time while forcing her to live in the closet. One of the other children in the home would sneak her food sometimes, but she lived like a prisoner for three months. This child went through hell but somehow was restored to a content young woman by the time she left."

Eyeing her, Roxy said, "Miss Holmes, that's how God works. Her transformation was one of new life in Christ. She changed because she made the choice to lay her afflictions, bad memories, scars, and troubles at the feet of Jesus. She discovered that she wasn't meant to carry her burdens because Christ's yoke is light. That's what reformed her, not medication or therapy sessions, although indisputably helpful."

Sandy looked stunned at Roxy's candor. "Well, that's for you to believe, but not me. Regardless, I don't think Cassandra could kill anyone. I'm assured she felt accepted and esteemed by the Blackwells, almost as if they were her kin. She never had a real family, and nothing could've possessed her to sever that bond."

Hours later, Roxy sat in her office, praying for Sandy and wondering how she could remain an unbeliever when God was so present in her profession as a therapist. After her prayer, she opened her eyes and felt a pang of loneliness. Seth occupied her mind, and she yearned to see him. She wanted to look into those eyes of his— as blue as the clearest sky, but changing depending on what he wore. She reached for her phone and nervously pressed the call button after reaching his number.

"Hey, you," Seth said, answering the phone. "How'd your day go?"

"Are you busy? I mean, have you left the office yet?" She inquired.

"I was just about to leave. Everything all right?" he asked.

"Can you come over for dinner? Or we can go out to eat. I just want to see you."

She heard the smile in his voice. "I can get take out and bring it over."

"Perfect."

What's gotten into me, she thought, running to her bedroom to change clothes. She couldn't explain her emotions but knew she'd not last days without seeing him.

When the doorbell rang half an hour later, she ran to the door, threw it open, and flung her arms around Seth's neck. After setting the food down in the kitchen, Seth wrapped Roxy up and kissed her.

"You couldn't stay away, could you?" He whispered.

"I'm sorry for the way I was on the phone this morning. I'll find a way to balance this out," she said, gazing up at him, meeting his eyes, and melting into them.

Almost in a whisper, Seth said, "I know this isn't easy and it's foreign for us both, but I'm willing to do whatever it takes for us to have a real shot at this." Grinning and speaking normally, Seth continued. "God's been working on me for some time now, and He has this under control."

Roxy busted into laughter and nodded her head.

"I know He does. If I'd just get out of His way and let Him run the show, we'd be smooth sailing."

Pulling the take-out boxes from the bag, Roxy looked over at Seth and noticed they moved like a well-oiled machine.

A memory flashed in Roxy's mind. She sat in the driver seat of Sam's Tahoe in the death row parking lot, waiting for Sam and Seth to return from their final visit with Raleigh. Despite Sam's efforts, Roxy couldn't visit Raleigh that day.

At twelve thirty, they climbed back in the SUV with red noses and puffy eyes. With one look, emotions spilled out. They put their arms around one another, creating a huddle. Seth began to pray for her, speaking words Raleigh told him to pray over her. Words she'd never forget.

"Comfort her, Father. Let her know this is Your will. Make her understand the system failed, not her. Give her peace that I'll be waiting to greet her upon her arrival into Your kingdom. This isn't my end, but my beginning."

Roxy bawled at the echo of Raleigh's words interceding to Christ on her behalf. That was Raleigh, always thinking of others even though his life was about to end. The trio met Rebecca and Cliff for lunch, although nobody ate.

During lunch, the victim's sister, Natalie Hope, stormed into the restaurant, yelling at Roxy. "Today your beloved murderer will die, just like my sister. Despite your pathetic attempts to free him, we get the last word. You don't deserve to breathe the same air I do for all you've done," Natalie said, through clinched teeth. Seth, her protector, stood up in front of her, blocking Natalie's spewed hate, and asked her to leave.

Seth jogged her out of her thoughts. "Everything all right?"

"I'm sorry. I was just thinking of how comfortable we are together," Roxy said, looking up from her plate at him.

"We've been through a lot together," Seth said, agreeing.

With dinner finished and cleaned up, Roxy took Seth to her back porch.

She told him about her interview with Patricia and her revelation about her illness.

"You're talented at what you do, even gifted. I know this seems heavy, but if anyone can exonerate Cassie and win her soul for Christ, it's you."

After watching the sunset, Seth stood up. "I better let you get to those journals. I won't be selfish with my time, even though I want to stay."

Kissing her sweetly, Seth showed himself out, and Roxy started a pot of coffee, feeling a slight twinge of exhaustion. Roxy sat on her soft rug, knees close to her chest, and opened the journal.

She struggled through the first three. Cassie's artistic abilities stunned Roxy. Her drawings were vivid, displaying what she went through as a child. The agony was palpable. Pictures portrayed her in pieces, like a puzzle, with various parts missing in each drawing, until finally she was a shell. Thought bubbles above the little girl said things like, "What did I do to deserve this?", "Keeping this secret in fear", and, perhaps the most painful one, "Why do people keep hurting me?"

Halfway through the fourth journal, her pieces came back together a little at a time. Roxy visualized the metamorphosis taking shape. The process was slow; first Cassie drew her head in full, with everything from the neck down still in pieces. In this drawing, the thought bubbles read, "Perhaps there's more to life than pain" and "If there's a God, maybe He loves me."

A few pages later, Cassie drew herself again, but she made her heart whole, and very pronounced, to display that it was intact. At the top of the page, in beautiful letters, she scrolled, "I'm God's chosen daughter!" A lump gathered in Roxy's throat as she read the beginning stages of Cassie's relationship with Christ.

Scripture appeared in her entries. Roxy wondered if Cassie did the same thing she did. When a verse jumped off the page at Roxy, she wrote it down. Cassie started with Psalms 25: "Lord, I turn to you. My God, I trust in You. Make Your ways known to Me, Lord; teach me Your paths. My eyes are always on the Lord, for He will pull my feet out of the net. Turn to me and be gracious to me, for I am alone and afflicted. Guard me and deliver me; do not let me be put to shame, for I take refuge in You."

The burn in Roxy's nose from incoming tears relented when she turned the page. Cassie expressed how alive she felt and detailed the foreign joy and peace in her soul.

Thus, began the baring of her heart. Cassie wrote:

> "Jesus experienced delight, harmony, and adoration, but also duplicity, oppression, agony, torment, and dread. I had no prior knowledge of what Christ went through on earth, but now that I know, the only logical response is to lay down my life before Him and trust Him.
>
> I feel like the lost sheep that You left the other ninety-nine to find, but You've been there all along. I just found You.
>
> There are no longer scales on my eyes because You restored my sight.
>
> My burdens are no more because I laid them at Your feet.
>
> My scars will be my testimony of Your great love.
>
> My joy comes from You and I have uncontaminated peace.
>
> Thank you for making me white as the falling snow!"

Cassie drew the most spectacular picture of herself, fully restored, sitting at the feet of Jesus. The expression on her face somewhere between awe and peace.

Roxy stared at the picture and wept, reflecting upon Cassie and her love for Christ that no longer existed. She read the remaining pages before she crossed the hall, climbed in bed, and prayed until she fell asleep.

CHAPTER 8

"ROXY, ARE YOU AWAKE? I have wonderful news," Seth asked, after Roxy answered the phone, early the following morning.

"What's going on?"

"We got the order back from the judge allowing us to test the bandanna, but there's a condition. The lab was selected by the prosecution, and it's in California," Seth said.

Roxy said, "That's great. Have you heard of the lab before? Who's preparing the package, and how's it being shipped?"

"Slow down. We received the order like thirty-seconds before I called you. Sam's on the phone figuring everything out."

"Okay, I can come by the office before my field work."

"I'll see you when you get here."

Roxy ran around her house, getting dressed, and gathering her files for the day's work.

Arriving at the law office forty-five minutes later, Roxy ran through the parking lot into the building. She rounded the corner, hearing Sam's raised voice, and saw his hand grasping the receiver.

She walked over to Seth. "What's going on?"

"From what I gather, Kenton won't allow us to view the packing of the bandanna."

"Are you kidding me? He knows that we have a right to observe the transaction, right? Especially considering that the state of the evidence when we found it was less than stellar."

Sam stomped into the office. "That guy's a solid jerk. The prosecutor will witness the packaging and see to it that the bandanna is mailed via Fed-Ex, but he's the only one."

"So, we're just supposed to trust the district attorney and the original detective who's still convinced of Cassie's culpability? We're not allowed to even watch how they handle the bandanna?" Roxy said.

"There isn't anything I can do, short of filing another motion to the judge, and I don't want to wait any longer," Sam said, putting his hand on her shoulder.

"I knew he was going to make this as difficult as possible for us," Roxy said, her eyes blazing.

"Look, this is the hand we've been dealt, and we'll deal with it," Sam said.

"I've got work to do. It'll do Cassie no good for me to stand here and stew over my frustrations," Roxy said, picking her purse up.

"I'll walk you out," Seth said, leading the way to the front door.

Roxy hugged Sam. "I hope this doesn't end badly. There's no telling if the dear sheriff knows what he's doing, and if he doesn't, then what?"

"Well, if it does, we'll figure out another way to the truth," Sam said.

Roxy stormed passed Seth, who held the door open for her.

Halfway to Roxy's car, Seth said, "I know that's not what you wanted to hear, but on a positive note, the lab is top-rated for DNA testing."

"Hopefully it arrives in a testable condition. Otherwise the quality of the facility won't matter," Roxy said, unlocking her car.

Seth put his hands on her cheeks. "Let's try to stay positive. It'll be in the mail tomorrow, so we should expect to hear of its arrival by the end of the week."

Roxy stood on her tiptoes to kiss Seth then said goodbye and drove out of the parking lot, watching Seth fade from her rearview mirror. Her pulse raced, and she was certain her blood pressure was through the roof. The audacity of Sheriff Kenton—to block them from monitoring how he handled their only viable piece of evidence was infuriating. Why would he put up such a fight?

Fantastic! I'm left with two people who couldn't care less whether the evidence arrives safely to the lab, and I just have to wait, Roxy thought, listening to the monotone voice of her GPS.

Greg Booker wasn't at all thrilled to partake in the interview, and Roxy wondered if this was an indication of his poor performance. Roxy didn't like to browbeat people or even be a finger pointer in other's shortcomings, but sometimes one's profession doesn't match his abilities.

"I don't know how much help I can be to you; my memory's not good these days," Greg said, attempting to clear the mounting paperwork on his desk.

"That's quite all right. I brought the material with me to jog your memory. I understand it's been a long time," Roxy said, getting her files out of her briefcase.

"I'd like to begin with documents you may have that we don't. Specifically, any interviews that your team did." Roxy paused, trying not to sound indignant. "Maybe of neighbors the police missed, group homes residents, or any follow up interviews," Roxy said, looking at Greg with a "did you do your job" look.

Chuckling, Greg said, "Miss Hollis, I'm a one-man operation. I didn't conduct any additional interviews because I didn't have the time to. This was a complex case, and as you know, triple homicides are difficult to work through alone."

Roxy strained, taking deep breaths and not wanting to lash out. Her instinct was to respond with,"Well, why didn't you hire a second chair?" or "So, what you're saying is you did a baseline job and received thousands for doing almost nothing."

Instead, Roxy asked, "So, what did you do to investigate alternative theories or suspects in preparation for trial?"

"I spent hours with Cassandra in jail and with Patricia. I sought out mental health experts to see if we could use the insanity defense but learned that wasn't a wise move. I did the best I could with what I had."

Roxy felt her cheeks flush with anger. "So, you thought she was guilty, or did you just hope everything she endured as a child would somehow benefit her presumption of innocence? Or was that the path of least resistance with your one-man operation? Your job was to defend her, not make her past somehow even out the crime."

"Look, Miss Hollis, like I said, I did the best I could. I'd be happy to give you my files and let you take a crack at what I had. Whether I believed in her innocence or not didn't matter and wouldn't have changed how I represented her. I did my job, and the cards fell where they did. Frankly, I think they would've fallen that way regardless. The state proved her guilt."

Roxy thought it best to stay silent to protect the threadbare bridge, should she need an affidavit from him in the future. Her rage was close to boiling over at his halfhearted expression. From where she stood, the state proved nothing other than Cassie's past aggressions and afflictions.

Roxy waited until Greg found his files, then took them, passed her business card to him, and let herself out. From the weight of her briefcase after taking his files, she felt another surge of defeat. The file he gave her wasn't the substantial one she envisioned getting from a triple homicide. It felt more like a file for a drug case or even a traffic accident.

***

Hamilton Baker still worked at the Treehouse shelter. She noted how gentle he was the minute he shook her hand, almost as if he was afraid of breaking her arm or something. His pleasant brown eyes, his smile full of very white teeth, and his ample belly created a resting place for his arms.

"Miss Hollis, I'm glad to meet you, although I don't know how much help I can be. My time with Cassandra wasn't favorable or even pleasant, for that matter."

"I read your interview with the police and your testimony at trial. I know her time here was before she met Jesus, but did you spend any time with her after that?" Roxy asked.

Mr. Baker flashed his teeth. "You know, I heard about her transformation and how God changed her, and to be honest, I wish I knew that Cassandra. As a believer myself, I know how God works within people, and from what I heard, she was no exception."

Roxy allowed the silence to hang in the air for a few beats as she studied the man. "Well, she isn't that woman anymore. I bet she's somewhere near where she used to be."

He nodded. "She spent a considerable amount of time in lockdown. She wouldn't let anyone in. None of the other girls could befriend her, and not a single staff member could get within arm's length." Hamilton stopped and shook his head. "I wish I could've done more for her. She probably feels like pain and injustice is all her life amounts to."

Roxy looked at him. "You think she's guilty, don't you?"

"I can't answer that. It's not my job, or even my business, to judge her for anything. All I can tell you is the girl I knew had more anger in her than she could contain."

Pointing to the windowsill, he asked, "Do you see those teeth marks?"

Roxy acknowledged.

"She did that the day she arrived because she was in handcuffs and couldn't use her arms. She crawled from about where you're sitting and ground her teeth into wood until we came back after finishing the intake paperwork with her caseworker. That's just the way she was back then—destructive in every way possible."

Roxy nodded her head. "What did you hear from Four Corners?"

The teeth again, like the frosting in an Oreo cookie. "That's where the magic happened—well, not magic, but God. I heard she found Christ and had an exemplary transformation. I never saw her, though, except in the courtroom. When I looked at her, I saw something in her eyes different from when I knew her. She had a light that wasn't there before."

Hamilton put his head down for a few beats. When his eyes met Roxy's, she thought he might cry. "I hated to talk about her past, but it was all true. I couldn't interject anything about her change because I wasn't involved in her life at that time, and saying what I heard wasn't allowed because of some silly law."

"It's hearsay," Roxy interjected.

Roxy really didn't want to ask this question, but she had to. "Although you didn't know her after she experienced salvation, do you think she really could have killed three people?"

Hamilton stared at his desk for what felt like an hour. "The girl I knew was more than capable of killing someone, but the woman I heard stories about and saw in the courtroom? No, I don't believe she could've. As believers, we have a keen sense of the spirit in people, and Cassie's was visible to me. I can't be certain, but that detective really had it out for her."

Roxy sat up. "Do you mean Detective Kenton?"

Hamilton nodded. "Yep, that's the one. He was aggressive with me when I tried telling him that many of our residents are hostile. He wouldn't have any part of me saying anything like that. He only wanted to know the bad things. He made some comment like if I didn't tell him everything she did, she may walk free, and he couldn't have that. He also asked me for names of residents she had beef with. When I gave him two names, he slammed his hand on the table and said he needed more than two. So, I gave him all the females who lived there when she did."

"Did you ever tell anyone how he treated you?" Roxy asked.

"Yeah, I told the prosecutor, and he blew it off, saying he'd talk to him, but that was just how he was. Oh, by the way, I'm surprised he got Amanda Hilltop to testify against Cassie. I heard that after Cassie's change, she found Amanda and apologized for her treatment of her, and they were friends for a while. Amanda went down a different path with drugs and prostitution. The girls were still on good terms from what I heard, which was why I was surprised when I learned she testified against her."

Roxy thought a moment. "Did she have a criminal history?"

"Amanda? Yeah, she was in and out of jail. In fact, she was released from jail a few days after testifying against Cassie."

Roxy wrote everything down, thanked Hamilton for his time, and ran to her car. She grabbed her phone and called Seth.

"Seth, please. It's Roxy," she told the receptionist.

"Hey, beautiful," Seth said.

Cutting him off, she said, "I need you to look up Amanda Hilltop for a plea deal she may have taken close to Cassie's trial. I was just with Hamilton Baker, and he said that Amanda was released from jail a few days after testifying. He also said she was in-and-out of jail for drugs and prostitution. This is the first I'm hearing about this. I know it wasn't in the documents I went through; I would've remembered. This could be a Brady violation."

"Okay, okay, slow down. Hang on," Seth said, putting the phone down.

Roxy heard typing and scrolling before he said, "I found it! She did get a deal. She had two felonies dropped and her sentence commuted on the one she was serving time for during Cassie's trial. Here's the bomb shell—she testified on a Tuesday and walked out of prison on Thursday."

Overcome with excitement, Roxy said, "Seth, this wasn't disclosed to the defense; ergo, we have a Brady violation. Hamilton said after Cassie found Christ, she sought out Amanda and made amends, which led to them becoming friends until Amanda strayed, but he still thought they were on good terms. I'm going to shift some things around and interview her this week. All right, I still have field work to do. Can you do dinner this evening?"

"Yep, I can. Just come over after you're done, and I'll cook."

"Okay, I'll see you then. Love you," she said, before realizing what just flew out of her mouth. Without thinking, she ended the call, not giving him time to respond.

She stared at the phone in her hand. *Stupid, stupid. Why did I just say that? I don't love him. I have love for him. Now I really screwed up.*

***

The jurors Roxy interviewed provided nothing. They all believed in her guilt and didn't regret convicting her. The panel struggled more with sentencing her to death than convicting her.

With a few hours left in the afternoon, Roxy decided to go home, pick up Amanda's file, check the validity of her address, and give it a go. Little did Amanda know that she could be the first appealable discovery in Cassie's case. Because the state didn't disclose this information, which was exculpatory in nature, they violated Cassie's constitutional rights.

Walking up to the small home, Roxy noticed a child's tricycle and a slide in the front yard. A lean, cleanly-dressed man answered the door. "Can I help you?"

Handing him a business card, Roxy said, "Hi, my name is Roxanne Hollis, and I'm a private investigator. Does Amanda Hilltop live here?"

"Amanda Coach now, but yes, she does. Please come in. I'm Robert, Amanda's husband."

Robert led Roxy into the living room where she saw a green-eyed little girl running around, the swooshing echoing from her diaper. "Can I get you something to drink?" Robert asked.

Shaking her head, she said, "Oh, no, thank you."

Roxy sat on the oversized-leather couch and waited for Amanda. Looking around, Roxy noticed the walls of the living room where packed full of framed photos. There were a few family photos but mostly pictures of Amanda's daughter in a variety of scenes, from professional pictures to everyday things little ones do.

"We're crazy about her," Amanda said, entering the room and pointing to the pictures Roxy was looking at. "What can I do for you?"

Amanda's appearance wasn't what Roxy had in mind. She appeared healthy with long brown hair, a clear complexion, and dull green eyes.

"Well, I was hoping I could talk to you about Cassie." Roxy explained.

At the mention of her name, Roxy noticed a pang of regret flash over Amanda's face. "What about her?"

"She was your friend, right? Well, after she tormented you— didn't you two make amends?" Roxy asked.

Amanda sat on the couch across from Roxy. "Yes, we were friends. She was good to me. She'd pick me up, take me to church with her, and teach me about the Bible. Even after I started using drugs, she'd search me out to bring me food and clean clothes."

"So, what happened?"

"What do you mean, what happened?"

"What made you testify against her?"

Amanda stared at Roxy, her eyes welling up with alligator tears.

"I was in a bind with charges pending, and after several meetings, the prosecutor and Detective Kenton offered me a deal."

Roxy allowed the silence and held her eye contact.

"At first, I refused to talk about what she did in the past because we had moved on. Detective Kenton wouldn't leave me alone, and after the third or fourth visit, he threatened me. He said he'd make it his life's mission to ensure I spent the rest of my days in prison if I didn't cooperate. I was terrified of him."

Amanda fiddled with her fingers.

"He made me a good deal and said it would be a fresh start, a clean slate, and a way to change the direction of my life. I fell for it and signed the deal. I never realized she'd get the death penalty. I can't believe I'm even talking to you. What will he do if he finds out I told you? He can't do anything to me, can he?"

Roxy didn't miss a beat.

"By all appearances, your life is together and on the up-and-up, so there's nothing he can do. It's been too long for anything in the past to stick. You don't have to worry about me telling anyone outside of my team. Did you tell anyone that he threatened you?"

She shook her head, biting her bottom lip.

"No. He was too smart for that. He knew nobody would believe me. I was a junkie and a whore. He was a cop."

Amanda shook her head. "He made me rehearse what I was going to say so many times, I could've testified in my sleep. He had the law behind him, and I had nothing but the prospect of a twelve-by-twelve cell. I was facing at least twenty years. I look at my life and I could've missed all this. I have a good life. I'm sober, happily married, and I have my daughter."

Roxy stared at her, mulling over her words. "So, did Cassie's attorney ever contact you?"

"Nope. Not a single word. Even when I testified, he never brought up anything. I saw Cassie writing notes to him and trying to get his attention." Amanda proffered this detail.

"There's a way to make this right."

"I didn't lie. I don't know what I could do, and what about Kenton? What if he finds out?"

"You're right; you didn't lie, but you omitted the truth, which, in this situation, was just as bad. Unless there was something in the plea deal about you speaking out in the future, which there rarely is, then he can't touch you. If he harasses you, I can help."

"Can I have a few days to think on this? I need to talk to my husband. She didn't do it, and I know that, but I have to think about my future and my family," Amanda said, standing up, indicating the interview was over.

"Okay. There's no pressure," Roxy said, putting her notebook back in her briefcase and standing up. She handed her another business card. "Contact me anytime, day or night, and we'll go from there. Thank you for your honesty, despite your fear."

Roxy sat in her car for several minutes, wanting to celebrate like she just hit pay dirt, but she'd be premature. Whether Amanda would facilitate bringing the corruption to the surface was another story.

Realizing how late it was, Roxy hurried home to get ready for dinner at Seth's. Then the memory came back to her like a flood.

I told him I loved him. How could I forget about letting that slip? I'll just explain that I was caught up in the moment, or better yet, I'll act like the whole thing slipped my mind and just play it off. That'll work out better than attempting to cover the words up.

She showered and slipped into a sweater and jeans before leaving.

When I get there, I'll tell him about my day, and hopefully the subject won't come up once we get caught up in the case, she thought, pulling into the parking garage of Seth's condo building.

Seth opened the door and stood inside with an enormous smile.

"You look wonderful."

"Thanks. I'm famished."

"The bandanna was put in the mail today. Kenton actually called Sam and told him after dropping the package off at FedEx," Seth said, leading the way to the kitchen.

"Did he by chance send a picture of the package or any visuals of the packing process?" Roxy asked, with sarcasm.

"Come on now, that's too much to ask," Seth said, chuckling. "And besides, what'd be the difficulty in that for us?"

"Of course not, but I gotta give it to the dear sheriff—at least he called. Do we know when the package will arrive?"

Filling Roxy's plate, Seth said, "Should arrive tomorrow or the following day, and they opted for delivery confirmation, too."

Laughing, she said, "Well, it's a miracle they took any precautionary measures whatsoever."

Once they sat down at the small table with plates of sautéed vegetables, baked chicken, and pasta, Roxy told Seth about her day, after he had blessed the meal.

"I had a lengthy interview with Amanda this afternoon. I didn't get anywhere with the jurors I found, and since I had the time, I decided to go for it. She was surprisingly forthcoming but didn't agree to help, yet."

After taking several bites, Roxy continued. "Get this, Kenton actually threatened her. She didn't want to testify against Cassie, but Kenton persisted in his pursuit. When she wouldn't budge, he threatened her with a long prison sentence. He told her she'd spend the rest of her life in prison if he had anything to do with it. Even today, she's terrified of what he could do to her, especially now that he's the sheriff."

"He can't do anything," Seth said, putting down his fork. "I hope you told her we'd protect her. He has no legal ground. It's been too long. Plus, he didn't put some iron-clad clause of secrecy in the deal; I already read it."

Nodding her head, Roxy said, "I know. I think she'll help us, but she needs time. She's still in fear of him all these years later. Oh, and Booker—It's no wonder he switched to probate because he was a lousy defense attorney. He provided nothing helpful but did give me a single file folder that he said contains his documents pertaining to the case. A single folder, Seth. It's honestly as thick as a traffic ticket file."

"Are we going to talk about the case all evening?" Seth asked, cutting a piece of chicken.

"No. We don't have to. Do you have something on your mind?"

Instantly she thought, *Please no! Please don't ask about the phone call.* She looked at him, awaiting his answer.

"Did I hear you correctly on the phone earlier, Rox? Do you feel that way?"

Knowing her face turned a paint-swatch of red, she answered. "Seth, I care deeply for you and I do love you, but not in that way, yet. We're just beginning, and I'm all in, believe me, but my feelings haven't grown to that level." She studied him as she spoke, watching for any amount of pain or disappointment on his face.

"Thank you for being honest with me. I had to ask one way or another, but I was determined not to be offended if that was your answer. You'll get there one day; I'm certain of that."

"Something else I wanted to talk to you about," Seth said. "We need to have a plan B in case the bandanna falls through."

"Okay, we're back on work now," Roxy responded, smiling. "I agree. Have you and Sam established a plan already?"

"Not exactly. I mean, we know we'll need newly discovered evidence of innocence, and if that isn't the bandanna, that burden falls on your shoulders, mostly. So far, we're doing well, particularly with today's breakthrough, if she decides to help us, but we need to have our ducks in order. We really don't know what's on the bandanna, if anything, and we can't put all of our eggs in one basket."

"I know that. Amanda's only one piece of the pie, but, Seth, there's something here, and it has to do with the sheriff. I don't know why I feel so strongly about that, but I do. From what I can tell, he knows what he's doing. It's our job to outsmart him in some way. Nobody can cover duplicity this long. Maybe he's afraid of what's to come, and that's why he's throwing such a fit about everything."

"Sam told me that Kenton is chummy with many judges and prosecutors in the area. I'm sure he's already putting feelers out to some of them. Minimally, this could tarnish his legacy and ruin his ego. That alone will make a man do crazy things."

"I know. He won't be the first power-hungry, egotistical man in my path. If he did everything correctly, he has nothing to worry about, but if he didn't, he should be sweating bullets, no pun intended," Roxy said.

CHAPTER 9

BEFORE THE SUN ROSE, Roxy drove to Mountain View. She'd certainly speak with Cassie about Amanda but didn't want to get her hopes up about the bandanna just yet.

After the guard released Cassie's handcuffs, she sat down with her arms crossed in front of her.

"Patricia told me you came to see her and took my journals."

Roxy nodded. "Has anyone told you how talented you are? Your writing is wonderful, and your artwork is breathtaking. I did read them, but I didn't expect them to provide evidentiary value. I wanted them, so I could know you better. Now, I feel like I've watched you grow up."

"All of that is down the tube now that I'm here. Who cares how I grew up or changed because at the end of the day, it no longer matters. I'm a convicted murderer—number 66435 to the Texas Department of Corrections."

"I'm sure that way of thinking is easier to live with in here, but that's not the woman I watched come alive in your journals."

"Right. Well, look how good Romans 8:28 worked out for me," Cassie said.

Roxy said, "Can you tell me about your friendship with Amanda Hilltop?"

Cassie's eyes hardened. "She betrayed me. I was always there for her, even going as far as looking for her on the streets to offer provisions. A lot of good that did because at the first opportunity, she threw me to the wolves."

"Detective Kenton threatened her with a lengthy prison sentence. He instructed her not to say anything helpful about you, but to focus on the negative things. She regrets it but admits she would've missed her life if she didn't testify the way she did."

With contention on her face, Cassie said, "Good for her."

"I talked to her, and she might help. I mean, maybe her voicing the truth will shed light on other things."

Cassie only shook her head, so Roxy changed the subject. "Anyone in the neighborhood that the Blackwells had an issue with?"

Cassie thought for a minute. "There was a family on Peachtree—which was the street behind the Blackwells—that had parties quite often. Always a lot of traffic, although we weren't certain the traffic came from that family. They had a daughter close to Faith's age, but Mrs. Blackwell wouldn't allow Faith to play with the child. Other than that, the neighborhood stayed quiet."

"Could anyone scale the wall at the perimeter of the neighborhood without notice?"

"I don't know if anyone ever has, but someone with upper body strength could easily climb over it."

"So, it's not out of the realm to believe someone ascended the wall, entered the home, shot the family, jumped back over the wall, and left before you got back?"

"Absolutely. That wouldn't be hard at all, especially for a man. The wall wasn't far from the house, either."

"Detective Kenton didn't get the security tapes in time, so we have nothing to view to make that case, but it's good to know. Amanda should get back with me in a few days to tell me if she'll sign an affidavit."

Roxy changed her tone to lighten the mood. "I have to know, what made you pick Mr. Booker?"

Cassie rolled her eyes. "His reputation from a few other inmates in county. That man did zilch for me. I suggested things to him constantly during my trial to no avail."

"Well, if it's any consolation, he changed his area of practice, which seems like a good move. He didn't offer much either. He said he spent hours with you in county?" Roxy asked.

"Yeah, he did, but more to convince me to plead insanity or whatever. He asked about my past more than anything. I guess he thought he could use that to my benefit."

"This is really none of my business, but how much did you pay him to hold the seat next to you?"

"Almost thirty-thousand when it was over. Cleaned me out, plus took some from Patricia."

Roxy shook her head. Criminal defense work pays, but the sad state of many defense attorneys mirrors the lousy work done in Cassie's case. Attorneys clean their clients out financially, do the bare minimum, and claim they worked tirelessly. Although not all defense attorneys were that way, too many of them were. Attorneys like Jake Bergance in *A Time to Kill* were few and far between.

***

The next few days went by in a flurry of paperwork and notes. Roxy spent little time in the field but managed to accomplish interviewing the rest of the jurors who would talk to her, which again provided nothing noteworthy.

From the office, she heard the phone ringing in the kitchen and took off in a sprint.

"Sam, are you there?" She asked, clicking on her phone at the last second.

"Yes, Roxy. Can you come by the office? We need to talk."

"Yeah. Is everything alright?"

"We'll talk when you get here, just come as soon as you can."

Roxy clicked the phone off and her head began to whirl.

What on earth? What if something is wrong with Seth?

Roxy put on the first pair of shoes she saw and left the house in yoga pants and a t-shirt. Racing to the office, she parked, ran inside, bypassed the receptionist, and went straight to Seth's office. Seeing him unharmed, she ran to him, threw her arms around his neck, and kissed him.

"I'm so glad you're all right," Roxy said, breathless.

"It's not about me. Let's go to the conference room," Seth said, taking her by the hand.

Roxy saw Sam sitting at the table with his head propped on one hand, staring at a piece of paper. Noticing Roxy, he stood up. "Rox, come in and sit down."

"All right, Sam, what's going on? You look like someone died."

Sam rubbed the length of his forehead. "The lab called today. The package they received was severely compromised in transit. The bandanna is no longer viable for testing."

That struck Roxy like a physical blow. The breath within her was completely knocked out. She couldn't form a comprehensible thought or even utter a word. She just stared at Sam as if she were waiting for him to say, "Just kidding."

She looked around the room for a camera crew to jump out and say, "You got punked," but Sam didn't speak, and, aside from Seth, nobody else was in the room. This really happened, and somehow, she saw it coming.

"He did this, Sam. You know he did because he's afraid of what was on that bandanna. Kenton purposefully packaged the bandanna improperly and probably even failed to label the box correctly to alert the handlers that there was evidence in the package. I knew this was going to happen." Her elbows landed on her thighs, and she put her head in her hands. "What are we going to do now?"

Seth squeezed her shoulder.

"We'll move to plan B. You still have witnesses to interview. We're not out of the game yet, but now we work harder. Our somewhat easy route is shut down. We're left with the road less traveled," Sam answered.

"I can't be here right now," Roxy said, getting up to leave. "I need some time to think."

Seth followed her out. "Roxy, we'll figure something out."

Roxy whirled around and yelled, "I can't lose again. I can't." She couldn't stop the flood of tears running down her cheeks.

"I know. This will work out," Seth said, in futile attempt to comfort her.

"Oh, yeah, and what if it doesn't? I need to go. I'll call you later." Roxy said, and opened her car door.

"No, no, no!" She screamed, hitting her steering wheel with the palms of her hands.

On the drive home, the inside of the car was painfully silent. Her thoughts went from rage to sadness to recognizable defeat.

What are you trying to do, Father? Are you giving me a clue that I'm done in this profession? Why is this happening?

Pulling into her garage, she noticed what looked like something written on her driveway. After parking, she stepped out of the car and walked to the words, and a gasp escaped her throat before horror hit.

In large white letters, the message read, "Stay away. Bow out."

Frantically digging in her purse for her phone, she called Seth.

"Someone's been here, Seth. I need you," she said, a quiet cry followed her words.

"I'm coming."

Roxy scanned her surroundings. there were no cars parked on the street, and nothing looked disturbed around her house. The only conclusion was Kenton. He tampered with the package and now threatened her to stay away from the case. She heard tires screeching and looked up to see Seth turning the corner.

"Are you alright, Rox?" Seth said, exiting his car at the curb.

"I'm fine, but look," she said, pointing to the message.

"That son of a—" Seth said, through clinched teeth. "I'll handle him. He won't get away with this."

"Seth, don't. Just let it go. I refuse to give him the satisfaction of putting me in a panic."

"Well, you can't stay here alone. I'll sleep on the couch, or you can stay with me," Seth said, putting his arm around her.

"I can't be away from my office. I have work to do and need my files. I really don't think he'll try to hurt me," Roxy said.

"We can't take any chances with this guy. He made sure the bandanna would be compromised in route to the lab and now this. He's desperate to keep the truth covered up."

"Okay. You can stay here. My couch folds out into a bed, so at least you'll be comfortable while you're in bodyguard mode," Roxy said, winking at him and jabbing his side playfully. "I bet he's already gotten to Amanda. He'll intimidate her again, and she won't talk."

"This just proves how afraid he is of what we're doing. He must be covering up something massive, like career-ending big, or he wouldn't risk getting caught. Yeah, you won't be left alone, even if it means going to the field with you until you uncover whatever is causing his fear."

"All right, let's call Sam. We can't exactly tell the police on Kenton," Roxy said.

Seth went inside first to check every room but found nothing to suggest anyone was inside.

Roxy felt uneasy and couldn't help but wonder how far Kenton would go to stop her.

With Seth in bed, Roxy shuffled socked feet down the hallway to her office. Now that Kenton had declared war, she had to step up her game to contend with the small-town sheriff. She stared at her whiteboard, reviewing the progress and contemplating her next move while noting who was left to interview. Kenton had managed to burrow himself into her bone marrow, nestling deeper with each layer she peeled back, taunting and gnawing.

CHAPTER 10

ROXY WOKE UP THE NEXT MORNING with a fierce resolve. Crawling out of bed, she smelled bacon—wait a minute, bacon? Roxy grabbed her robe and proceeded down the hallway to find Seth looking like a professional chef in her kitchen.

"Good morning, beautiful," he said, sliding a cup of coffee to her on the counter. "Sit down. Let's eat, and plan our day."

"Be careful, Seth. This is something I could get used to. Waking up to a handsome man in my kitchen and breakfast cooked. I never knew you were so domestic," Roxy said, taking a seat at her breakfast bar.

"Anything for my girl. Just think, this is what the future looks like, but I'll never have to go home. You'll be where my heart calls home."

"Getting ahead of yourself a bit, don't you think?"

"Nope, not even a little bit. You see, God and I have this all worked out, and you're the only one who has to catch up."

"Well, then, I suppose the boat's out of the harbor, and I'm still standing on the dock."

"You're driving the boat, Roxy," Seth said, eyeing her.

Over breakfast, Roxy said, "On the agenda today is Cassie's caseworker, Suzanna Parker, a phone interview with Michelle Crocker, whom Cassie first worked for as a nanny; hopefully, she'll provide contact information for her twins. They're twenty-eight now. They were six when Cassie looked after them, so they may not remember anything, but it's worth a try. If we have time after that, I wanna attempt Holly Franklin, which was Cassie's roommate at Treetop. She didn't have anything good to say, and she testified against her at trial, but with the latest intel from Amanda, there's potential for her."

"A full day's work. I figured we'd hit it hard after yesterday. Are you going to reach out to Amanda today or give her more time?"

"I don't want to overwhelm her, especially if Kenton already paid her a visit. I'll reach out early next week, but for now, my focus is finding the truth. We have nothing for physical evidence." Roxy drained her coffee.

"Oh, I still need to find neighbors the police didn't interview," Roxy said, washing her plate off in the sink before loading it in the dishwasher. "I'm going to get dressed and get my files together. We can leave in twenty minutes."

Seth walked over to her. "Keeping today completely professional is a challenge we've yet to embark on. Are you up to the task?"

She walked away from him, down the hall, and turned her head. "I won't have a problem with that. You know me: when I'm in the field, it's all business. My mission is imperative right now," she said and turned into her bedroom, laughing.

Taking Seth's car, they drove to the county's child protective services office to meet with Suzanna Parker, who was now the county director. As Roxy was entering the building, the strong odor of musk hit her. After she told the receptionist she was there, she sat next to Seth in an uncomfortable-hardback chair.

"Roxy," a grey-headed, slightly plump woman called from the door leading to the personnel area.

Seth and Roxy stood to greet her and followed her through the cubical farm to her office.

Suzanna had a spacious office with comfortable furnishings and a back wall of windows. Her certificates, awards, and college degree hung on the wall behind her massive-mahogany desk.

Pulling a notebook and pen out of her briefcase, Roxy said, "Thank you for meeting with us. This is Seth Carmichael, an attorney on my team." Roxy tilted her head toward Seth. "As I mentioned on the phone, I figured you more than anyone else could tell us the most about Cassie's adolescence in custody."

Suzanna acknowledged Seth and moved her chair forward, folding her hands together, almost in a position of prayer.

"Her case stays with me because the ending wasn't like most others. Cassie lived half her childhood bouncing from one place to another, suffering abuse at the hands of foster families. I wasn't the original worker who removed her from her mom, but I stayed with her the last six years. Naturally, Cassie's problems with trust kept a barrier between us for several years, until she realized I wasn't against her. After she let me in, we forged a pretty good friendship, though not without setbacks. I'd make progress with her, but then something would happen at a placement, and she'd blame me, which caused us to start from square one. I understood her logic because I took her to new placements."

Roxy watched the woman making gestures with her hands as she spoke. She could tell by her tender words that she cared for Cassie.

"What about her dark side?" Roxy asked, adding, "We can't be caught off guard when we take this case back to court, so we need to know as much as you can remember. I have the trial transcripts recounting the instances with Hamilton Baker, Amanda Hilltop, and Holly Franklin."

"Cassie had severe bipolar disorder and PTSD, which only added to her distress. She never treated me the way she did others. In fact, the times she was mad at me, I got the silent treatment. Her peers and those in positions of authority were a different story. She didn't like people telling her what to do or getting in her way for that matter."

Suzanna stopped for a moment. "In her first foster home, she attacked the biological child, putting her in the hospital. After that, we placed her in homes without children. Sometime later, we discovered that Cassie was forced to live in the closet without food for several days at a time. Cassie admitted to attacking the girl because the parents treated her normally, while Cassie lived like an inmate. She had two foster homes after that, before her six months of sexual abuse. The two families elected to remove her because of her reluctance to participate in anything or follow rules."

Suzanna paused and took a drink of water.

"The easiest way to explain Cassie back then, in a comprehensive manner, is to compare her to a jaguar. Jaguars prefer to be alone for fear of competition against other members of their own species. Cassie was very much that way, especially with those closer to her age. The older she got, the worse this mentality progressed. At Treehouse, she lashed out at anyone who got too close to her, which made her roommate a prime target. The facility finally ended up rooming her alone because she assaulted every roommate she had. When her behavior could no longer be controlled in that level of a facility, we transferred her to Four Corners, which is the closest thing to prison without serving time. Four Corners is reserved for children with severe mental or behavioral problems. Sometimes the program is successful, like in Cassie's case, and other times it fails. Cassie graduated the program a completely different person, and I mean a through-and-through transformation. I'd never seen one of my kiddos change so much, and to tell you the truth, I haven't had another experience like it."

Suzanna stopped and bowed her head.

"When I discharged Cassie on her eighteenth birthday, I knew she'd make it. She wouldn't be a statistic. She'd be the girl who'd change the world someday. I truly believed that."

Her eyes welled up. "We stayed in touch the first few years, but the time got away from me, and before I realized it, I heard the report about her on the news. I didn't accept it at first, but after a Google search, I found it was true. There it was in black and white, screaming at me through the screen, accused of triple homicide. Cassandra Lovejoy, my golden kiddo. It's still difficult to swallow. I had kids I knew would end up in prison at one point or another, but Cassie wasn't one of them." She shook her head. "I can't see her committing murder, Miss Hollis; even at her worst, she wasn't capable of killing anyone."

"Were you ever contacted by Greg Booker?" Roxy asked.

"The only person I heard from was a jerk of an investigator with the police department out there, but never anyone from Cassie's team. That detective who handled her case had it out for her. When I went to the station, he slammed his hand on the table every time my answer wasn't what he wanted to hear. He finally cut me off and kicked me out."

Seth and Roxy exchanged a look before Seth said, "We've heard that more than once about Detective Kenton, who, by the way, is now the sheriff. That tactic is apparently something he used on everyone. Perhaps he'd benefit from anger management or something."

Roxy chuckled and said to Suzanna, "Is there anything else you can think of that might help us?"

"Only that she couldn't have done this to anyone, much less people she loved. Because she never really had a family, when acceptance did come, she poured herself into whoever they were. I know she did a wonderful job with those twins she watched because they loved her. I just hope you're able to get justice for the family and for Cassie."

Getting into Seth's car, Roxy said, "Can we use the conference room at the firm to call Michelle? That way we'll have plenty of space, and the office phone is better quality."

"I was going to suggest that but didn't know if we were staying in the field until later this afternoon or not," Seth replied.

Walking into the conference room, Roxy pulled the phone closer to the chairs she and Seth selected and sat down. Pulling out everything she needed, she dialed the number.

"Michelle?" Roxy asked when a woman answered.

"Yes, is this Roxy?"

"Yes, ma'am. Thank you for taking my call. I also have my partner Seth Carmichael in the room. He's an attorney working on the case."

"Okay. What can I do for you? I don't know what else I can provide other than what I told the police, but I'll do my best."

"The difficult part about investigating old cases is ascertaining the validity of the material in the files. We have no real way to establish whether we received the entire case file without talking to everyone again", Roxy said and went headlong into her questioning. "I understand Cassandra worked for you for four years, correct?"

"Yes, she did, and I hated to lose her when we moved, but I couldn't convince her to come along with us."

"She was that good of a nanny that you asked her to move with you?"

"Oh, I begged her—pleaded, really. Everything short of hitting my knees in front of her. She was stellar, top of the line, and I haven't had a nanny as good as her since. Luckily, my boys are grown, and I don't have that worry anymore."

"Did she ever become aggressive in any way?" Roxy asked.

"Never, and if she had, I would've fired her. My boys adored her and cried for weeks after we moved because they missed her. She went beyond what I asked of her. My boys learned more about scripture and Jesus than I could ever teach them."

Dumbfounded, Roxy choked out, "So, there was never anything negative or out of line about her performance?"

"Nope. That's why the whole case boggled my mind. I could never wrap my head around the theory that Cassie killed an entire family. The Cassie I knew would never have done anything like that. Would you like to talk to my boys? I have them here just in case they could help in anyway. They were young, but they remember her. I'd like Timmy to go first, but before I hand the phone over, you do know he's autistic, right?"

"Uh, no, I didn't know."

"No need to worry. He's high-functioning and brilliant. What makes his feelings for Cassie remarkable is individuals with autism typically don't engage or form relationships with others. He bonded with Cassie and took to her as if she were me."

"Okay. Thanks for telling me," Roxy answered, glancing at Seth with compassion on her face.

As the phone switched hands, Roxy heard Michelle say, "Timmy, why don't you go first, honey. This is the sweet lady I told you about who is trying to help Cassie."

"Okay, Mom," Roxy heard Timmy answer meekly before he took the phone.

"Hello, Roxanne," Timmy said.

"Hi, Timmy. I'm so glad I get to talk to you. How are you?" Roxy inquired.

"I'm well, ma'am. How are you?"

"Doing fine, thank you. I wanted to talk to you about Cassie. I hear you two were pretty close."

"She was such a wonderful person. She always made me feel so much love and care. She was more than just a nanny; she was my friend. She read the most fascinating stories to us from the Bible. My favorite book is still Daniel. She'd always tell us something new every time we read it. Did you know that Isaiah prophesied about King Cyrus years before he ever set the Jewish people free?"

"I did know that. I love the book of Daniel, too," Roxy said.

"Cassie also taught us about the 483 years in chapter nine. This blew my mind, but over the years, I learned even more. Do you have time for me to share this with you?"

Roxy looked at Seth and shrugged her shoulders. "I'm always open to learning about Scripture."

"Okay. First, it's important to know that the Hebrew word for week is seven, so in some translations, the verses in Daniel nine will refer to seventy weeks, but it's really saying seventy sevens. Also, the

Jewish calendar year is based on a 360-day lunar year, which makes the 483-year period in Daniel equal 173,880 days." He paused. "Are you following so far?"

"I think so," Roxy said.

"Okay. Between reviewing commentaries and watching videos, I learned that the 483-year clock started ticking when the order to restore and rebuild Jerusalem was issued. This is found in Nehemiah 2, which notes the time as the month of Nisan, in the twentieth month of King Artaxerxes, which was March 5, 444 B.C."

"Are you ready for this?" Timmy asked.

Roxy held her pen ready after already noting a few things. "My pen's ready."

"Here's the mind-blowing part; 173,880 days after March 5, 444 B.C. was Nisan 10 or March 30, A.D. 33. That was the day of Jesus's triumphal entry, penned in Luke nineteen. You know, when Jesus publicly proclaimed Himself Messiah, riding down the Mount of Olives into Jerusalem, and finally, the temple. His disciples praised God joyfully, saying, 'The King who comes in the name of the Lord is the blessed One. Peace in heaven and glory in the highest heaven.' The final seven years is saved for the seven-year tribulation. Isn't that remarkable? I mean really, how phenomenal is God's timing? And some say He doesn't exist," Timmy said.

Roxy starred at Seth across the table, her jaw gaping. She shook her head and mouthed, "What do I say to that?"

Seth shrugged his shoulders, a smile lifting the corners of his mouth.

"Here I thought I knew my Bible well, Timmy. That's amazing. I took notes to study myself."

"I could tell you more, but I know that's not why you called. Back to Cassie—she altered my life. I've never known anyone as compassionate, loving, and unique as her, other than my mother, of course. She was my best friend, which may sound peculiar, but at that age, I was astute beyond my years, making it easy for me to participate in intelligent dialogue with people older than me. We'd spend hours talking about God, life, and history. I don't think I'd be the man I am today without from her devotion to us. Is there anything I can offer you specifically that might guide you in helping her?"

"Was there ever a time that her behavior frightened you or made you uncomfortable?"

"Never. Even in the beginning, when I'd normally pull away from people and go into a shell of sorts. She studied how to approach me in a way that made the transition exceptionally easy. I could tell early on that she was well-intentioned with no ill motives. I'm good at reading people and can tell if someone means well, because my emotions are sensitive and my senses heightened. I never felt off about her or around her; in fact, my feelings were precisely the contrary. My mother said it took me months to get over our move and her absence in our lives."

Roxy could sense his sincerity and love for Cassie. She couldn't help but hurt for the once young and heartbroken boy. "Thank you so much, Timmy. You've helped more than you know."

"Will you be able to save her before she dies, Roxanne?"

With great effort to choke back the lump forming in her throat, Roxy said, "I hope so, Timmy."

Tommy took the phone and offered his greeting with a deep and matured voice. "Hello, Miss Hollis. I don't think I can provide much more than Timmy did. I agree with everything he said, and I'm not even half as smart as he is with biblical discernment."

"He taught me something I didn't know, so I have to agree with you, sir, but I appreciate your insight."

"Cassie is dear to me and I hate what's happened to her. Frankly, there's no way she killed anyone. If she loved that family the way she did ours, she'd have died to protect them from harm. Her heart was pure gold. She's one of those people you look at and think, I want to be just like that. I want to love like her, live like her, and keep her close. I hope you're an answered prayer. We've prayed for her all these years and perhaps, at the eleventh hour, God's working a miracle that'll glorify Him on a greater scale."

"Thank you, Tommy. I appreciate your time. Would the three of you be willing to sign an affidavit and testify if needed?"

"We'll do whatever we can to help Cassie, Miss Hollis. You know how to get ahold of us."

Roxy ended the call and sat back in the chair.

"Whoa, that was intense. I know the boys were young, but their recall is incredible. I think they're invaluable evidence toward her character."

"You're right, but this isn't newly discovered evidence of innocence. The family is solid for character references, but nothing more. At best, they establish Cassie's ability to love beyond most people," Seth said, shaking his head.

Roxy put her head down. "This isn't going to end well, is it?"

"Don't do that to yourself. We aren't out of the fight yet; there's still time," Seth said, planting his hand on the top of her head.

Roxy heard the door open and looked up to see Sam, his face a blotchy mess. His fingers clutched a piece of paper.

"Sam, what is it?" Roxy asked, standing up.

"Roxy," Sam said, through deep sobs. "We were right, honey."

Roxy took the paper. Her eyes scanned the text, and her throat threatened to close, the anger rising first and quickly piggybacked by deafening sorrow.

"He's innocent now," Roxy managed to get out before she crumbled, landing on the hardwood floor, her knees clanking like bricks on contact.

Seth took the paper and saw that CODIS, the national FBI DNA database, had notified Sam regarding the DNA match on the knife used to stab Raleigh's girlfriend. As the three of them knew, it wasn't Raleigh's but that of a man recently arrested for rape in Arlington.

Sam wiped his face and grabbed Roxy's arm pulling her up.

"There's more. Brison Gale confessed to killing Keren after raping her. He knew about Raleigh and his execution but said he never felt bad about letting him take the fall. He agreed to a plea deal including Keren's murder, coupled with his more recent rape."

Roxy could only stare at him with her lips clenched to maintain control of her emotions. Rebecca's face entered her mind.

"We have to tell Rebecca and Cliff," Roxy said.

Sam put his arm around her. "We'll go together. We're a team, and this isn't something we'll do alone. Let me call Heather and tell her I'll be late for dinner."

Sam left the conference room, and Seth sat, pulling Roxy on his lap. She slid into the acquainted throbbing of Raleigh's death. She closed her eyes, her tears landing on Seth's pale green button-down shirt. Before fully losing it, she stood, wiped her cheeks, and excused herself to freshen up before leaving.

In the bathroom, she pulled her phone out and called Cliff, knowing she'd fall apart if she dialed Rebecca.

"Hey, Roxy," Cliff said.

"Hey, Cliff. Are you guys home?"

"I'm getting off work now. I'll be home in about thirty minutes."

"Sam, Seth, and I wanted to come by. Is that all right?"

"How exciting. The five of us haven't been together since—well you know."

Roxy closed her eyes. "We'll be there soon."

She stepped in front of the sink, placed her hands on the edge of the marble countertop, and stared at her reflection.

Get yourself together, girl. Come on. This is an answered prayer. Stand up straight, she told herself, turning on the water to wash her face. After drying off, she decided against reapplying more mascara because it was fruitless with the tear shedding ahead of her.

CHAPTER 11

ROXY WATCHED THE WORLD passing by the front-seat window in Sam's Tahoe. How would she say it? This was supposed to happen before the needle, prior to him speaking that defining sentence to her, and before he entered heaven's gates. Nevertheless, for whatever reason, God wanted it this way, and knowing that pulled Roxy out of her self-pity.

Once the house came into view, Roxy saw familiar rocking chairs and a pitcher of tea with five glasses situated on the wicker table.

"Are you ready for this, Roxy?" Seth asked.

"No, but let me tell her. I need to be the one to say it. Where's the document, Sam?"

With the Tahoe parked, Sam pulled his briefcase from behind the seat, opened it on his lap, and grabbed a manila folder. She took the file in her hands and thought, for such a weightless file, the contents could've been earth-shattering at the right time. Now this feather-light file would cause instant pain but, at some point, relief.

Roxy took a deep breath when she stepped out of the car. With Sam and Seth on either side of her, she walked toward the porch. Roxy heard the screen door open and saw Rebecca and Cliff walking out to meet them. Rebecca's full-face smile went slack when she saw them. Roxy tried to maintain a decent facial expression but failed the minute she locked eyes with Rebecca.

"Honey, what's the matter?" Rebecca asked, stopped in place.

"Let's sit down," Roxy said, leading Rebecca to the middle rocking chair. Roxy sat on one side of her with Cliff on the other. Seth, and Sam sat across the table.

"Rebecca, I don't know how to say this," Roxy said, sucking in a breath, "but we received a CODIS hit on the knife today."

Rebecca put her hands over her face and wept, rocking back and forth. Cliff reached for the file, opened it, and studied the contents.

"So, this proves he didn't kill Keren, right?" Cliff asked, looking at Sam with tear-rimmed eyes.

"Yes, it does. We'll file a bill of innocence for Raleigh next week, but we still need the rest of the documents," Sam answered.

Rebecca's head shot up. "What other documents, Sam? What's he talking about?" She asked, turning to Roxy.

"The man's name is Brison Gale, and he confessed to the murder in a plea deal. He only had a rape to contend with, but once his DNA was discovered on the knife, he struck a deal. We have to wait on that paperwork to add to the bill," Roxy said.

"Why didn't this come sooner? What good will this do now? He's already gone. What are we supposed to do?" Rebecca asked, as quickly as an assault rifle.

As the inevitable tears came, Roxy said, "We can clear his name, and that's what we'll do. We'll also exonerate him and have peace with the world knowing he's innocent."

As silence hung in the air, a black Dodge Charger came up the driveway.

"Who's that, Momma?" Cliff asked.

"I'm not sure, honey," Rebecca said, watching the door open.

A torrent of horror washed over Roxy when the car door opened. Natalie got out of the front seat, but Roxy saw something different on her face. The anger usually a fixture on Natalie's face wasn't there. In its place, her eyes were red, and her face was every bit as grief-stricken as theirs. Seth stood up, taking his place in front of Roxy, his eyes glued to Natalie. Seconds later, a small boy, probably eight or nine, got out of the backseat and took Natalie's hand.

The moment Rebecca saw the child, she stood and gasped. They watched Rebecca run down the porch steps. Natalie stilled and hung her head.

"Miss Jacobson, this is your grandson, Martin Raleigh Hope."

Rebecca fell to her knees in front of the boy. "Oh, my sweet Jesus, I knew You had a reason behind all this, and now You've made it known to me."

Roxy calmed, afraid to move as Cliff walked over to Natalie. He embraced her, and the two stood, weeping. Roxy glanced at Seth and noticed tears streaming down his cheeks. Sam had his handkerchief to his face, wiping tears and blowing his nose. With a simple nod toward the Tahoe, the trio got up and walked away from the newfound family.

Before reaching the vehicle, Natalie ran to Roxy. "Roxy," Natalie yelled.

When Natalie reached Roxy, she grabbed her shoulders with both hands and stared into Roxy's eyes. "Can you forgive me?"

Roxy let out a quick sob. "I already have."

Natalie looked at Roxy, confusion causing her eyes to dart back and forth between her and Seth, who stood close enough to pull Roxy away if need be.

"But how can you say you already forgave me after everything I've put you through?"

A smile spread Roxy's cheeks. "Jesus told me to. He's forgiven me many times over, and it's my honor to forgive as He forgave me."

Natalie smiled and opened her arms. The women hugged, sobs shaking their bodies before they parted.

***

Rebecca's mind whirled with the sight of Martin sitting across from her. "He has Raleigh's eyes," she said.

Several minutes passed since Natalie brought the boy to her, and her mind hadn't caught up with her heart. The minute she laid eyes on him, she knew he was her grandson, without question. She saw so much of Raleigh in Martin. First, Roxy tells her that Raleigh was finally cleared, although it's a year late, and now she has a grandson—a grandson, a piece of Raleigh here to enjoy life with.

"Tell me about yourself, Martin," Rebecca said, sitting up and offering the boy a slight grin. "I have what, nine years to catch up on?"

In a quiet voice, the bright-eyed boy said, "I'm almost ten; my birthday's next week. I'm in fifth grade, and I play football. I live with my aunt."

Natalie spoke up. "Martin came to us nine months before Keren died. Raleigh never knew about him, for whatever reason. I honored my sister's wishes and felt obligated to do so, until we found out about Raleigh earlier today. I couldn't let him miss another minute of a family who'd love him the way we do. So, the only thing I knew to do was bring him here and hope you'd forgive me."

Natalie paused to compose herself. "I never knew how burdened I'd feel until I learned the truth. I figured at the very least you can tell Martin about his father, but if you're willing, I'd like both of you," she said, glancing up toward Rebecca and Cliff, "to become active in his life. My mother isn't doing so well and it's hard on me juggling school, work, and taking care of him."

Rebecca covered her mouth for a moment. "Honey, whatever you need from us, we'll do. You know, when we lost Raleigh, we knew he was innocent but couldn't fathom why he was taken in this way. Today, I know why and feel like I can move on from my grief to embrace what's next."

She turned to Martin. "Young man, your father is dancing in heaven. I know this is a lot for you, but would you like to see some pictures of your daddy?"

A full tooth smile broke out on Martin's face, and with his hand reaching for Rebecca's, the two went inside.

CHAPTER 12

"I DON'T KNOW THE IMPLICATIONS of all this, but you still don't need to be alone," Sam said, glancing back and forth from Roxy to the road.

"I haven't thought about that because I'm still in disbelief over what just happened. Raleigh has a son! And did you see him? He's a 'mini me'," Roxy said.

"It's surreal. The logical response is God knew what He was doing. What better outcome, other than the obvious, could've happened than what just took place?" Sam asked.

From the backseat, Seth answered, "Nothing really. Rebecca has a piece of her son and Cliff his brother. I hope Natalie will allow them to be involved in Martin's life. I wonder if Raleigh knew."

"He didn't know. Martin's last name is Hope, not Jacobson. Raleigh would've insisted on him carrying his last name, and the fact that it's not tells me he didn't know," Roxy said.

"Okay, Miss Investigator. I didn't think of that," Seth said.

"That's why you pay me the big bucks."

Turning to Sam, Roxy said, "On a serious note, when can we file the bill of innocence?"

"We'll start working on it this week, Rox. I want that bill as much as you, but like everything else in the justice system, it takes time. You know the wheels of justice move slowly."

***

Roxy couldn't put the day's events out of her head long enough to throw dinner together, nor did she have an appetite. The state of Texas had executed another innocent man, which brought the total to a staggering fifteen people, that they knew of. The United States didn't have just a wrongful conviction epidemic but also the—unspoken—wrongful executions, especially in Texas. How can 'we the people' not bat an eye at their state killing innocent people?

A lump gathered in her throat so thick she felt like she needed to clear something from her esophagus. Raleigh was innocent, and although she had known that long ago, the world would now know.

She closed her eyes and saw Raleigh in the cherrywood casket. Friends from Rebecca's church, a handful of Raleigh's family members, Sam, Seth, and Roxy occupied the first few rows of the small chapel. The brown pews, white carpet, and cream-colored walls, the smell of flowers and death in the air. She remembered lacking the ability to look at Rebecca, so, for most of the service, she had stared at the lectern. Rebecca had requested the pastor to read from Psalm 23, and while she knew the passage from memory, the first four verses broke her composure.

> "The Lord is my Shepherd
> There is nothing I lack
> He lets me lie down in green pastures
> He leads me beside quiet waters
> He renews my life
> He leads me along the right paths
>   for His name's sake
> Even when I go through the darkest valley,
>   I fear no danger
> For You are with me, Your rod and Your staff –
>   they comfort me."

Roxy collapsed into Seth, her sorrow uncontained. Seth pulled her to her feet and walked her to the lobby, hoping for privacy. His tears landed on her shoulders, splashing with microscopic ripples of pain as he held her close, whispering prayers in her ear.

At the graveside, a gospel choir sang 'It is well with my soul' as they lowered his casket into the ground. Roxy assembled under the tent, stone-faced, refusing to break until she got home. As the brokenhearted mother grieved the unjust death of her son, Roxy patted her back, taking deep breaths to stomach her own pain. After everyone left, except Seth, she sat in the same chair observing the mound of dirt.

"What are you thinking about, Rox? You've been wiping the same spot on the counter for like five minutes," Seth said, coming in the kitchen.

"I was calculating how many innocent people the state of Texas has executed. I think he makes fifteen, but I could be wrong."

"That's close, if not spot on. Remember the case of Cameron Willingham, convicted of killing his three children in a house fire?"

"How could I forget about him? I remember the protests of his execution in February, and the investigator shredded the old findings less than a year later."

"Is your memory even human? How can you remember the month of his execution? Wasn't it like a decade ago?"

"It was 2004, actually," she said, smiling.

***

Before dawn Roxy was sitting on floor in her office, piles of folders scattered around her, looking through each document. Unbidden thoughts from the previous day wrecked her mind.

"What're you doing?" Seth asked, popping his head in the doorway.

"You scared the crap out of me, Seth. I couldn't sleep, so I figured God had a reason. I'm going over the files again. I feel like something's missing, but I don't know what."

Roxy stretched and reached for the next stack of files. "There were several neighbors Kenton never interviewed, which are still on my list. I'm getting close to the wall again, and I'm worried our options are dwindling."

"I wouldn't say that. Kenton's clearly nervous, otherwise he wouldn't be bothering you. You're close. I need to go by the office for a bit to help write the bill for Raleigh. You're staying home today, right?"

"Yeah. You know, I feel like a kid again with the constant watchful eye of you and Sam, but, yes, I'm staying home, buried under this mountain of paperwork."

Seth walked across the room, bent over, placed a kiss on the top of her head, and said, "I love you, Roxanne Hollis."

Roxy smiled and shook her head. *That man.*

She heard the front door close and his car start and back out of the driveway and realized she was alone for the first time since the message on her driveway.

She flipped through each page of the neighbor's files. She remembered the family Cassie had mentioned and located the file with the enlarged aerial photo of the neighborhood. After stretching it out, she found Peachtree Street and noted the addresses. Without names, she'd conduct a reverse search and find the information, which shouldn't be difficult.

She powered up her computer and navigated to the database used to track down witnesses. Keying in the two addresses, she found two names; Philip and Kate Nichols; and Chris and Megan Stars. To her delight, the Nichols family still lived in the same house, which meant she had a way into the neighborhood.

She jotted down the phone number of the Nichols family and the new addresses for the Stars family. With a jolt of excitement, she found her phone and called the Nichols residence, holding her breath while it rang.

"Hello, Nichols residence," said a shaky female voice.

"Hello, is this Kate Nichols?" Roxy inquired in the sweetest voice she could muster.

"Yes, dear. Who's calling, please?"

"Hi. My name is Roxanne Hollis, and I'm a private investigator. I'm working on the Blackwell case. Are you familiar with that case, ma'am?"

"Paul, Sarah, and sweet Faith. Yes, I knew them. What do you mean you're working on the case?"

"I work for a firm that considers questionable cases. May I come by and visit with you and your husband sometime?"

"Sure, darling. When can you come?"

"Well, what's best for you and your husband? I can work my schedule around that."

"I don't think we have anything to do today. Phillip's in the garden right now, but he shouldn't be much longer. Can you come this afternoon?"

"Yes, I can," Roxy said, trying to contain her excitement at the access to the neighborhood. "Will you tell the guard to expect me?"

"I'll call him. Tell me your name again and what vehicle you'll be in."

"It's Roxanne Hollis, and I'll either be in a black Honda or a silver BMW with my partner Seth Carmichael. If it's all right that I bring him along."

"Sure thing; we'll expect you later today."

Without missing a beat, she called Seth.

"Hey, honey. Miss me already?"

"Well, yes, but that's not why I'm calling. We can finally get into the neighborhood."

"Seriously? Wait, what'd you do?"

"I set an interview with the Nichols family, who still lives behind the Blackwell home. Mrs. Nichols said she knew the family and agreed to meet with us, which includes telling the guard to allow us in," Roxy said, squealing. "We're in, Seth. Can you come with me, or I can go alone?"

"Oh, no, you don't. I'm coming with you. When's the interview?"

"Later this afternoon. I was thinking about leaving here at one thirty or so. Will that work?"

"Yeah, that gives us several hours."

"Perfect. Okay. And, Seth, I have a deep regard for you, too," Roxy said, and hung up the phone without giving him a chance to respond.

Announcing his homecoming hours later, Seth walked in Roxy's front door, saying, "Honey, I'm home."

Roxy laughed. "How original. I'm almost ready."

"Are you decent?" Seth asked at the beginning of the hall.

"Yeah, I'm in the office."

She heard his big feet hitting the floor in his dress shoes and then saw him standing in the doorway. She lost her breath looking up at him from her spot in the middle of the floor.

"You're too handsome, Seth Carmichael."

"You're pretty easy on the eyes yourself."

"I want to park on the Blackwells street and walk from the house to the perimeter, timing how long it takes."

"The timing's a great idea. Surely, it's not too far from the house, right?"

"On the map, it looks like it's a few hundred yards, but I could be way off."

"Let's go and see for ourselves. You ready?"

"Yep. Let me get my files and my briefcase."

After they showed their IDs, the guard opened the security gate and allowed them in.

"Drive slow, Seth. There," Roxy said, pointing to the left. "That's the street. Park here, and let's get out."

Roxy took her time scanning the houses on both sides of the street. She looked at the trees and what they would block if someone climbed the wall. She noted the windows on the houses and their potential views of the Blackwell house. The whole time, her phone was clicking with photos for her to dissect later.

The wall was about two football fields from the Blackwell house, but in the dark, if the shooter stayed close to the trees, his path to the house was a straight shot. The brick wall that surrounded the neighborhood was about three and a half feet tall by her estimates.

"Are you seeing what I'm seeing?" Roxy asked.

"Probably not. My investigative skills aren't what they used to be," Seth said, elbowing Roxy.

"Look at how easy the path would be, especially in the dark, with the trees for cover. I imagine he ran and ducked behind trees to ensure nobody saw him."

"I see what you mean with all these trees, but were they this big fifteen years ago? I don't know much about forestry, do you?"

"Not a clue, but even if they were a few feet shorter, they'd still be enough cover, I think," she said, taking pictures of the trees to find out what kind they were later.

She surveyed the streetlights and wondered how bright they were on the street corners. If they were like most lights, more for curb appeal than for actual lighting, that helped the shooter even more. The lights were typical—tall, black towers, a cover, and a light at the top. If she guessed, the light only beamed out about ten to fifteen feet at the most, and there was one on each corner but none down the street. The lights were six to eight feet taller than the small black street signs with white letters.

"Only two street lights," Roxy said, pointing up the street. "You'd think, in a neighborhood with security gates, there'd be more lights on the streets."

"Once again, I never would've thought of that."

"You're an attorney, Seth. You don't go door-to-door or have the task of looking at a murder scene fifteen years later, while trying to imagine every detail you can think of."

Roxy patted his arm. "Moving on, there's no sidewalk, which means if a guy was walking down the street that night, nobody would be too alarmed, because where else would he be walking? He could've appeared to be on an evening stroll if he decided to play it that way."

"You keep saying he. Are you convinced the killer was a man, or is that just automatic?"

"Well, no, I guess you're right. I shouldn't assume it was a male, but I'd bet on it," Roxy said, walking back to the car.

They pulled further down the Blackwells street, parked and got back out.

"Seth, use the stopwatch on your phone and time me."

Roxy took off and ran to the brick wall and back three times, asking Seth to hit the lap button each time she reached the Blackwell's home.

"Roughly sixty-three seconds," Seth said, facing the phone toward Roxy.

"Okay. Now, the Blackwell house. Look at the gate—I wonder if it's the same." Roxy studied the home. The side of the house driveway and garage were adjacent to the gate, meaning it was easy enough to assume the killer ran up the driveway and straight into the backyard. "I remember from the crime scene photos that the back door is right around the corner from the gate. The bandanna was dropped right inside the gate."

Roxy eye-balled the path from her position at the end of the driveway to the gate. *It really was a straight shot.*

Ten minutes later, and after several trips through the same few streets, Seth said, "Someone's going to think we're casing the place. We better stop and head to the Nichols' house before Kenton shows up."

A burst of laughter escaped, Roxy said, "Oh! Would he love to catch us doing something wrong or, at the very least, slow us down! He probably wouldn't be too happy to learn that we're in the neighborhood."

Seth parked on the curb, and after gathering up what they needed, they walked to the door. Roxy stood staring at the beautiful home with its light brick, bright red shutters, and matching red front door. The yard was pristine, with shaped shrubs lining the house. There were four windows on each side of the front door on both levels. She imagined the view from the upstairs window provided another angle to the neighborhood because of the elevation of the house.

A petite, elderly woman answered the door, wearing khaki pants and a red-collared shirt. Roxy noticed her frail hands and well-put together face.

"Come in, dear," Mrs. Nichols said, opening the door wide enough for them to walk inside.

"Thank you so much for having us, Mrs. Nichols. This is my partner, Seth," Roxy said, motioning in Seth's direction.

"Nice to meet you, ma'am," Seth said, taking her hand.

"Would you like to sit in the sunroom?"

"That'd be wonderful. Is your husband done in the garden?" Roxy asked, following Mrs. Nichols down a narrow, white-walled hallway.

"He's finished and by now is done making the lemonade. He'll meet us in the sunroom."

Moments later, Roxy, Seth, and the Nichols were seated in black wicker chairs in the large, breezy sunroom, sipping iced lemonade from glass tumblers.

"What is it exactly that you're trying to accomplish here, Miss Hollis?" Mr. Nichols asked in a deep, twanging voice. He'd crossed his arms over his bulging belly, which was covered with a red shirt that, by all appearances, could burst at any moment.

"We're reinvestigating the case just to ensure the state convicted the right person before her execution. I understand that you weren't interviewed," Roxy said, poising her pen over the legal pad propped on her knee.

"Well, no, that's not right. I went to the police station to tell my story," Mrs. Nichols said.

Roxy's heartbeat increased. "What do you mean? Did they not listen?"

"Oh, they did, dear, but they didn't believe me because I never heard back from them."

"Do you remember who you spoke to, Mrs. Nichols? I need a name."

"Of course, I do. It was our dear sheriff. Well, he wasn't sheriff then."

Roxy looked up from her pad, after writing Kenton and underlining it a dozen times, to meet Seth's intense gaze.

Kenton, again. Why does everything lead to him?

"Okay. What was your interview about?"

"Before I tell you, will you come with me?" Mrs. Nichols requested, standing up. "I want you to see something first. What I'm about to say will make more sense."

Seth and Roxy followed Mrs. Nichols out of the sunroom, through the dining room, and out the back door. Standing on the porch, Mrs. Nichols pointed her finger, "Look that way. I can see the Blackwells backyard, if I stand close to my house."

Roxy peered down, following Mrs. Nichols' direction, and looked to where her finger pointed. Although, from where she was, she had to stand on her tiptoes to see over the fence, she did have a direct line of sight to the backdoor of the stone-faced house. Seth looked over at her and nodded, seeing much better than she did with his height.

"At first, I was unsure of what happened, but I heard a loud scream when I was in the sunroom and came out here to listen. I didn't hear anything else until I saw the Blackwells' backdoor fly open, and a man darted out and ran up the street toward the front of the neighborhood. He lost whatever it was that covered his face. He paused, turned around to come back for it, but I guess he changed his mind because he turned back around and ran for the exit."

With her left arm holding her legal pad, Roxy took copious notes, using shorthand to write everything down, while listening to Mrs. Nichols' account.

"I was slightly alarmed, but I went back inside and didn't think much of it until I heard the news report the next morning. I called the police department the next few days but never heard back. When I saw the news that they had arrested that sweet woman who worked for the Blackwells, I made Philip drive me to the police station. I finally got the detective to hear me out."

"Do you remember if he took notes or recorded your interview?" Roxy asked, looking up from her pad.

"He did. He had a small pad that he pulled from his front shirt pocket." She patted the left side of her chest.

"He asked me what felt like a hundred questions. I stayed with him for over an hour. When he dismissed me, I asked him if they were going to let the nanny go. He looked at me and said, "No, why would I do a thing like that?" I said, "Well, because of everything I just told you" and he said, "Ma'am, how good is your eyesight?"" She shook her head. "I was so mad I stormed out."

"Let's go back in, dear," Mrs. Nichols said.

Before following Mrs. Nichols and Seth back to the sunroom, Roxy stood closer to the house and looked down at the backdoor of the Blackwell home. She was shocked at the ease with which she could see the door and the street from this vantage point.

Roxy reclaimed her seat. "Was there any lighting at all, whether in your yard or the Blackwells?"

"When the man ran out the door, the motion light that hung on their patio triggered and the yard lit up like a helicopter's spotlight. Believe me, dear, I could see well enough to know it was a man and not the nanny."

Roxy nodded. "I'm not doubting you, but how did you know it was a man?"

"Men are built differently and often carry themselves unlike women. This man was massive." She held her arm up over her head. "Towering and bulky. It was roughly fifty feet from where I stood to the man running from the home, but with the motion lights, I had a good visual."

"Did you see Cassie come back from the grocery store?"

"No, I didn't, but I did hear some screaming. I was already in my pajamas and didn't go back outside; however, I learned later that it was the nanny outside."

"Did you ever hear from a Greg Booker? He was Cassie's defense attorney."

"I sure didn't, but I'm guessing he never knew about what I saw; in fact, I bet nobody outside of Philip and the sheriff knew."

"Did you know the neighbors on either side of you?" Roxy asked.

"Not really. They were both much younger than us, but we did have to call the police on the neighbor across the street," she said, pointing toward the front of her home. "But thankfully, they moved a few weeks after the murders."

Roxy thought back to Cassie saying there was a family with crazy parties and a daughter around the same age as Faith.

"Do you remember their names?"

"The Biggs family," Mrs. Nichols answered.

"Mr. Nichols, did you see anything?" Seth asked.

"No. I didn't go outside with her, and when she came back inside to inform me, it was too late because he was already out of sight."

"I have to ask," Roxy said. "Why didn't you call the police after you saw the man?"

"I did," Mrs. Nichols said. "They said they'd send an officer out."

Roxy nodded, adding a note to check the 911 records.

"Mrs. Nichols, would you be willing to sign an affidavit with everything you just told us?" Seth said. "This could help Miss Lovejoy."

"I certainly will, and I want you to add that I talked to the sheriff. That man should've listened to me. I just hope it's not too late. I had no idea someone else was working on her case, otherwise I would've contacted you."

Seth nodded. "We'll type up everything you just told us, verbatim. When you read it, if there's something you want to add or change, we'll make the corrections before you sign it," Seth explained. "We can have the affidavit ready in a few days and bring it by. Roxy's a notary, so we can handle that as well."

"Will you call before you come, please?"

"Yes," Roxy said, closing her briefcase before standing up. "We'll let you enjoy the rest of your day. Thanks so much for your help, it's invaluable."

Back in Seth's car, Roxy said, "Are you kidding me? Did that just happen? Can you believe Kenton withheld this from the defense—heck, that he kept this from everyone? No wonder he's fighting us so hard—this is career-ending huge."

"That's a glaring Brady violation, and he could face criminal charges as a result, or at least be reprimanded. Of course, that won't look good for the county sheriff. The question is, can we prove her story?" Seth said.

"Seth, I saw the back door. So did you. Why would she make up something like that? To me, she's a credible witness, and I think Kenton knew that, which is reason enough for him to be nervous. I wonder what he did with his notes."

"As smart as he is, he probably trashed or shredded them. If he spoke to her in an interview room, he would've deliberately ensured the recorder wasn't on, which shows motive of malice intent to suppress evidence. Having that tidbit of knowledge goes a long way in court."

"After talking with Mrs. Nichols, I know Kenton wrecked our opportunity to test the bandanna because he knows the killer isn't Cassie."

She looked out the car window. "All the pieces are falling together, and Kenton's at the center of everything. The frustrating thing is we still lack enough reasonable doubt to prove her innocence. Her story's a great start, but it doesn't meet the necessary burden," Roxy said. "What're we missing, Seth?"

"We're getting closer. What about those other two neighbors and Jackie Sparse?"

"The Stars family moved three years after the murders to just a few miles from here. The Biggs family moved across town a few weeks later, according to Misses Nichols. I want to save Jackie for the end, but the court doesn't value a snitch recanting their testimony at the last minute. We'll need more than her caving to prove Cassie's innocence."

Diverting the subject, Roxy asked, "Are you going back to the office to finish the bill?"

"Sam should be finished with it by now. We figured you'd want to file it yourself. We'll send it electronically, but for good measure, you can take a hard copy to the court clerk."

With a new light in her eyes, Roxy turned to Seth. "You know me so well. I'd love nothing more than taking a hard copy down. Rebecca will sue the state for wrongful death, too, right?"

"We wanted to give her some time to process everything. We also need the bill before we file suit, but Sam and I agreed to handle it pro bono. We decided that's the least we can do, considering we couldn't save Raleigh."

Roxy's heart swelled. "That's great, Seth, really. A suit like that won't be cheap, and eating the cost is noble. I'm proud of you guys."

"It's the right thing to do. We couldn't carry a clean conscience any other way. I'll take you back to your car, and you can follow me to the office to pick up the bill. Plus, we need to get your notes from the interview and prepare the affidavit."

CHAPTER 13

PULLING INTO THE PARKING GARAGE of the county courthouse, Roxy's pulse picked up. She had no real reason to be nervous. The tensions probably came from potentially having to face anyone of her many adversaries with this paper in her hand.

After going through security, she walked up the marble steps, running her fingers across the smooth white wall, to the main floor of the courthouse. She wasn't dressed for this whatsoever—her hair in a bun and wearing jeans, a fitted T, and flats—but that didn't matter. Her outer appearance couldn't touch what this would provide for her heart. Of course, the wheels of justice move like muddy pond water, but this would set off a crescendo of events.

With her head high, one arm at her side and the other clutching the folder, she opened the glass doors to the court clerk's office. She found the section of the long countertop she needed and waited, not drawing attention to herself.

The court clerk's office was large with several individual desks in the center of the room. Nothing remarkable, other than the potential of each piece of paper shuffled between hands. Indictments, protective orders, payment for fines, divorce degrees, marriage licenses, arrest warrants, lawsuits, and criminal complaints all traveled through this room. The patrons were in various points of life when they entered the glass doors. The stories the women occupying those desks must have.

"Can I help you, ma'am?" A woman with a heart-shaped face and piercing blue eyes said, shaking Roxy out of her wondering.

"Yes. I'd like to file this for Rollins and Carmichael, please."

"All right, what's the filing?"

Clearing her throat, Roxy pulled the thick packet from her file and laid it on the desk in front of her.

"It's a bill of innocence."

With sudden excitement, the woman said, "Oh, I've never seen one of these before."

Roxy answered in a firm but somewhat elevated voice, "Well, it's not a happy occasion when the state of Texas executes an innocent man. Perhaps that's why you've never filed one before." Roxy could feel every eye turn toward her, but she didn't care.

Behind her, a tall, lean man with chiseled cheeks entered the room.

"Roxanne Hollis," the unnamed man said. "I thought we should expect you here after the electronic filing my office just received."

Roxy whirled around and took his outstretched hand with a firm handshake, noticing his long eyelashes above hazel eyes.

"I'm Clark Benton, the newly elected District Attorney of Dallas County."

"Nice to meet you, sir." *What do you want with me,* she thought.

"Would you accompany me to my office once you're finished here?"

"She's done, sir," the clerk uttered. "Here's your file-stamped copy, hun." She handed Roxy back a copy of the bill with the clerk's seal on the front.

"Thank you," Roxy said, as she slipped the file into her open briefcase.

Following Mr. Benton into the hallway, Roxy said, "We can talk here, if you don't mind."

"Miss Hollis, believe it or not, I'm on your side. I wanted you to come with me and discuss this case, if you have the time. From what Mister Carmichael tells me, you're the expert."

Well, this is interesting. Roxy felt intense determination to plead Raleigh's case. "I have time. Lead the way."

They were silent on the elevator ride to the eighth floor.

Roxy's mind whirled. *Give him the benefit of the doubt. Who knows— he could be different.* She shook her head. *Yeah, right.*

"Roberta, hold my calls, please," Mr. Benton said to his secretary as they walked passed her desk and into his large office.

Roxy noticed the simplicity of the man's space. An ample blond desk and large black office chair. Behind his desk, a mural of Lady Justice, with the balanced scales on one hand and a blindfold over her eyes. A quote printed above her head read, "May justice be done even if the heavens fall." Two standalone white tufted-back chairs sat in front of the desk.

"Please have a seat. Can I have Roberta get you something to drink?" Mr. Benton asked, hanging his suit jacket on a coat rack in the corner. "I hope you don't mind me getting more comfortable. This is a casual meeting."

"No, thank you on the drink, and I don't mind; this is your meeting," Roxy responded, as she took her seat.

Mr. Benton brushed off his emerald dress shirt, ran a hand through his brown hair, and sat down.

"Well, Roxanne—oh, may I call you Roxanne?" With a perfunctory nod from her, he continued. "Tell me about the case of Keren Hope."

Roxy breathed in deep, telling herself to stick to facts and not add commentary.

"Keren was stabbed to death on March 1, 2005. A man walking his dog found her four days later. The man's story was that the dog found the machete first when he stopped to relieve himself. It wasn't until the dog persisted to go off the trail that the man saw Keren's fingertips, sticking out under some large branches thrown on top of her. Once the homicide detectives arrived on scene, they noticed a blood trail on the edge of the path that looked like someone had dipped the bottom of a mop in blood and whisked it across the pavement. What we figured out later was the blood was from the perp dragging Keren into the woods. With the time gap, the police found nothing after they canvassed the area."

"Okay, how did they get Raleigh?" Mr. Benton asked.

"Do you want my theory or where they went wrong?" Roxy asked, confused with where this was going.

"I haven't gone through the case file, and Mister Carmichael said you have the entire file memorized, so all of the above," he answered, appearing genuine in his hunt for information.

"Raleigh was Keren's long-time, on-again-off-again boyfriend. Naturally, the police work from the inside out as far as suspects go, so after ruling out her family, they moved onto Raleigh. His fingerprints were in her vehicle, which was reasonable, but not on the murder weapon. There was DNA on the knife, but it wasn't his, so the source of the DNA remained a mystery. They had one witness who thought a car that looked like Raleigh's was in the parking lot around nine p.m. "We can't excuse the lineup,"" she said, including dramatic air quotes. "The lineup was conducted by the investigating detective, with Raleigh smack in the middle, and the one witness, who hardly knew the color of the car, chose Raleigh. You may not know this, but recent studies in the wrongful conviction community suggest that lineups administered by the detective assigned to the case aren't free from bias or hints to the witness. Anyway, once the witness picked Raleigh from the lineup, he became their prime suspect. He had an alibi, but because it was his mother, the police dismissed it. Keren's family told the police about the couple's frequent fights, and it's my opinion that, after that, the police developed tunnel vision and built a case to fit their theory. Sometimes this occurs without fault because in the detective's mind, he's the favorable suspect and the community demands justice. There's no way to know in Raleigh's case."

"All right." Mr. Benton looked up from his legal pad, where he was feverishly taking notes. "What do we know as fact now?"

"The game changer is Brison Gale's full confession. His version of events is that he was intoxicated in the parking lot of Willingham Park. He said he watched Keren running around the pond in the middle of the park. He's a hunter and had binoculars, which he used to maintain a visual of her. After several laps around, he got out of his truck, wielding a machete, and attempted to rape her after forcing her into the woods on the backside of the pond. He managed to rip her shorts off, but she fought to keep him off her. He said after knocking her unconscious, he managed to get her nude but couldn't perform because of the alcohol—his words, not mine. Afterward, he killed her, stabbing her roughly twenty-seven times from what the medical examiner's report said, because he knew she could've identified him. He wore gloves during the attack and had on a long-sleeved shirt, which explains how she put up such a fight, but no DNA was found on her. He then dragged her body deeper into the woods, covered her with foliage, and left the scene, but forgot the machete. If he'd taken the knife, it would've been a perfect murder, but thankfully, he handled that knife so often that the gloves did him no good."

"Is all of that information in the petition?"

"Yes, sir, with the added legalese," Roxy said.

"Please, call me Clark, Roxanne. I want us to remain civil here."

She tried hard not to laugh. "That would be a first. Others in your position make the civil part difficult, but I'm willing to give it a try for Raleigh's sake."

"Thanks for your candor. I'll read over the petition and get a hearing scheduled as soon as I can. I don't want to delay matters any further. The point is that the state of Texas screwed up, and we can't put off accepting responsibility for our errors."

Roxy laughed. "I'm sorry, but the state has yet to admit fault in any exoneration. In this case, there's nothing anyone can do to correct this blunder because Raleigh's dead. This is more than wrongdoing; an innocent man was executed."

"I'm more cognizant of that than you know. My office won't challenge the bill and will expunge his record. I'm also willing to hold a press conference with you and your team after the hearing to apologize to Raleigh and Keren's family for this momentous injustice. I'm trying here," Clark responded, a look akin to desperation in his eyes.

Roxy had no more fight in her, and for whatever reason, she believed Clark. "Call the office with the hearing date, and we can coordinate the news conference at that time," she said, handing him her business card.

Before closing the door, Roxy turned to Clark. "Have you seen *To Kill a Mockingbird*?"

"Hasn't everyone?" He responded, a lopsided smile etching his face.

She smiled. "As Atticus Finch said, in the name of God, do your duty."

With that, Roxy closed the door.

CHAPTER 14

"I'M NOT CONVINCED WE CAN win this one," Seth said, leaned back behind the desk in his office. "Mrs. Nichols recalled, with remarkable clarity, I might add, that she saw a man, not Cassandra, running from the home that evening. She also said she told this information to Kenton, but he never followed up, nor did he disclose the interview to the defense. With that, we have two Brady violations, if Amanda comes through."

Seth leaned up, stretching his arms over his desk. "I'm worried for Roxy because I don't know if she can handle another loss."

Sam stayed quiet for a few beats, his fingers tapping his mustached chin. "Seth, we've had close calls like this before, and she still has witnesses to interview. Don't lose faith in her yet; she still has work to do."

"Who still has work to do?" Roxy asked, stepping into Seth's office without knocking.

"Hey, Rox, did you get the bill filed?" Seth asked.

"Here's the file-stamped copy," she said, tossing the documents on his desk. "Now, you didn't answer my question."

"We were just discussing what other possible angles we have in the case," Seth said.

"You're a terrible liar, Seth. Seriously, what's going on?"

"Roxy," Sam said, turning toward her, "we don't want to see you hurt, and with the track this case is on, we aren't sure we can win."

Roxy nodded. "We have two Brady violations—well, I hope so—and I still have witnesses to interview. This isn't over."

Roxy brushed the thought of a loss off and changed the subject.

"Onto better topics; I had an interesting conversation with Clark Benton while I was at the courthouse. For the first time in history – well, in my experience—the DA agreed to acknowledge culpability, not contest the bill, and expunge Raleigh's record. He'll call at some point to give us a date for the court hearing. Oh, and he wants to hold a press conference after the hearing to apologize."

Crickets. Not a single word in response. Roxy looked at Sam and Seth, waiting for some excitement or something.

"This is a good thing. We couldn't have asked for a better outcome."

"I know. I guess I'm shocked," Sam said. "Where was he sixteen months ago?"

"Exactly," Seth said. "Have you talked to Rebecca?"

"Not yet. We should wait to call her until we have a date for the hearing, don't you think?" Roxy suggested.

"Good point," Seth said. "What are you doing for the rest of the day?"

"I'm heading home, after stopping by Amanda's house to touch base."

"Please be careful. I'm staying here to finish up a few things, and I'll see you at your house."

Roxy had called Amanda three times over the last few days, leaving messages each time, but hadn't heard back from her. The radio silence frightened Roxy. She had the mounting fear that Kenton had harassed and silenced Amanda, and Roxy wouldn't be able to contend with whatever damage he'd done.

Roxy knocked on Amanda's front door after driving by the house twice and seeing movement inside. Finally, Mr. Couch stepped out on the porch and closed the door behind him.

"She doesn't want to help you, Miss Hollis. Please, leave her alone," he yelled.

"Did Kenton get to her because if he threatened her? If so, we can help," Roxy said. "She can't be prosecuted for anything because she didn't lie."

"Leave, please, or I'll be forced to call the police," Mr. Couch said, before leaving her alone on the porch.

The realization of Kenton's constant intervention in the case took the wind out of Roxy's sails. Whatever his reasoning was, it gnawed the edges of her mind without making sense. Mrs. Nichols' discovery had definitely shined a negative light on Kenton, but why was he persistently meddling in the case over that?

Back in the comfort of home, Roxy grabbed her Bible, situated herself among the oversized pillows, and searched God's word for comfort. Her fingers found the book of Ephesians, a small book full of invaluable gems. The specific declaration of chapter three jumped off the page and right into her soul.

> "I pray that He may grant you, according to the riches of His glory, to be strengthened with power in the inner man through His spirit and that the Messiah may dwell in your hearts through faith. I pray that you, being rooted and fully established in love, may be able to comprehend with all the saints what is the length and width, height and depth of God's love, and to know the Messiah's love that surpasses knowledge, so you may be filled with all the fullness of God."

Roxy flipped to Philippians, landing on a passage she knew so well, and allowed the words to seep freely into the frightened places in her heart.

"Don't worry about anything, but in everything, through prayer and petition with thanksgiving, let your requests be made known to God. And the peace of God, which surpasses every thought, will guard your hearts and minds in Christ Jesus."

"Father, I'm unaware of your plans for me, and I'm clueless as to the reasons behind these things, but one thing I'll never let go of is my trust in You. Nothing could make me question my faith or Your unwavering commitment to ensure my life gives You glory. Lavish me with wisdom, bestow my heart with discernment, and pilot my steps. Reveal truth to me, Father. Help me exonerate Cassie," she whispered. "Lord, I'm afraid."

"Are you alright, Roxy?" Seth asked, entering the room as if he had been standing at the doorway awaiting the conclusion of her prayer.

"How long have you been here? I didn't hear you come in."

"Not but a few minutes, Rox. Who are you afraid of? Talk to me." Seth crossed the room and sat next to her.

"Kenton. He got to Amanda. She wouldn't even talk to me, and her husband threatened to call the police if I didn't leave her alone. There's no other sensible reason to explain her actions. I know she wasn't on board to begin with, but now she won't even communicate with me. He's up to something, Seth, and I don't like this."

Seth put his hands on the top of his head, sprawling his arms to look like wings. "We have some resistance, but we can't quit. She's innocent, and I'm convinced now that Kenton knows that, too, which is why he's doing everything within his power to derail our work. Not to change the subject, but have you eaten? I grabbed some Mexican take-out?"

"Now that you mention it, I'm starving," Roxy admitted.

He stood and put his hand out to help her up. She wrapped her arms around him and laid her head on his chest. She breathed the scent of his cologne and felt butterflies flutter about her stomach. Roxy had to concede to herself that the more she spent time with

Seth, the more she felt for him. Dare she say that she loved him because she wasn't so sure anymore that she didn't.

"Clark called, and our court date is next Thursday at nine a.m. in Judge Grey's courtroom," Seth said, between bites of fajitas.

"Of course. I mean, why not in his court when there are a dozen other judges who could've signed the bill?" Roxy said.

In the past, Judge Grey had expressed his disdain for Roxy and her faith. Judge Grey had also presided over Raleigh's trial, which added to the consternation Roxy felt at facing off in his courtroom, again.

"Clark assured Sam and I both that he won't contest the order either. Although he's not excited about signing it, with the district attorney's submission, he has little choice in the matter. He also alerted the media and scheduled the press conference for the courthouse steps at nine thirty."

***

The day before the hearing, Roxy managed to get away alone and drove to the cemetery. She found Raleigh's resting place easily in the massive land of graves by the war memorial adjacent to his plot. Stepping from her vehicle, she held a bouquet of yellow roses at her side.

I haven't been here in so long, she thought, taking measured steps in the dew-filled grass.

She laid the roses atop his headstone and brushed off the dirt and grass clippings before sitting down. The silence in the cemetery was eerie. There wasn't a breath of wind. Roxy stared ahead, seeing flowers, balloons, and arrangements left on other graves. The peace in the air rested Roxy's pain, and she put her head down and closed her eyes.

When she opened her eyes, she stared at his name and shook her head as the inevitable tears trickled down her cheeks. Her gaze hung on the dash, representing the years of his life, and she wept.

"Oh, Raleigh, why couldn't this have come sooner?"

She chuckled. "I'm talking aloud as if you're right here. I'm losing my mind."

Almost like it was rehearsed, a flock of geese flew overhead, their honks causing Roxy to look up and see the new gravestone next to Raleigh's. The laugh that escaped her lips came from her toes and released a flood of emotion from her soul.

Whatever has been taken from us, we know will be restored in God's own time, the inscription read. *Well, how about that?* She thought.

When Roxy walked away from Raleigh's grave, she left her feelings of defeat and failure and her cloak of remorse there. Carrying that around the last year had exhausted her, but she'd carry it no longer. Healing comes in strange ways, and this must be God's time to restore what's been taken.

CHAPTER 15

JUDGE GREY'S COURTROOM was unremarkable with cherry pew seating for spectators and two matching tables for the prosecution and defense teams before the identically colored judge's bench. Roxy sat between Cliff and Rebecca with Martin, Natalie, and Sylvia, Keren's mother, on Rebecca's other side.

"All rise for the Honorable Judge Grey," the bailiff exclaimed, before the chamber door swung open and Judge Grey's plump frame ambled into the room.

"Court is now in session," Judge Grey said, his index finger pushing up rimless glasses, his voice deep and raspy. "We're here to dissolve State v. Jacobson. Mr. Benton, you may begin."

Clark rose, revealing a tailored black suit.

"Thank you, Your Honor. I'd actually like to give the floor to Mr. Rollins, if it pleases the court."

"Sure thing. Mr. Rollins, you have this court's attention."

Standing to his feet, manila file in hand, Sam stepped to the lectern in splendid fashion wearing a couturier blue suit and bright orange tie and handkerchief.

"Thank you, Judge. Today we're here in a futile attempt to right a deplorable injustice committed by the state of Texas. Raleigh Jacobson received his death sentence in this very courtroom over nine years ago. Seven years and some months later, that sentence was imposed, despite my team's relentless attempts to overturn his conviction. A few weeks ago, everyone else learned the truth that my colleagues and I already knew. Raleigh Jacobson is factually innocent in the murder of Keren Hope."

Stepping back from the microphone, Roxy knew Sam fought to maintain his professional bearing.

"I witnessed Raleigh's execution as did each person sitting behind the defense table, minus the child. For illustration's sake, Judge, I'd like to set my watch for 184 seconds, which is the length of time I counted, while I watched my client's chest rise and fall, until it stopped."

With the Judge's nod, Sam set his watch. "Let's go back to the execution chamber in our minds. The twelve-by-twelve square room with the gurney in the middle. Raleigh wore a crisp-white prison uniform, laying on white sheets, unnecessarily restrained with tan straps. The small microphone was removed from above his mouth where he gave his last words, with which he still maintained his innocence. The warden received the green light from both phones, which have direct lines to the governor and the attorney general and issued the death order. The first drug, five milligrams of sodium thiopental, poured into Raleigh's veins, making him unconscious in ten seconds. Second, one hundred milligrams of Pancuronium bromide entered an already unconscious Raleigh as a potent muscle relaxer. Last, the one hundred milliequivalents of potassium chloride, which stopped his heart. May we observe that span of time in Raleigh's memory."

Roxy bowed her head as the allotted time began and the quiet in the room hung like thick fog. Roxy felt Rebecca's body quaking beside her as she recounted Raleigh's last words.

"To my mother, I'm sorry you've gone through this and carried the burden all these years, but Momma, it's almost over. I love you, and I'll meet you at heaven's gate. Cliff, my brother and my dearest friend, take care of Mom. I love you, man. To Keren's family, I'm sorry for the loss you endured, but I was not the cause of that loss. I loved Keren, and I'd never hurt her. To my attorneys Seth and Sam, you guys fought the good fight, and I know you would've done anything to stop this. Thank you for the many hours you spent trying to right this grave wrong. I love you both, dearly. My sweet Roxy, continue your work, thank you for your dedication, and I love you. Always fight for veritas! I'm an innocent man seconds from execution by the state of Texas. Receive my spirit, Lord."

The words echoed as she looked down at her right wrist and saw the small tattoo with simple lettering of a single word: *veritas*. Every time she saw the ink, she remembered not only Raleigh but also her passion to unearth truth.

"Albeit dramatic, Your Honor," Sam said, acknowledging the end of the 184 seconds, "I couldn't think of a better illustration to mark the injustice than that. As members of the criminal justice system, we're perilous when we don't consider the consequences in our judgment of others. This case is unlike other exonerations because Raleigh is not sitting in this courtroom today, moments from attaining his freedom. Raleigh lays under six feet of dirt at Rest Haven Cemetery, and that's an error we're unable to fix or justify. We cannot provide restitution for the many years of wrongful incarceration because the state murdered an innocent man."

"Watch yourself, Counselor," an irritated Judge Grey said.

Clark stood. "Judge, what Mr. Rollins is saying is the truth, and he's right. It's incumbent of us not to just deliberate the truth but to pursue it, discover it, and live by it. To begin that expedition, I'd like to grant Raleigh's bill of innocence, and to further illustrate our efforts, I move to expunge his record."

Roxy swore she saw the judge roll his eyes before he slammed his gavel.

"Very well, Clark," Judge Grey said, and left the bench after signing the order.

Roxy left the group to put herself together before the cameras would broadcast her face. After washing her tearstained cheeks, Roxy reapplied mascara and lip gloss.

Gathering with Seth and Sam, the three shared a look that said more than words could. They'd done it. Though late, they'd exonerated another client.

"Roxy," Clark said, walking toward her. "I'd like to give you the floor after my speech. I think you've earned this."

Me? Roxy thought. "Yes, I'd love to speak. Thank you."

"It's not about me. This is for Mr. Jacobson," he said, leading them out to the front steps of the courthouse.

Roxy gulped at the sight of the media trucks covering the street. The podium had so many mics taped to it she feared it'd fall over. She glanced over at Seth who nodded at her as if to say, "You can do this."

They allowed Clark to step in front of them toward the multitude of mics, and he cleared his throat.

"Thank you for coming. My name is Clark Benton, and I'm the District Attorney of this great county. One of my goals here is to right wrongs, as well as make our cities and towns safer. The first remains more difficult than I thought; however, today, my office is taking one step in the right direction. About thirty minutes ago, we declared Raleigh Jacobson innocent. He was convicted of murdering his girlfriend nine years ago and executed by the state of Texas sixteen months ago."

Audible gasps sounded in the crowd, but Clark carried on. "The state of Texas, along with my office, would like to extend our deepest condolences to Keren's family and to Raleigh's for this egregious mistake. I accept full responsibility for the death of Raleigh and will do whatever I can to help these families heal."

Clark turned to face toward Natalie, Sylvia, and Martin. "Please accept our apology, and may your daughter, mother, and sister finally rest after the long-awaited truth surfaced." Turning the other direction to address Cliff and Rebecca, he blinked. "Mrs. Jacobson, there's little I can do to express my sorrow at what happened. I rehearsed these lines to get it right, but meeting your eyes is more difficult than I prepared myself for. I cannot bring Raleigh back, but I vow to you that I'll put forth every effort to ensure this never happens again."

Clark bowed his head, stepped back, and relinquished the platform to Roxy.

With as much professionalism as she could assemble, Roxy clutched each side of the podium, smiled her best smile, and over a flurry of hidden emotions, she addressed the crowd.

"My name is Roxanne Hollis, and I'm a private investigator. Two years ago, I began working on Raleigh's case. Early on in my examination of the evidence, it became clear that Raleigh didn't murder Keren Hope."

Scanning the many faces in a sea of focused eyes staring back at her, she mused the gasps and inaudible responses. "In an already flawed justice system, the task of proving innocence is more difficult than many know. Shouldering the burden of exonerating an individual serving life in prison is one thing, but death row adds a more complex layer to the already arduous assignment. My team and I labored for months to free Raleigh; however, we failed, though not for lack of every effort known in this line of work. All that aside, today justice is here, and Raleigh is exonerated. His memory is restored, and the closure we needed can begin. We are grateful to Mr. Benton for his quick support and rendering the bill of innocence. Please allow the families to have some privacy during this difficult time. Thank you!"

Reporters shouted questions as Roxy turned around to join Sam and Seth for a victorious embrace. "Roxanne, is it true you're working on another case?" A woman with a microphone shoved in her face. "Will the family sue the state for wrongful death?" Another reporter asked. Seth walked around Sam and stood behind Roxy as a buffer between her and the media.

"Don't worry, Rox. I'm right here," Seth said, closing the circle of hugs, his joyful tears mixing with his team's outward display of emotions.

"Now the healing begins," Roxy said, basking in the moment. Although she never doubted his innocence, she wasn't quite sure this day would ever come, and now that it was over, she didn't know what to feel—joy for truth; grief at its tardiness; happiness that her investigative abilities were no longer in question; guilt that Raleigh wasn't here to live through his vindication.

"Let's go home," Seth said. "I mean, to your house."

She stood on her tiptoes, wrapped her arms around his neck, and looked into his ocean-blue eyes. "I'm in love with you. My home is wherever you are."

Without missing a beat, he pulled her off her feet and kissed her. "I have a deep regard for you as well." He let out a howl of laughter, "Who am I kidding? My love for you started nearly a decade ago. I've waited for reciprocity, and now that you've caught up, does this mean you'll marry me?"

"I'm in the slow lane over here," she responded, taking his hand in hers. "Let's go!"

CHAPTER 16

ROXY'S STEERING WHEEL SLID through her hands, her car trailing behind Seth's. When she turned onto her street, she saw a scene of endless blue and red from what looked like a dozen police cars and fire trucks. Her breath caught in her throat as terror rippled through her mind. She closed in on the scene and realized her home was disintegrating into smoldering ashes. Flashes of dancing flames, black smoke, and water skyrocketing out of large yellow hoses like Niagara Falls consumed her field of vision. She jumped from her vehicle and took off in a sprint toward what was left of her house.

"Roxy! Roxy!" Seth yelled, running after her.

Two firefighters stopped her before she made it to the front yard. "Ma'am, you cannot go any further. Is this your house?"

Roxy's mouth wouldn't work. She nodded her head, not taking her eyes off the shell before her. In a flash, she thought about her files and tried to get a glimpse of the office, but she couldn't. She felt Seth come up behind her and put his arms around her neck.

She turned around to face him. "Do you think he could've done this?"

"Who? Kenton?" Seth asked.

Nodding, she locked eyes with him, and without a sound, she knew he thought the same thing. Pandemonium ignited within her. *Why would he burn my house down? What would he have to gain? Did he break in first?*

"Your file cabinet's fire resistant, right?" Seth asked.

A sense of solace hit her, and she relaxed. "Yes. Yes, it is. Sam talked me into spending the extra money." A boisterous laugh escaped her lips. "I bet Kenton never thought of that. Oh, what a relief. I can replace everything else."

"The best investment you've ever made. Your files are secure despite the fire, and your insurance will cover everything else. On the bright side, you get everything new," Seth said.

"Miss," a stocky firefighter said, walking toward her.

She turned to acknowledge him. "Yes?"

"Your home's a total loss. We'll have an arson investigator here soon. Not saying there was foul play, but it's mandatory for house fires. The hot spots are extinguished, but I wouldn't recommend going inside until after the investigator clears the scene. You should call your insurance company as soon as possible."

"Good thing I have a really comfortable spare bed at my house," Seth said, with a shrug. "We can go by the store on the way to get whatever you need for the next few days."

***

Although Roxy should be upset, or at the very least frazzled by the loss of her home, roaming through the aisles with Seth to purchase incidentals made her feel docile.

"I need pajamas, under garments, which you cannot see—" a shy smile crested her lips "—a few outfits, toothbrush, makeup, shampoo, conditioner, deodorant, hair ties, a hairbrush, a straightener, phone charger."

Throwing one arm over her shoulder and laughing and motioning with his other arm, Seth said, "We'll take one of everything."

"Very funny, Seth. I have nothing aside from what's in my car."

"Well, let's load this buggy up. We need to call Sam, too."

"After I call my insurance company—or better yet, while I call them, you can phone Sam."

"Whatever you need, my love; I'm here to serve you."

"I like the sound of that."

After filing the claim with the insurance company, Roxy listened to Seth finish talking to Sam. Looking out the car window, she noticed a man of average height with salt and pepper hair in a white collared shirt and blue cargo pants taking unrushed steps around her house with a clipboard in his hand.

She pointed and motioned to Seth that she was getting out of the car to talk to what had to be the arson investigator.

"What's your gut telling you?" she asked, walking up behind the man.

He whirled around, startled. "Are you the homeowner?"

"Roxanne Hollis," she said, offering her hand. "I didn't mean to scare you. My apologies. It's just that I'm an investigator also, so I figured I'd come over and pick your brain a bit."

Taking her hand in a firm shake, he said, "Caleb Graves. At first glance, this is arson. Follow me around back."

Walking behind him, Roxy stepped through the remains of the wooden gate into her backyard. Matching his gaze, she saw a gaping hole under what was once her office window.

"See this here?" He asked, pointing to the obvious starting place of the fire. "If I had to guess, someone came through the alley here and threw a Molotov cocktail, or something similar, trying to break the window, but missed. The damage is done, although I see you took precautions." She followed his hand that was pointing to the file cabinet.

A smile broke across her face. "Like I said, I'm an investigator, and I can't afford to lose my work. I heeded sound advice from someone wiser than me. When will your report be finished for my insurance company?" Roxy asked, rounding the corner to return to the front of her house.

"I can have a preliminary report to you by close of business today, but my full report will take a few more days. You're free to go through and take whatever you want from the home. Here's my card if you need to reach me," Caleb said, placing his card in her hand before leaving.

"What'd he say, Rox?" Seth asked, jogging toward her.

"We were right. Come look at this."

Returning to the same spot Caleb had showed her, Roxy felt the anger rising in her throat. It seemed that Kenton was taking great lengths to halt her investigation, but the question remained. Why?

"He's becoming determined; maybe dicey is a better description."

"Right, but what's he trying to do? He must have a tie to the truth, or he knows Cassie's innocent. Otherwise, he's going after me for some unilateral reason."

Knowing she sounded insane, Roxy guffawed. "He's out of his mind, but he fails to remember that I'm no dummy. He destroyed nothing that can stop me. Look at my file cabinet. It's a darker shade of grey with the soot, but everything within the drawers is intact. I bet that never even crossed his mind."

"I love you, you know that? Your house sits here in ruins and you're standing there laughing like you just won the lottery," Seth said.

"No, I'm chuckling because he thought this would wreck me, but all he did is delay the inevitable. That's hysterical, you have to admit."

"You're right, Rox. Oh, by the way, Sam said you can stay in his guest room."

She met his gaze. "Maybe I should stay with there. That's the responsible and less risky choice to make. I mean, I trust myself, but I also know temptation can roar its ugly head."

Seth looked down. "The voice of reason and truth. You're right. Will you at least come over for dinner?"

"I wouldn't pass that up for anything in the world. We need to get my files out of here. I don't want him discovering his failed efforts. Do you think I can store them at your office?"

"Sam also offered to set you up a temporary office in one of the conference rooms. We can put your files in there."

After dinner and a shower, Roxy's mind wouldn't settle. The million thoughts swirling around, engrossed in the day's events, were exhausting. She tried to piece together the fire and the reasons. Of course, Kenton knew many were focused on the press conference, so his timing was perfect. Perhaps that even enraged him more. He saw her success in one case and made this plan to demolish her triumph in Cassie's case. Everything pointed to him: Amanda, Mrs. Nichols, surely Jackie Sparse, the previous threatening message on her driveway, and now the arson. His fingerprints were tangled in every web, but she circled around to the same question—why? What was his stock in this? Could the truth dismantle his career or, worse, make him criminally culpable?

"Where's your head, Roxy?" Seth inquired, walking down the hallway and towel drying his hair. "Does the color of my walls intrigue you or something?"

She shook her head. "No. I can't process why Kenton's so involved in everything. I mean, everyone embedded in this case has something to say about him, and now this. It just doesn't add up. I have Jackie Sparse and the two neighbors left, but beyond that, I don't know where else to go."

"We have Mrs. Nichols now."

"Right, but it's her word against his. Without clear and convincing proof, I'm afraid the court will believe him." She shook her head. "That's not enough, and you and I both know that. Now the insurance stuff will slow me down some, but I need to find a way to keep moving. I'm thinking of not rushing the rebuild. I can stay at Sam's as long as I need to. Plus, now that we have the bill, I'm sure you and Sam have Rebecca's lawsuit as top priority."

"We've handled cases with high stress levels. Sam and I litigate our own cases on top of the pro bono work we do. Although this is a different kind of stress, we'll manage. This is what Kenton wanted; his goal wasn't only to destroy your hardcopies but also to distract and overwhelm you." He put his index finger under Roxy's chin. "You're tough. Don't forget that."

***

After getting less sleep than she needed, Roxy bought a Mac laptop and headed to the back conference room of the law firm. She set up her computer and obtained the three witness files left to interview. Amanda was out, thanks to Kenton, and with the single affidavit from Mrs. Nichols, the burden of proof was miles away.

Roxy perused the files, noting detailed questions to ask. Armed with the addresses needed for her interviews, she left the office and headed to the field. Chris and Megan Stars were first, only because of location. She found the house without issue. She was puzzled that the family had left such an upscale neighborhood and moved to a much older one.

Roxy walked up three concrete steps to the front door and rang the bell. After three more rings, she settled with leaving a business card and a note scrolled on the back. Against her better judgement, Roxy headed to Jackie's house for an unscheduled interview. She learned that it was a toss-up between scheduling interviews ahead of time and showing up for a cold interview. With people like Jackie Sparse, she thought it suitable to arrive unannounced.

Jackie lived in a seedy area, in an apartment complex Roxy wouldn't visit after dark. The complex was made of six forest green-sided buildings. The fallen paint chunks from the brown hallway crunched under Roxy's feet on the crusty green carpet. The odor of stale cigarette smoke and foul body odor hung heavy in the air.

Roxy found apartment 3B and knocked on the door. An eerily thin woman with frizzy blond hair answered the door. Although Roxy knew Jackie was in her early forties, the woman looked eighty; her green eyes were tinted with yellow, broken capillaries covered her nose like a road map, and she had a mouth full of decaying teeth. Judging by appearances alone, Jackie's sobriety ended after her release.

"Can I help you?" Jackie said, in a raspy voice.

"Jackie Sparse? My name is Roxanne. Can we talk for a minute?"

"About what, and who are you? Are you a cop?"

"I'm a private investigator, and I need to talk to you about Cassandra Lovejoy."

At the mention of her name, Jackie's defenses went up. She crossed her arms but didn't shut the door. "I don't have anything to say about her. I testified a long time ago, and I haven't been involved since. Is that it? I have things to do, so—"

Jackie tried to close the door, but Roxy's forearm held the door open. "I know you testified. I read the transcript. This won't take long. I only need a few minutes, please," Roxy said.

"Wait, you're the one he told me about. I can't face perjury charges and go back to prison. The sheriff suspected you'd come here for me to change my story or whatever. Besides, I can't go against the deal he gave me."

Keep her talking, Roxy thought. "What deal?"

"My plea deal? Aren't you supposed to know these things?"

"I know about your deal, but there's nothing that prohibits you from talking to me or telling me the truth. If Kenton told you that, he lied."

Jackie chuckled. "He can afford to lie, to say whatever he wants because he knows I have to do what he says. I'm not going back to prison. Just because he bribed me to li—I mean, to seek a confession out of Cassandra doesn't mean I broke the law."

"Do you understand Cassandra's months from the death chamber for a crime she didn't commit? You just admitted to lying, even though you stopped yourself from finishing the sentence. It's too late. I know you lied. You have an opportunity to make this right. You walked out of prison with a slap on the hand after killing someone, and you haven't even quit drinking or used your freedom to do something constructive."

"You have no idea what you're talking about," Jackie said.

"Oh, I think I do. You're in the bottle attempting to block out what you've done because it's too much to live with. Think about how much worse the sting will be when she's executed. Do you want to live like this forever?"

"Look at you with your put-together life thinking you know anything about me."

"Jackie, I know more than you think. I'm giving you an opportunity to make this right. The law firm I work for will represent you from anything the sheriff may try to prosecute you for, whether it's perjury or breaking anything in the plea agreement. Can I come in, please?"

Without acknowledging the question, Jackie stepped back from the door, allowing Roxy to enter the musty apartment. The furnishings were sparse and dingy—a love seat and a lawn chair in the living room and a queen-size mattress on the ground in the back corner of the studio apartment. Mountains of clothing and towels littered the floor, and a tower of dirty dishes covered the Formica kitchen countertop. Roxy regretted not putting a fine layer of lavender oil under her nose; the aura of filth enveloped her.

"Excuse the mess. I live alone, and the clutter doesn't bother me," Jackie said, clearing the love seat.

"No problem. I'll stand, though. I've been sitting all day." Roxy said, sticking to her standard line in situations like this.

"Sure, okay. So, how much do you want me to tell you?"

"Why don't you start with how the 'deal' came to you? Who presented it to you? What were the parameters of the agreement? Things like that," Roxy said.

"So, I went to prison for the accident. I knew I faced heavy time and couldn't stand the thought of spending years there. That place is hell."

It's supposed to be, Roxy thought.

"Detective Kenton handed out flyers in county lock-up to certain inmates. When I asked to talk to him, he told me he could persuade the DA to be loose on my charges. He was really nice and pretty much prepared me before moving me into her cell. I sort of made stuff up because he kept telling me he wouldn't do anything for me unless I gave him something."

"Are you saying you fabricated the story of your own accord, or did you have help?"

"He told me a lot about the case beforehand, and yeah, I made up the rest. Cassandra befriended me but never told me anything. I had to give him something, or I would've spent half my life in prison. I know it's wrong, but you have to understand."

Roxy nodded "He manipulated you in a vulnerable situation, presenting you with a 'get out of jail free' card, and you took the bait. I've never been in your shoes, so I can't say what I would've done, but I bet the guilt gnaws at your conscience, doesn't it?"

When Jackie responded, her voice cracked. "More than you know."

"What are you going to do about that?"

"Can I tell a judge or something?"

"Well, yes, but the first step is signing an affidavit, which we can draw up right now."

Jackie put her index finger in her mouth and nibbled on her nail, staring back at Roxy. "Um, well. I dunno."

"Jackie, you have the ability to release your remorse right here, right now. The pit in your stomach that plagues you could begin to go away with this single gesture of integrity."

Still biting on her fingernail, she nodded her head, indicating she'd sign an affidavit. Roxy pulled the preprinted affidavit sheets from her briefcase and handed one to Jackie with a pen. Although Roxy preferred typed affidavits, she couldn't gamble losing her, considering Amanda's reluctance to speak with her.

"How much have you had to drink today? I can't legally have you sign this document if you're under the influence."

Jackie laughed. "Only a few drinks, but believe me—it takes more than that for me. I'm lucid."

"Okay. Write your full name after the word "I" and begin writing everything you just told me in the lines below. If you need more space, the second page can become a continuation of the first. Don't sign your name until I tell you to."

As Roxy watched the woman write a few lines, dry her face with the back of her hand, and begin writing again, she felt an urgency to work harder, but she wasn't sure how. Jackie's admission brought one more piece to the puzzle, but it wasn't enough.

There had to be more. She had the two neighbors left, but if they didn't provide much information, the case would remain where it stands. Something was missing. Where's the link to the killer?

"Here you go. I think this is all of it," Jackie said, pulling Roxy from her pondering.

Roxy took the papers, read both sheets, and nodded her head. "Now, I need you to sign here," she said, pointing to the signature block at the bottom of the page, "and I'll notarize it afterward."

Jackie looked at the signature line for several moments before lowering the pen to the paper. Roxy notarized the affidavit and placed the document in Jackie's file before putting everything back in her briefcase.

"You did the right thing, Jackie."

"I hope so. What do I do when Kenton starts harassing me?"

Pulling a business card out of its holder, she handed it to Jackie, after underlining her cell phone number. "You call me at this number. I don't care what time it is, day or night, and we'll handle it."

"Okay. Can you go now?" Jackie asked, standing to her feet.

Once a layer of hand sanitizer covered her hands, Roxy called Seth.

"Hey, sweetheart. Any luck?" Seth said.

"Were you sitting on it or what?"

"With everything going on, yes, I've kept my phone close all afternoon."

"What a man you are. I got a signed affidavit from Jackie if you consider that luck."

"Really? That's excellent, Rox. We need to go by Mrs. Nichols' this evening and get hers signed as well. What about the neighbors?"

"I went by the Stars house, but they weren't home, so I left my card. I'll try the Biggs family soon."

"I'll go with you. Didn't you say they live on the other side of town? I don't want you going that far alone, and I feel better when I'm working with you. I was worthless today, but Sam made great progress on the lawsuit petition. How about a nice quiet evening with a home-cooked meal and strategizing on the case?"

"Sounds perfect. I'm headed that way anyways. I want to get this affidavit locked up and study the case from a few different angles before wrapping up."

Roxy switched off the radio and drove to the firm in silence. Well, her car was quiet, but the inside of her head raged with tumultuous thoughts.

Jackie and Mrs. Nichols had both signed affidavits, plus the Crocker family for character witnesses. Kenton remained that gigantic link, but his piece didn't correlate with anything obtained thus far. Where was the bridge? What element was she overlooking? Something Seth had told her when she was new at investigations entered her mind. "Don't narrow your area of objectivity so much that you miss something that doesn't appear to fit. Remember, that's what good detectives do, which results in wrongful convictions."

Without her white board, she felt lost. Roxy asked to borrow one and spent the next thirty minutes reconstructing what she remembered from her board at home, adding new key points. She wrote Kenton's name in massive letters at the bottom and circled it in red. She sat back and ran a hundred scenarios in her mind—a random robbery gone bad didn't fit because the possessions within the home remained intact. Mrs. Nichols saw a man leaving the home and even observed him lose the bandanna. Two witnesses admit to basic bribery and coercion by Kenton. The individuals within Cassie's past cannot see her committing this crime, although there were plenty of cases where people do things that surprise those closest to them.

Glancing at her laptop, she realized she'd never put Kenton through her database. She found his birthday, keyed in his information, and pressed enter with a fresh wave of glee.

While the search wheel turned on her screen, she tapped her nails on the table. Over her monitor, she saw Seth striding down the hallway and turning at the sight of her.

It must be casual day at the office, she thought when she saw he was wearing faded jeans and a bright green polo shirt with white shoes.

"What're you doing?" he asked, and the question made her whirl back to her computer screen.

"Seth, look at this! I never did my background on Kenton until now, and I feel like it's Christmas. Our sheriff isn't so lily white. He has several letters of reprimand for disobeying orders, insubordination, and not following protocol. Here, we have a complaint of excessive use of force during an interrogation, sexual harassment, and one for stealing narcotics from a drug bust. Did he work narcotics before homicide?"

"That's normal in small towns, so that makes sense," Seth said, reading the complaint sheet.

"Seth, this is my intuition speaking, but do you think he had something to do with all this in a roundabout way? Maybe he knows the killer and is connected somehow to him, which would explain why he ignored Mrs. Nichols' lead?"

"You have superb gut instincts, Rox. You could very well be onto something here. We can talk more about that this evening. Print all of that off, and we'll take it with us."

The visit to Mrs. Nichols' house was quick and to the point. Roxy didn't even want to accompany Seth because she felt she was onto something, but she had to notarize the document. Roxy talked nonstop about possible sequences of events that included Kenton. The most profound to her was Kenton's possible acquaintance with the gunman, but the how and why were still unknown. Nothing she processed fit the crime because the Blackwells' records were clear as glass.

"I want to see Cassie tomorrow before we visit the other families. I need to talk to her about our new findings and see if anything rings a bell. Maybe Kenton slipped something in an interview about Mrs. Nichols or alluded to something that sticks out. I'm overdue a visit."

"I'll feel safe with you driving to Mountain View."

After calling the prison to schedule the visit, she and Seth ate Chinese food and tossed possibilities back and forth like an active volleyball game.

Swallowing the last of her beef and broccoli, Roxy said, "Now you sense my frustration. It's like there's a hole with the finishing pieces hidden in somewhere that I've yet to turn over the stone or something. It's so frustrating."

"Remember Mike Kristoff?"

Roxy nodded and chuckled.

"We weaved the web of that case for over a year. The conversations were similar in that case, too, until the final shoe dropped after we found the journal."

Mike Kristoff was a seventeen-year-old closet homosexual. His neighbor, Malcolm Page, had had several mental health issues and befriended Mike about a year before his murder. Mike's stepfather, Gabriel King, was running for a senate seat and believed his stepson's lifestyle hindered him. Mr. King broke into Malcolm's house, stole his gun, shot his stepson with one fatal round to the heart, and put the murder weapon back in Malcolm's house.

What Mr. King, who was at that time a very established senator, didn't count on was Mike's best friend having his journal. Reading the journal had turned Roxy's stomach inside out because of the horrid treatment the boy endured at the hands of his stepfather. Armed with that information, Roxy interviewed Mike's mother, although the woman refused for months, and she broke her silence after reading her son's grief and pain from his accounts of emotional abuse.

"We did drive ourselves crazy with that one," Roxy said.

Early in the case, Seth and Sam were able to release Malcolm from death row because of his documented mental illnesses, which paid off, because proving his innocence took much longer than anticipated.

"Your persistence won that case, Roxy. You refused to give up on Malcolm or on Mike for that matter. This is the same way."

"Except we don't have much time with this case, and Cassie's life is on the line, which puts the desperation to solve this case much higher. A matter of months, and it'll be too late for her."

"I know, but don't get hung up on that because you have plenty of time. The other shoe will drop in this case, too. The truth always has a way of revealing itself."

CHAPTER 17

ROXY PACKED HER FILES in the backseat and stuffed her purse with snacks for the journey. Just as the scenery became dull, Roxy put her earbuds in and started a book to pass the time. Out of nowhere, a black suburban came close to her bumper before jerking the wheel to the left to pass her, or so she thought.

In quick succession, she looked down at her speedometer and noted that she was going five over. She scanned the road around her, noticing no other vehicles nearby. Under her breath she said, "Okay big guy, go around me," but instead, the suburban matched her speed, and before she could think of what to do, she saw black soaring toward her and felt her grip on the steering wheel go slack as fear overtook her.

In a flash, her car was rolling like a matchbox car thrown by a four-year-old. She heard glass shattering, metal bending and breaking, and her own screams. The car finally stopped rolling over, landing upside down, sixty feet from the road, with an unconscious Roxy inside, thrown around like a ragdoll. The black suburban didn't even pause to watch the aftermath of the crash.

***

"Seth Carmichael," a man asked.

"This is he. Who's calling?" Seth asked.

"This is Sergeant Branson with the Texas Highway Patrol. Roxanne Hollis has been in an accident. She's being transported via helicopter to Baylor University Medical Center. Do you know where that is?"

Seth's pulse increased and the bile in his stomach lurched to the back of his throat. "Yes." That's all he could manage to say before he started yelling for Sam.

"Sam! Sam."

Sam heard his pleas and ran to the door of his office, and what he saw stopped him cold. Seth was bent over his desk, his face red, with tears rolling down his cheeks. All he was able to get out was, "Roxy—Baylor Medical Center—can you drive?"

"What do you mean, Seth? Is she in the hospital? What happened?" Sam asked.

Seth shook his head and handed Sam his keys.

"Let's go. I'll explain in the car, but we need to leave now."

Seth's heart felt like a cinderblock as he watched the mile marker signs whiz by on the highway. Without looking, he knew Sam was driving much faster than the posted speed limit signs.

What if she was dead? Oh, God, please don't take her from me. Our life together just began. Seth thought of how she'd look in a wedding dress. How radiant she would be pregnant. Her glowing face the instant she laid eyes on their child.

"Come on, Seth. Pull yourself together. Can you tell me what the officer said to you now?"

"He said she was in an accident and they medevacked her to Baylor. That's all I know."

In record time, Sam pulled into the hospital's lot and parked the car, but before Sam could even retrieve the keys, Seth jumped out of the car and sprinted toward the emergency room entrance.

Barreling through the doors, Seth yelled, "Someone, anyone, please."

A petite nurse in hot pink scrubs approached him. "Sir, are you injured? What's wrong?"

"No, it's not me. My girlfriend was in an accident, and he said a helicopter brought her here," Seth said, looking back and forth for Roxy's red hair.

"Sir, look at me," the nurse said, waving her hands in front of his face to get his attention. "What's her name?"

"Roxanne Hollis."

"Stay here. I'll check our system."

Seth stood frozen, his eyes darting around the white cubed room and searching for anything familiar. People were bustling about him, going through swinging doors, and that's when he saw Roxy burst through the doors, bandages wrapped around her head, tubes coming from every part of her upper body, and blood—so much blood.

"Roxy! Roxy!" Seth shouted and ran to her side.

All he felt were hands pulling him back. "Sir, she's going into surgery. You have to wait here."

He watched the massive amount of people attaching and pulling tubes from her as they rolled her bed through the trauma doors.

Sam came up behind him. "What did you find out? Seth, say something." Sam yelled, shaking Seth.

"She came in on a gurney and went through those doors." He pointed before the sobs started.

"She had tubes everywhere, and there was so much blood, Sam. She was intubated, and her eyes were closed." Seth managed to get the words out before he crumbled.

The horror rose in Sam's chest. "Okay, let's find the chapel."

Sam grabbed Seth's arm, and although Seth had several inches on Sam, he felt like he was leading a child to Sunday school. Walking down the halls with the smell of antiseptic and death hanging in the air, Sam followed the arrowed signs.

Pushing open the wooden doors, Sam saw two rows of three pews, a raised altar, and a beautiful stained-glass display of Jesus. Seth walked to the alter, fell to his knees, put his face on the floor, and wept. The sound of despair penetrated Sam's heart, and his knees weakened. Sam gave Seth a minute to grieve before joining him to pray.

Laying his hand on Seth's back, Sam prayed. "Father, we come to you with heavy hearts. Lord, we know You're in the operating room with Roxy just as we know that You go before us in everything we face. Father, we ask that You pour wisdom into the surgeons as they operate. We petition that the doctors in that room with Roxy are gifted at what they do, and that with Your help, their efforts would be successful. Father, we desire her full recovery. We plea for you to put Your hands inside her, that You would put her back together, that You would mend whatever is broken or damaged. You are the ultimate healer, Father. Please, do what only You can do."

Before Sam could say amen, Seth spoke. "Yes, Lord, I agree. Father, You told me she'd be my wife. Please don't take her from me before that comes true. She has so much life to live."

After several minutes, Seth stood and sat in the first pew, staring at the stain-glass image.

"Seth, she's a fighter. Don't lose faith. God's in control."

Turning his head to look at Sam, his eyes swollen and red, his voice hoarse. "I can't lose her."

Neither spoke but sat silent, in and out of prayer for the next hour. Seth's crying did the same, starting and stopping, off and on. Sam never knew these emotions could have such distinct sounds to them, but he heard various levels of grief and pain in Seth's cries.

"We better go to the waiting room," Seth said, straightening his pale blue shirt as he stood up. His pants had a white hue on the knees, but he didn't care.

He ambled back down the hallway on autopilot, replaying the image of Roxy on that bed, lifeless and broken. Taking a seat, he looked around at the various people in the waiting room with him and wondered what news they anticipated. Was their loved one teetering between life and death? Were they here because of an injury, accident, or illness?

"Would you call Rebecca, please," Seth asked.

"Yes, I will," Sam said, pulling his phone out of his suit jacket pocket.

Minutes later, Sam said, "Rebecca will be here soon."

"All right."

***

Rebecca dropped her phone on the counter, grabbed her purse, called for Cliff upstairs, and threw him the keys as she ran out the door.

"Momma, what is it?" Cliff asked, buttoning his shirt.

"It's Roxy. She's been in an accident and is in surgery at Baylor Med. I need you to drive."

Turning the car after backing out of the driveway, Cliff punched the accelerator and asked questions in rapid succession.

"What happened? What surgery? What're her injuries?"

"Cliff, you're not a nurse right now. I have no answers for you. Sam told me what I just told you because he knows nothing more. We need to pray."

"I can't pray, Momma. I'm driving."

"Son, don't you know that a position of prayer is in your heart and not bowing your head or closing your eyes. Just agree with me."

"Okay, Momma."

Rebecca prayed perhaps the most eloquent prayer she had ever prayed that lasted much of the hour trip to the hospital. She had a habit of reciting scripture while praying and, as she called it, covering Roxy with specific promises found in God's word.

After they said amen, Cliff asked, "How do you do that, Momma?"

"Oh, my boy, when your brother was still alive, I'd pray all night sometimes. You see, most people believe prayer should be short, sweet, and to the point, but I feel some prayers are conversational between God and me. I always ask for the Holy Spirit's direction at the beginning of my prayer, and I let Him take over. You should see my friends at our prayer group. We pray for hours, sometimes."

"When I grow up, I wanna be just like you, Momma."

"You have a full-time job, me to take care of, and now our precious Martin. God understands that, but you should try starting your prayer off the way I do and let Him take the reins. You'll be amazed if you don't rush it."

"We're almost there. You gonna be all right?"

"God's in control, and I believe He isn't finished with Roxy. She may have a long road of recovery ahead of her, but she'll be all right."

Rebecca stepped inside the sliding glass doors, met Seth's tortured gaze, and opened her arms.

"Seth, honey, she'll be okay," Rebecca said. Seth collapsed into her embrace.

"Who's here for Roxanne Hollis?" A doctor in navy blue scrubs asked.

Seth jerked from Rebecca, wiped his eyes with his palms, and walked toward the doctor.

Sam jumped to his feet and followed Seth.

"Would you come over here, please?"

The group rallied around the doctor.

"My name is Dr. Clocksly, and I've been operating on Roxanne. She's one tough woman. Initially, we thought she had enough intracranial pressure that a craniotomy was necessary, but after further examination, that avenue was ruled out, although she did suffer a serious concussion on top of the swelling. Her right cheekbone shattered, which caused severe distension in her eye socket and pressure to the front part of her skull. We opened up that area to remove some bone fragments but will wait on reconstructive surgery to repair the damage to that side of her face."

He took a deep breath, glanced and made brief eye contact with Sam, Seth, Cliff, and Rebecca.

"That was the least of her problems. Her right lung suffered a puncture from one of several broken ribs. We inserted a chest tube to eliminate excess fluid. She also has a vertical shear pelvis fracture; specifically, the right half of her pelvis bone shifted upward."

After Seth had a puzzled look on his face, Cliff said, "Seth, most people don't realize how crucial the pelvis bone is to other areas of the human body."

Cliff used his body as an exhibit, pointing to various places as he explained.

"The pelvis bone starts at the bottom of the spine and consists of the sacrum, which is a large triangular bone, the coccyx or tailbone, and the hip bones. In its totality, the pelvis bone aids in securing the muscles of the hips, thighs, and abdomen, and offers protection to the organs in the lower abdomen. In addition, parts of the bowels, bladder, and propagative organs go through the pelvic ring."

Seth's face turned polar-bear white at mention of Roxy's reproductive organs. "Is there a chance this could affect her ability to have children?"

Dr. Clocksly looked at Seth. "The injuries to her pelvis could modify her ability to give birth the natural way, but we found no signs that her female anatomy was compromised in anyway."

He continued. "I do want to stress that this injury led to significant blood loss. We performed an open reduction and internal fixation to repair the bone, which means we placed the bone in its original place and held it together with screws. Because the fracture tore her skin, there's concern for infection, so she's on a high dosage of antibiotics. There was muscle damage around the break, which is common, but makes the recovery more difficult. She has extensive bruising and deep lacerations all over her body."

"But she's alive?" Seth asked.

"Yes, she is, and we managed to put her back together. She has a long road ahead of her, but she'll survive."

Seth put his hands on his knees, trying to contain his relief. He asked, "Doctor, do you know what happened?"

"The medical team that brought her in said a man passed an overturned vehicle on I-35 E and called 911. He said the vehicle was about sixty feet off the road and was practically unrecognizable. The first responders were there in minutes and managed to pull her out through the windshield. No other vehicle was involved. Seems fishy to me, but I'm only a doctor."

"When can we see her?" Seth inquired.

"I'll have a nurse come and get you in a bit. She's just now coming out of anesthesia and needs a few minutes to orient herself. Plus, we need to ensure she's not feeling anything. The pain will be excruciating if she can feel it."

After the doctor departed, the group moved back to the waiting room.

Half an hour later, a nurse appeared. "Seth Carmichael?"

Seth jumped to his feet. "Yes, I'm right here."

"She's asking for you," she said, walking ahead of him.

The nurse stopped in front of room 117. "She's right in here."

Seth took a deep breath, dried his face off, ran his fingers through his hair, and pushed open the door. He walked passed the bathroom and turned right at the end of the wall. His eyes met Roxy's, and he froze. She looked so small in the hospital bed amidst a dozen wires and tubes. Her swollen face almost made him second-guess her identity. Her right eye was covered with a bandage, along with the dressing wrapped around her head, which he deduced was protecting the incision from her cheekbone fracture. Her neck had a rainbow of red and purple from seatbelt burns and bruises. Her upper chest displayed several scratches and additional bruising, with her arms covered in cuts and bandages. Blankets hid her lower body, and deep down Seth was thankful for what he couldn't see because what was already before him was almost too much.

Roxy opened her mouth, wincing at the pain, but managed to say, "Seth."

With that one word, he moved to her side. He pulled a chair as close to the bed as he could get, grabbed her hand, and kissed each finger. He put his head down on the side of the bed, still holding her hand, and bawled.

"Oh, Roxy, you have no idea how afraid I was. I thought I lost you."

Roxy pulled her hand from his grip, placing it on the top of his head, stroking his hair.

"Shh, Seth, it's all right, honey. I'm right here; look at me."

Seth lifted his head up, his face a blotchy mess. "I love you, Roxy. I love you so much. I'll be here every step of the way. I'll take you to physical therapy and every doctor's appointment. You don't have to worry about anything."

"I love you, too, Seth, and I know you'll take care of me. God ordained you for me, and His plans are never wrong. We'll get through this."

"And after you recover, you'll see that marrying me is the logical thing to do," Seth said, and the smile on his face reached his eyes.

"I think I already know that, but this doesn't count as your proposal."

Seth's expression flattened.

"What is it, Seth? Why are you looking at me like that?"

"The doctor said this might affect your ability to deliver children naturally."

"If I can still carry a child, I don't care how I deliver. I'm alive, Seth."

"Do you have any memories from the accident?"

"I remember a black suburban with dark windows rammed me off the road. He came up beside me, and I thought he was going to pass me, but he hit me instead. Then, the sounds are loud in my mind. Crunching metal. Breaking glass. My own screams. I don't think those will ever leave me."

"Wait, are you saying you think the crash wasn't an accident?"

"No, I'm not saying that. I'm only telling you what I remember. Did you ask the first responders if there was another vehicle involved? Maybe the other driver lost control or something."

"I don't think I saw them. Nobody else come in before or after you, though, so that might indicate enough."

Hearing a quiet knock, Roxy's eye shot to the left of the room, waiting for whomever opened her door.

"Hi, Roxanne, my name's Cora. I'll be your nurse for the rest of the day. How are you feeling?"

Roxy admired the short, petite woman with purple-rimmed glasses that covered light brown eyes and a fit frame clothed in colorful scrubs.

"Please, call me Roxy. I feel okay right now. Am I allowed to eat?"

Cora said, "Yes, you are. I suspect you're quite hungry. Would you like a menu from the cafeteria?"

Seth interjected himself in the conversation. "Honey, I'll get you anything you want; just name it."

"The choice is yours." Cora shrugged.

Clearing what must've been dirt from her throat, Roxy said, "I think I'll let him pick something up for me."

"Okay, hun. You press that call button if you need anything, and I'll be here in no time. What's your pain level?"

Level? Roxy thought. *What kind of question is that, and how on earth do I answer?*

"Um, I'm not sure what you mean by level. I think I'm still numb because I can't feel anything."

"That's what we like to hear. I bet you'll start feeling something in the next few hours, and we gotta stay ahead of the pain. You have a pain pump, and here's the magical button that releases the pain meds into your IV," Cora said, handing Roxy the tan cord with a red button on its head.

"Okay."

"What do you want to eat, love?" Seth asked, pushing a strand of Roxy's hair out of her face after Cora left the room.

"I'd kill for some Japanese spring rolls with peanut sauce," Roxy said, laughing. "I almost died, and I want peanut sauce."

"Let me get Sam. Rebecca and Cliff are here, too."

"I want to see them."

Seth leaned over and kissed her on her forehead. "I'll be right back."

Seth headed back to the waiting room, and his world righted itself again. An hour ago, he was feeling literal pain in his chest, as his mind spun with thoughts of Roxy's death. Nothing could've prepared him for that outcome, and now that he knew she'd heal, he rejoiced and praised God for His goodness.

He rushed back to the waiting room. The anticipation on everyone's faces reminded Seth of children waiting in line for an amusement park ride as they surveyed him coming toward them. He noticed Heather next to Sam and knew she had arrived during his time with Roxy.

"She's really banged up, but she wants to see you guys. And, per Roxy's character, she wants some Japanese spring rolls."

Everyone guffawed. "Leave it to her to be so specific about a food choice after what she just went through," Sam said.

Sam closed the door behind him, took a deep breath, and turned the corner to see Roxy. He was grateful he wasn't claustrophobic with everyone crammed in the small room. He connected with her, and his heart felt panged at the sight of her broken and bandaged body.

Sam and Heather were unable to have children, but God had given them Roxy several years ago, and even though she was an adult, their connection remained special. They considered themselves her surrogate parents. Sam heard Heather's audible gasp when she saw Roxy and knew she felt similar despair.

Joining everyone else standing around her bed, Sam reached out his hand and grabbed Roxy's. Without anyone asking, the circle linked, and Rebecca began to pray. After Rebecca concluded, Sam started, and after Sam, Seth finished.

"How are you feeling, sweetheart?" Sam asked, drying his eyes with a baby blue handkerchief.

"I'm alive, and that's what's important. I do need some food, though."

"I called in the order, and I'm leaving right now," Seth said, putting his phone back in his pocket. "I found a place not far from here. Sam, do you have my keys?"

***

After Roxy ate and everything calmed down, she began to feel unimaginable pain in her lower abdomen. Breathing hurt, moving sent agonizing pain signals to her brain, and the slightest twitch propelled a sensation of what near-death must feel like. She gripped the pain pump button and pressed down until the machine beeped.

After the meds hit, Roxy drifted into a heavy sleep with Seth by her side. When Cora came in to check on her, Seth attempted to rid his face of tears.

"She'll come through this, right?" he asked.

"It won't be easy, but with enough support and physical therapy, I think she'll make it."

"Do you know how long the process will take? I mean the physical therapy and stuff."

"A few months at the very least. She suffered a serious fracture, and that will take time to heal."

CHAPTER 18

SETH SAT BACK IN THE HOSPITAL CHAIR and looked at Roxy, mangled and broken but asleep. He realized, after some thought about Cassie's case, that he'd be forced to do some of the investigation himself, but he couldn't go alone. As an attorney, he'd need a witness to anything obtained during his investigation because he couldn't put himself on the stand. He and Sam could do the legwork, while Roxy directed them. She wouldn't like it, but they had no choice.

As if a revelation from God punched him in the gut, Seth sucked in a breath and remembered what Roxy said. A single vehicle—matched her speed—slammed into her—what if it was Kenton? What if he tried to kill her?

Seth stepped out of the room and walked down the corridor seeking a quiet place to call Sam. Looking at his watch, he shook his head at the thought that it was too late to call him; he had to tell someone.

"Sam, are you awake?" Seth asked, pacing in small circles.

"Yeah. Seth, is it Roxy? Is she all right?" Sam asked.

"Sam, I think Kenton tried to kill her."

"What?!" Sam yelled. "Explain yourself."

"She said a black suburban matched her speed and rammed into her. Nobody else came into the hospital from that accident, Sam."

"How did he know where she'd be, Seth? Come on. This is a far stretch."

"Think about it. She called the prison to schedule her visit. He's the sheriff, for crying out loud. Surely he knows people working at Mountain View. It's not too far off, considering he burned her house down."

"You really think he did this?"

"He probably has other people doing his dirty work, but, yes, I do. There's something in Cassie's case he doesn't want out, and he's trying to stop her from finding it."

"This slows down the investigation. If it was him, he succeeded, at least partially."

"No, Sam. You and I will pick up the baton from here. We can't stop the progress. There wasn't much left to do."

"Whoa, Seth. I'm not an investigator; I'm an attorney."

"I know, but you forget, before I graduated law school, I was an investigator, and I mentored Roxy. Don't worry; I'll do the talking, but I need you as a witness."

"All right. You win, but we can't start right away. I have cases at the firm I need to work on next week. After that, we can wrap up the field work."

"This'll be great, Sam; you'll see."

Seth had an extra pep in his step walking back down the hallway to Roxy's room. When he slipped in, he turned the corner and saw her awake.

"Hey, you," she said.

"Why are you awake, love? You should be sleeping."

"I opened my eyes and saw that you were gone, so I waited for you to come back. Where'd you go?"

"I went to call Sam." He placed her hand in his. "I need to tell you something. Sam and I are going to finish the leg work in the field, while you recover."

Her eye opened wide. "Seth, but—"

"Roxy, we have no choice. Plus, I know what I'm doing. Remember, I taught you everything you know," he said, winking at her. "And you'll be directing the way the investigation goes. We'll talk by phone or in person before Sam and I do anything."

Roxy put her head down, fiddling with the sheet. "You're right. I just wanted to finish this for Raleigh, but there's no other way with me injured."

"We're a team. If we finish this, then you do, too. We do what we have to with our situation. We can't just quit."

He kissed her forehead, and she smiled.

***

Roxy's medical equipment consumed the spare bedroom at Sam and Heather's house. Her rented hospital bed was against the middle of the back wall, with physical therapy and workout gear covering the floor. Her medications were on the nightstand, within reach, along with her computer, multiple files, and her Bible. The living arrangements were perfect; Heather was available during the day, and Seth came over after work, even sleeping on the pullout sofa during weekends.

Over the next month, Roxy threw herself head-first into physical therapy and fitness regimens. She worked herself sick with her therapist and an additional session with Seth in the evening. Five weeks after her release from the hospital, she could tolerate weight on her feet, though not for long. She refused to use a wheelchair, insisting on her crutches instead. Her desire to regain her ability to walk unassisted kept her working as hard as she could. She longed to run again, to put her earbuds in and feel the wind gracing her cheeks with the rhythmic pattern of her feet on the blacktop.

The reconstructive surgery on her face restored most of her previous look, although a perceptible scar remained. The plastic surgeon instructed the use of vitamin E oil on the scar to reduce the pigmentation of the affected skin.

Meanwhile, Sam and Seth tried twice to interview the Biggs family, without success. With Roxy on the phone via Seth's Bluetooth headset, Seth and Sam walked to the front door for the third time and rang the bell. Seth noticed each time how the outside of the home was an absolute wreck. The grass was a foot tall, and everything in the flowerbed was shriveled and dead.

"What do you want?" A deep male voice choked out.

Sam and Seth looked at each other before Seth said, "Mr. Biggs, my name is Seth Carmichael, and I'm an attorney. Can we talk?"

The door opened and a sloppy, big-boned man with pudgy cheeks and hollow gray eyes stood on the threshold. "About what?"

"We know your family lived in Whitehead Estates several years ago. Specifically, your address was 206 Peachtree Street. We are re-investigating the murder of the Blackwell family, who lived at 206 Pear Tree Street."

Mr. Biggs's face paled, and he shook his head. After a few moments, he moved to the side and allowed Sam and Seth to walk in.

Roxy, laying in her bed, listened without making a sound, even though her phone was muted.

Seth sat on a cluttered brown couch with clawed feet below. Sam stood beside him without a word, merely observing his surroundings. The room was dark and dreary with shades closed, not allowing a smidge of sunlight in the shadowy room.

"What do you want to know?" Mr. Biggs asked, sitting in the matching brown recliner across the coffee table from Seth.

"Did you know the Blackwells?" Seth asked.

"Not much," he said.

"Do you remember their murders?"

"Yep."

Seth tilted his head, sensing the man knew more than he was telling. "You moved pretty quickly after that."

"Yeah. After something like that happens, I felt my family wasn't safe."

Roxy unmuted her phone, asked, "Where are his wife and daughter?" and put her phone back on mute.

"Is your family here?"

Mr. Biggs put his head down. "They're dead."

Roxy perked up so fast that the healing wounds on her body panged with discomfort. Dead. She unmuted again. "What happened to them?"

"I'm sorry to hear that. May I ask what happened?" Seth inquired, genuine concern in his voice.

After what felt like thirty minutes of silence, Mr. Biggs lifted his head, revealing a blemished mess. "They were murdered on June 25, 2001."

Roxy arched her body to reach her laptop, threw open the lid, powered it on, and her fingers flew to the search bar. She typed their names in, and the amount of hits was in the thousands. Her eyes scanned the more recent articles and scrolled down the page until she found the story announcing their murders.

"Kay and eight-year-old Elizabeth Joy Biggs were shot in their home yesterday evening, while Peter Biggs, the third member in the small family, was on a business trip out of state. Police are combing the area for evidence and canvassing the neighbors for witnesses. If anyone has knowledge of the murders or the family, the police are asking for your help. Call the tip line at 555-3TIP. The story is developing, and News Channel 8 will bring you the latest as we obtain the information."

"Seth, they were shot in their home, while Peter was out of town. Keep him talking. I'll dig for more information."

Roxy muted her phone again and clicked on a more recent story.

"Cain Pierce, convicted of gunning down Kay and Elizabeth Biggs in June 2001, withdrew his appeal this week and requested that the state set a

date for his execution according to his constitutional rights. His attorney said they will honor his client's wishes and petition the court for a date."

She navigated to the Texas Department of Corrections website and keyed his name in for his mugshot. Her breath caught. Cain had dark brown eyes and black hair and was six feet tall and 280 pounds. She looked at his shoulders and upper body, wondering if he had only bulked up in prison.

Clicking her phone again, Roxy said, "The man convicted of killing them is on death row and requested an execution date nine days ago."

Seth cleared his throat. "Did a motive ever come out?"

With Roxy back on mute, she went to the Texas Supreme Court website to read the court pleadings. Again, keying in his name, she located the docket. Combing through the long list of pleadings, she found the appeal response. She read the guts of the case laid out at the beginning of every pleading, and her blood went cold.

"Cain Pierce was convicted of two counts of criminal homicide on September 5, 2003, in Tarrant County. The jury sentenced Mr. Pierce to the death penalty for the crimes. Mr. Pierce shot Kay and Elizabeth Biggs execution style in their home because of a drug debt. This was an orchestrated hit to resolve said debt, and whether Mr. Pierce was just the hitman is undetermined, although the state has its theories of third-party involvement. Mr. Pierce remains silent on the matter, not offering any information, despite the state's offered plea deal for his cooperation. He declined to take the deal and invoked his Fifth Amendment rights during his interrogations with Homicide Detective Dale Kenton."

"I was a drug addict and got mixed up with the wrong people," Mr. Biggs admitted, hanging his head. "The murders were my fault because I couldn't pay my debt." Mr. Biggs ran his hands up and down his face. "I spiraled out of control, and my family paid the price. This was some sick attempt at making me suffer, and let me tell you, it's working."

Noticing a break between questions, Roxy hit the button and jumped in. "Seth, Kenton's involved in this, too. He was the detective, and Cain Pierce, the hitman, pled the fifth during every interrogation. The courts suspect he was a hitman and someone else was pulling the strings."

Clearing his throat after listening to Roxy, Seth asked, "Do you remember dealing with Detective Kenton during any of this or any time for that matter?"

Shaking his head, he said, "I don't think so, but I'm not good with names."

Seth pulled his phone out, went to the Google search bar, and typed Kenton's name in. "Here's his picture. Does he look familiar?"

Mr. Biggs gripped Seth's phone and studied the picture. "Vaguely, but I have no idea where from. Maybe the trial or something connected to the case."

Roxy chimed in again. "Seth, go out on a whim and ask him if he thinks the murder of his family was connected to the Blackwell's deaths."

"Mr. Biggs, did you move because you thought the Blackwell murders were associated with you?"

Making eye contact with Seth, his voice shook. "I won't lie, the thought crossed my mind, but after we moved, I didn't worry about it."

"Did you see or hear anything the night they were murdered?"

"I was high every day back then. Even if I had heard anything, I couldn't remember it the next morning."

"All right, Mr. Biggs, before we leave, is there anything you can think of that I need to know?"

Without a word, he shook his head and stood to walk them out.

"Here's my card, Mr. Biggs. Please call if you remember anything. Maybe your memory will trigger something."

When he and Sam closed the car doors, Roxy unmuted and let loose. "Put me on speaker, Seth."

"You're on," Seth said.

"Okay, guys. Seriously, this is linked in some way. The timing, the manner of death, and you know what just occurred to me? We have no ballistics report in our file, apart from pictures of the shell casings from the crime scene. We have no paperwork from the bullet fragments or any indication that the casings were sent through Nibin. Can we get access to the Biggs murder file?"

"What about the autopsy report, Rox?" Sam asked.

"It indicates finding fragments during each autopsy but nothing further. Would the police elect not to run the fragments through the national database because they had their suspect already, or did Kenton facilitate excluding them on purpose? We need the Biggs file. We know it's still at the courthouse. What about interviewing Cain? His attorney is Butler Philsey, if that helps."

Sam spoke up. "I know Butler. I'll call him and see what he thinks. Did you find an execution date for him yet? We may not have time to interview him."

Hearing Roxy's fingers hammering on her keyboard, they waited. "We have seven days. His execution is scheduled for next Thursday."

"All right, Rox. We'll take care of the arrangements. Are you okay?" Seth asked, feeding his car fuel and exiting the neighborhood.

"Yep, I'm good. Doing some exercises before physical therapy. I'll be fine; you go save the day, and let me know what happens."

When the call ended, Sam said, "When are you going to propose, Seth? You need to marry her already."

"Since you brought it up, I wanted to talk to you about that. I'm thinking of waiting until she can walk again. Perhaps setting up something at the lake with candles, or a fire and lights, but having everyone waiting somewhere to celebrate afterward. What do you think?"

The joy in Sam's voice exploded in the car. "That's perfect. How much longer do you think?"

"I asked her therapist, and she said at the rate Roxy's going, another three to six weeks and she'll be walking. After we figure out a narrow window of time, I'll start making plans."

"What about a ring?"

"I found a company where I can design it myself. I want it unique to her. I have the final call set for next week, and it'll take three additional weeks for them to customize it and get it to me."

Sam looked at Seth and smiled. "Here's the bigger question: are you going to call her father?"

Seth took a deep breath, wishing he could have this conversation somewhere other than his car. "Well, I thought I'd ask you. You know she has nothing to do with her father, besides, I wouldn't even know where to find him. She considers you like a father, so what do you say? Do I have your blessing?"

Sam thought through the agony Roxy had experienced over the years because of her father. He was the only immediate family member she has left but a raging alcoholic. Coming back to the present, Sam said, "I wouldn't want anyone else for her, Seth. I trust that you'll take care of her."

"Okay, then, that's that," Seth said, breathing deeply to suck back the thump in his throat.

Sam walked passed Seth's office and entered his own, closing the door behind him.

He sat at his desk and picked up a framed picture of him and Roxy at one of their many brunches. He traced her face with his thumb and relished the goodness of God for giving him the ability to stand in as a father for her. Over the years, Sam had remained a proponent of Roxy mending the bridge with her father, even facilitating a trip to visit him.

Sam had driven Roxy to the state-funded apartment complex in southern Oklahoma. He watched her saunter down the narrow sidewalk, noticing the initial stiffness in her frame before she straightened her back, stuck her chin out, and finally, knocked on the forest-green door. A man answered—he assumed it was her father—

and after a few minutes of talking, she stepped inside and out of his sight. Sam studied his watch, but her visit didn't last long. Three and a half minutes later—not that he was counting—she threw the door open and ran to his car.

After shutting the car door, Roxy said, "Drive. I told you this was a terrible idea," her voice teetering between hysteria and rage.

He found a gas station a few miles out of town, parked, and turned to her. "Talk to me, sweetheart. What happened?"

"I tried to tell him I forgave him for killing my mother, and he said I should be forgiving myself because I was the reason he started drinking and, if not for me, he would've never driven drunk with my mother in the car."

Sam's insides curled up, and he wrestled with the urge to drive back and give the man a piece of his mind; instead, he comforted Roxy. In the following moments, he made the conscious decision to be the father she needed, and for the better part of a decade, he'd been doing that. Heather also reveled in the role of stand-in mom, but carefully, as not to take the place of Roxy's real mother.

"Hey, Sam, you gonna call Butler today or Monday?" Seth asked, popping his head in Sam's doorway.

"It's almost three; I'll wait until after the weekend. You go ahead and head out. I assume you're staying at my house this weekend?"

"You know it. I'll see you later."

***

Seth heard Roxy grunting before he even knocked on the door. When he walked in, he saw her deep in her therapy session and joined Heather in the kitchen.

"One more set of ten, and you're finished," he heard Whitney say.

"All right." Many uncomfortable noises followed from Roxy.

He retrieved a bottle of water from the fridge and headed into the living room. Whitney was journaling Roxy's progress. Roxy's face was crimson, and the sweat on her forehead gleamed in the overhead light, visible to Seth from across the room.

"How's she doing?" Seth asked, facing Whitney.

"She's making steady progress. Today, she took four steps, unassisted, so the number is climbing, daily. I do think she's overworking herself when I'm not here, though. She needs to allow her muscles to rest because of how hard we work during our sessions. I told her she can only do one mini-session a day outside of our time together."

"You hear that, Rox? Only one session from now on."

"Mini-session," Roxy said. "You know best, but I don't like this new rule."

"I know you don't, but remember, you're relearning everything, and as the old saying goes, you must crawl before you walk and walk before you run. We'll get there, but it takes time. I'll see you tomorrow."

"Do you need me to help you to the shower before dinner?" Seth asked, after Whitney left.

"I can't believe she said that. She acts like I don't know my own body. I had incredible endurance before this happened, and now I can't even work out by myself."

"Honey, she's not saying that to punish you or even to slow you down. You've been spending more than half your days working out. She isn't even saying you can't work out, just to dial it back a bit. Besides, with all these new things happening in the case, I need your help. Let's just give her advice a try for a few weeks and see what happens, all right?"

Kissing the top of her head, he handed her the crutches, helped her up, and walked behind her into the bathroom. He fell right into caretaker mode, turning the water on, grabbing two towels, and a fresh set of clothes.

"I'm going to help Heather finish up dinner, but I'm not far off if you need me."

CHAPTER 19

WHEN ROXY'S EYES OPENED the following morning, she felt a weight like a mac truck on her heart. She dreamed of Cassie and the nightmare that she might not come home alive. Her brain rattled like a pinball machine with endless thoughts, such as the realization that she had had a visit scheduled the day of her accident, and she didn't show up. She stared at the celling, following the lines of texture, when the revelation hit her. *I'll write to Cassie.*

Ever so slowly, Roxy nudged herself upright and scanned the room for her notebook. She chuckled, looking at the mess around her bed—her computer, papers, various medical equipment and supplies—and the disorder of the furniture to make room for her hospital bed.

Remembering that it was the weekend, she yelled for Seth.

"Good morning, sweetie. Did you sleep all right?" Seth said, hurrying down the hall, looking completely disheveled.

A loud laugh fled from the pit of Roxy's stomach. "Did you just wake up?"

"Yeah, how can you tell?"

Roxy pointed to the mess on his head.

Seth put both hands threw his hair in a bad attempt to brush it back. "See what you have to look forward to when we get married," he said with a wink.

"You keep saying that, but I've yet to hear a proposal." Roxy shot back sarcastically.

Sitting next to her on the bed, Seth pushed her hair behind her ear. "I will when you least expect it, believe me. Now, what did you call me for?"

"I want to write a letter to Cassie, but I can't reach my notebook. And now that you're in here, I'm starving."

"A letter, huh? That's a good idea, but what're you going to tell her without revealing what we have to whoever processes her mail?"

"You can put it in the firm's preprinted envelope, so it has the appearance of legal mail, which it pretty much is, if you think about it. It's a case update from a member of her legal team."

Seth shook his head, teasing Roxy. "Look at you actually bending the rules, just a hair. I never thought I'd see the day."

"Hey, now, I'm not breaking the rules; I have no other way to communicate with my client in my present condition. What would you do?"

"No, no, I think it's brilliant. I just had to take the jab for old times' sake."

"Good, I'm glad you agree with me. I'll have it written for you to mail off Monday morning."

They sat for breakfast after Seth cooked.

Roxy swallowed and took a drink of water. "We have to interview Cain. I feel like he has more to do with Cassie's case than we think, but I can't put my finger on it."

Seth nodded in agreement. "I know. It's ironic, isn't it? I mean, how coincidental that both his daughter and wife were shot execution style just like the Blackwells. The only thing I can't figure out is the difference in the two with Mister Biggs alive, but not Paul. That doesn't add up, but the rest makes sense."

Roxy pondered that, holding her fork. "Then there's Kenton. How does he fit? Is there a link between him and Cain? Kenton investigated the Biggs' murder, too. How convenient for him if he had something to do with it. I need my white board to lay it out, add this new piece, and study."

"Well, Sam's calling his attorney Monday, and hopefully we can go visit him early in the week since his execution is scheduled for Thursday. I'm going to the courthouse first thing Monday morning to pull the file. I want to absorb as many of the details as I can and track the similarities before I interview him."

Roxy's head perked up. Things seldom made her pulse elevate like sifting through the paper trail of a case file. She imagined herself following a tight underground tunnel with a small light, while she picked her way through to the other side.

"Look for positions of the bodies, whether the house was ransacked after the murders, how he got in the house, the murder weapon, the defense theory of the crime, and how involved Kenton was in the investigation and the trial. I'm sure his presence in the file will be as overwhelming as it is in Cassie's case."

"I love you, you know that?"

With a smile as big as a banana, Roxy said, "What?"

"You know what. I've never met anyone who loves paper like you. A the mention of me checking out the file, your cheeks flushed, and the pace of your words flew out like machine gun rounds. You'd be content buried in case files all of your days."

"I can't help it, but it's your fault."

"Is that so?"

"Remember what you always said—you cannot properly work an investigation until you know everything there is to know about the case."

"That's my girl! If I taught you nothing more than that, you'd still be as dangerous as you are with a case."

"Can you make copies of the file, and I'll go through it for you? After all, my recall appears to be much better than yours."

"You're right, but I can handle it. No need to bill the firm for the copies when it's not necessary."

***

A loud crack of thunder woke Roxy Monday morning. The heavy rain sounded on the roof, and the gray sky peeked through the window. She fought back the feelings of inadequacy plaguing her. The uselessness she endured suffocated her, but the case seemed to move along despite her confines.

Roxy struggled with how much to reveal in the letter because, regardless of how she sent it, there was no guarantee of confidentiality. Settling on vagueness, she scribbled out the first page. Turning to the second sheet, her pen halted just above the page. She wrestled with trying to minister to her again. Deep within her heart, she felt the nudge. *All right, Lord. Here goes.*

> *"I'm going out on a limb here, but I have to try again. When I think about the trials we face in life, not only do I think about Paul and Job, but also Daniel. Ripped from his home; surviving on only vegetables, fruit, and water; ordered not to continue his normal Jewish tradition of praying three times a day, facing Jerusalem; and thrown into the lion's den. When Daniel first entered Babylon under captivity, he was a young man, not yet an adult. He endured many trials and tribulations in his days, but God remained faithful. Cassie, my point is there aren't many stories in scripture of an individual not suffering in some way, whether it's Abraham and Sarah's infertility until old age; Joseph being traded into slavery; Moses in the book of Exodus attempting to free the Israelites from Pharaoh, and their subsequent forty years of wondering in the wilderness; Job losing everything and suffering through debilitating*

physical pain; David's enemy's constant pursuit; or Jesus and the incomprehensible suffering He endured on our behalf. The book of James says, "A man who endures trials is blessed because when he passes the test he will receive the crown of life that God has promised to those who love Him." I don't believe in coincidences, Cassie, and I need to acknowledge that God gave me your case for a reason. He's still pursuing you, which is why He sent me because He wants you back. Did you know that scripture illustrates the miracle of turning anguish into joy? John 16 paints an image of how agony is meant to lead to the birth of something. Jesus illustrated how painful childbirth is, but once the child is born, the mother forgets about the pain and focuses on the blessing of her child. If we trust Christ in our pain and don't turn our backs in defiance, He will see the agony through to the end. We don't see the whole picture like He does; in fact, our feeble brains cannot fathom a fraction of His plans, which is where our faith comes in. For whatever reason, this is a part of His plan, and trusting Him with this season of your life changes everything. Just because you're mad doesn't mean He won't listen, nor does it indicate that He doesn't love you. I heard a preacher say that our faith should not be anchored in our circumstances, but rather in a person, Jesus, who came and walked among us, experiencing life the way we do, and gave His life as a ransom for us. Put your faith in Jesus, not your situation."

After praying over the letter, Roxy folded the pages and placed it back inside the notebook.

***

Sam lifted the phone from its cradle and dialed Butler Philsey's number, mumbling a prayer under his breath.

"Philsey and Cummings, how may I help you?" a chipper female voice said.

"Yes ma'am, this is Sam Rollins. Is Mr. Philsey available?"

"Let me check for you, Mr. Rollins."

Listening to the soft saxophone and piano melody in his ear, he closed his eyes, getting his thoughts together, before Butler picked up the phone.

"Sam, how are you?" Butler's ancient voice rang out over the line.

"Doing well, Butler. How are you?"

"Oh, you know me. I can't complain. What can I do for you?"

As there was no point in being indirect, Sam said, "Cain Pierce is your client, correct?"

Butler seemed to hesitate. "Uh, yes, sir. Why do you ask?"

"Well." Sam chuckled. "That's complicated. My firm's investigating a possible wrongful conviction, and we're going on gut instinct that Cain may know something about our murders."

"What case?"

"It's the Blackwell murders from 2001."

There was no answer. Sam looked at the read out to ensure Butler remained on the line.

"I can't remember the case. Who tried it?"

"Greg Booker."

Butler chuckled. "No wonder you're looking into it. So, what does Cain have to do with this? His execution's in a few days."

"That's just it. He may have nothing to do with our case, but the Biggs family lived the next block over from the Blackwells back in 2001, and apart from Mr. Biggs enduring the murders, the criminalities are objectively comparable."

"Huh. Well, I can ask him if he'll consent to a visit with you. I assume your investigator will be tagging along to take point on the interview?"

"Roxanne's out of commission, but my law partner, Seth Carmichael, is substituting for her on this one."

"Okay, I'll see if I can get him on the phone later today, and I'll let you know."

Sam gave Butler his cell phone number and ended the call. Now all he could do was wait and see what happened.

***

Seth pulled the cardboard lid off the first banker box from the Biggs case. He had to tug a few cards before he could access the information, but the open records act always remained in his favor, even when he had to fight.

Retrieving the first pile of documents that was rubber-banded together, he took out his pen and legal pad and turned the first page. In his head, he thought of Roxy and her infatuation with this very tedious part of investigations. Some people had the knack for this and some didn't, but Roxy—well, let's just say she was overqualified in this area. He shook his head and pulled his runaway mind back to the case.

The crime scene photos halted his movements. Mrs. Biggs sat on the couch, her arm draped over her daughter, Elizabeth. The gunshot wound, visible in the head from the position of the photographs looked nearly, if not exactly, identical to those of his victims. The stippling around the wound suggested the shooter had shot at close range. Seth could see the reflection of the television on the glass coffee table in front of the victims. A blue bowl of popcorn sat tipped over between Kay and Elizabeth. The next photo was a close-up of the mother, her dull green eyes staring lifeless back at him, and a perfect hole between her eyebrows.

Dreading the next photo, he sucked in a breath and turned the page. As he thought, it was of Elizabeth's face, inert and innocent, with hazel eyes lacking the glow of life, and a similar hole, stippling also present, from the bullet in her forehead. The next several photos portrayed the house, seemingly untouched. The crime scene report stated no forced entry, fingerprints lifted from the front and back doors, no spent casings, Mr. Biggs nowhere in the home, positions and conditions of each victim, and a log of minimal evidence.

Attached to the report was a list of each person who had entered and left the scene, followed by the badge number and times. Scanning the list, he locked on Detective Kenton, one of the first to respond to the shots fired call. Taking feverish notes, he put a star beside the similarities to and a dash by the differences with the Blackwell's murder.

From what he could tell, Mr. Biggs had caved after he learned about the murders. A transcript of an interview conducted by Kenton with Mr. Biggs recorded the heartbreaking details of his addiction, the large sum of money owed, and the probability that the murders of his wife and daughter were the result of his debt. He provided the names and numbers of his dealers, and one thing led to another, which ended with Cain Pierce. More notoriety for Kenton, but one thing nagged at Seth; if Kenton was connected somehow, what's he holding over people to keep them quiet?

Scanning through the state's opening statement, he remembered what Roxy had told him about their theory that Cain didn't work alone and about his refusal to answer questions or give up his boss. The case was really a slam-dunk. Cain didn't stand a chance. The defense had tried to claim that Cain feared for his own life, and so he had done what he had to do; since he didn't provide a name, however, Cain's jury took less than an hour to convict him and less than that to sentence him to death.

The pieces didn't add up. He stared at his notes and ran various scenarios through his mind, but each time, something didn't fit. The Blackwells weren't addicts; there wasn't an enemy of either Sarah or Paul. They had Mrs. Nichols and her description, which was eerily close to Cain, but why the Blackwells?

The revelation hit him with the velocity of a train: Cain screwed up. It was an accident.

The address numbers were 206, but on different streets. Both families had three people, and each had a daughter close in age. Seth put his theory to the test, his pulse racing; he knew he was right, but proving this was the difficult part. Without Cain's admission, his fight upstream would be almost impossible. Seth took the boxes back to the clerk and ran out of the courthouse to his car.

Thinking of Roxy's session with Whitney, Seth elected to text her. On shaky fingers, he typed, "Call as soon as your PT session's over" and hit send.

Hopeful, he waited a few minutes, but no reply came. He'd tell Sam in front of the whiteboard and connect all the dots. Perhaps that was better anyway, given the potential interview with Cain.

When Seth entered the glass doors, he said, "Where's Sam?" to the receptionist.

"He's in his office. Just got off the phone with Butler Philsey."

"Thanks."

Hurrying down the hallway, passed Sam's office, he said, "Sam, come to Roxy's conference room, please," with urgency oozing in his voice despite his effort to conceal the excitement.

Sam walked in the room to see Seth sorting notes and pointing at Roxy's whiteboard.

"Sam, thanks. Please close the door, and draw the blinds."

Following Seth's instruction, he sat down and, obviously confused, said, "You look like a crazy person. What's up?"

"I had a—a revelation of sorts," Seth said, pacing in front of the whiteboard. "I used to think Roxy made this stuff up, but I think I had one. I think Cain killed the Blackwells on accident."

Sam reared back like a force of energy rushed his face. "That's a strong statement. Fill in the blanks."

Seth stepped in front of the whiteboard to illustrate his theory. "Okay, go with me here. Both families were made up of three people," he said, holding up three fingers, "and each had one daughter close in age. The crime scene photos are ridiculously similar, minus Mr. Blackwell."

The receptionist's voice came from the phone on the table. "I'm sorry to interrupt gentleman, but Roxy's on line two."

"Thank you," Sam said, and pushed the button, patching Roxy through.

"Seth, are you there?" Roxy asked.

Sam said, "We both are, sweetheart. Seth had a breakthrough and is in the beginning stages of articulating his apparent revelation."

A hearty laugh came through the line. "You thought I was insane when I told you about mine. I told you. It's the "aha" moment. All the pieces align, and God pulls the sheet up, exposing the finished puzzle. Oh, I can't wait," she said, with a squeak. "Let's hear it, but start over."

"I think Cain's our man. He killed the Blackwells on accident and finished his intended target months later, after the dust settled."

Before Seth could say another word, Roxy's voice burst over the speaker. "What?"

"Let me finish, honey."

"I was telling Sam about all the similarities. Okay, so the crime scene photos and manner of death are pretty much mirror images of the Blackwells, minus Paul. Nothing disturbed in the house at either scene. Both couples had one daughter, close in age. The house number of both homes was 206. Kenton was involved from the beginning on each case."

Roxy interrupted. "Wait. According to the state's timeline of the crime, Paul was leaving the room to turn the bath water off at precisely the same time the gunman entered the room. Paul caught him off guard, and once he killed him, he had to finish the job. He probably thought he met his mark, even though he killed Paul, too. It fits, Seth. How do we prove it?"

"That's the kicker. It's not what I believe but what I can prove that matters," Seth said.

Sam spoke up. "We have an interview at Polunsky tomorrow afternoon. Butler called back shortly before Seth arrived."

"Well, I'm going, too. Who's picking me up?" Roxy said.

Sam and Seth shared a look, and Seth shook his head.

"I don't know if that's such a good idea," Sam said.

"Sam, I'm not paralyzed. If they won't let me bring my crutches in, Seth can carry me to my chair before Cain comes in. This case is too important. I'm a big girl, and I'm going. It's not open for discussion."

Shaking his head in defeat, Seth said, "All right, Roxy. We need to call the prison first and make sure they'll allow the crutches."

"That's fine."

After the call ended, Sam looked over the table at Seth. "Don't alert the prison that Roxy's coming with you. We don't want another attempt on her life. I asked Butler to keep names off the list and just tell them it's a legal visit. It's safer that way, don't you think?"

"I didn't even think of that; good point. I guess I'll carry her if she can't bring in the crutches like she said." Seth shook his head and looked at Sam. "I know I can say this to you, but I don't think she's ready for a trip like this. Too much moving around involved, but she's a force all on her own, and arguing with her about her abilities is something I won't do."

"If Roxy believes she can make the trip, let her go, and be thankful that you'll be with her. She can sleep on the way back if need be. Promise me you'll keep your eye out for sabotage like before."

Seth nodded. "She and I will head up in the morning. I promise to keep you updated throughout the day, and Sam—I won't let anything happen to her."

Seth and Roxy talked over the new conclusion of the crime a hundred times that evening. Roxy's satisfaction with the results grew, but one glaring, titanic-sized iceberg remained unsolved: Sheriff Dale Kenton. That alone ate at Roxy well into the night as she struggled to sleep. An unanswered question for an investigator was the equivalent of missing a million dollars to an accountant. No matter how big or small the absent information, the search remained until the facts surfaced.

CHAPTER 20

GROGGY AND TIRED, Roxy hobbled to the car with Seth for their drive to Polunsky. Seth packed for her like a mother's first trip out with a newborn. You had to love the man for his overachieving signs of devotion toward her. That was her conclusion, anyways.

"So, how do you want to handle this?" Seth asked, steering through the preposterous Dallas highway system.

"I want to get a good look at him before I say a word. Mrs. Nichols provided a pretty good description of the guy. Well, nothing precise, but she said he was massive, remember? His mugshot demographics seem spot on, but I want to see for myself. We'll maintain control and ask our basic questions. Maybe he'll be forthcoming since he's days from death. Who knows?"

"I'm not counting on him spilling the beans, but we could get lucky. I'll just say I'm not holding my breath. Most criminals aren't honest about past crimes unless they benefit from the transaction, and we have nothing to offer him."

"A clear conscience, maybe?"

Seth belted a laugh. "Rox, he probably won't care about that, but you're always the optimistic one."

"I'm not confident in man, but in Jesus. He can turn anyone around, and I've seen Him do that. Look at you, Seth. You're a radical change if I've ever witnessed one."

Smiling and eyeing her between surveilling the wide-open road ahead of him, Seth said, "You're going to witness to him, aren't you?"

"He's hours from death. I'd feel worthless if I didn't at least ask the question. He deserves the same amount of grace and forgiveness I do."

After getting on 175-East, the highway turned into two lanes, and the trip was quiet. Although this was the slower of the many routes to take, Seth preferred this way because of the little towns they'd go through. Roxy admired the trees and the snowy, cotton-candy clouds above. There was something about a long journey in a car that ruptured the cognizance right open, bringing forth pent-up raw emotions. Maybe it was life fleeting by outside the window or the absence of anything to concentrate on that forces the brain into overdrive. Alternatively, perhaps it was just her; feasibly, she could be the only one who descends into an ocean of considerations while in the car. Her thoughts went from Rebecca and their unforeseen friendship, to Martin and the goodness of God, to Seth and her unequivocal affection for him.

Painfully, her myriad of emotions took her to Raleigh and her upcoming saunter into the last place she had spoken to him. She remembered the indescribable odor, bright white walls, bulletproof glass, small green counter, and black telephone linking the condemned man to the outside, all in the small visiting room.

A waterfall of emotion hit the marrow of her bones at the sight of Raleigh's hand pressed on the glass as her own trembled on her side, and their tearful prayers over the phone. Echoes of her heels ricocheting off the hard floor as she exited the room and her melting into Seth's arms when the door closed behind her. Her last image of

Raleigh when she turned away was his head in his hands, as if it were weighed down.

When her mind settled, the black metal sign that read "Allan B. Polunsky Unit" in white block letters backed by lush, emerald grass entered her field of vision. When they entered the prison, Seth took her to the first chair available before he checked them in. The immediate atmospheric conversion of the facility struck her the minute she sat down.

After the check-in process ended, Roxy took a deep breath, closed her hand around the handle to open the visiting room door, and faced the dread head on. Hobbling the best she could while trying to look dignified at the same time, she almost fell into a brown-backed plastic chair in front of the glass pane.

Roxy heard the bars clattering and closed her eyes. No other sound in the world mirrored that of those solid metal tubes knocking together. She heard shuffling feet and chains jangling from the ankle shackles worn by Mr. Pierce. When she looked up, her eyes processed the monstrosity of a man standing before her. Like John Coffey in the Green Mile, Cain Pierce towered over the guard unlocking his handcuffs in order to turn him around and secure him to the visiting table. Cain's expression stayed in a state of confusion as they waited for the prison officials to finish securing him.

Roxy studied the man as he stared at his lap, seeming to refuse eye contact with her. He certainly qualified as the massive man Mrs. Nichols saw.

She picked up the phone, rubbing the ends on her shirt before bringing the connected line to her ear.

"Mr. Pierce, my name is Roxanne Hollis, and I'm a private investigator. This is my partner, Seth Carmichael, an attorney. We just need to ask a few questions."

Finally, his head lifted just enough for his eyes to meet Roxy's and freeze her blood. His eyes were nearly all black, revealing the smallest ring of golden brown at the edge of his pupils. She'd seen full-blown methamphetamine addicts with massive pupils, but

Cain's eyes were different; his pupils lacked immense dilation, and his eyes were simply black, almost lifeless. The dark circles around them gave him a raccoon appearance. His high cheekbones protruded out from under his eyes, and his large nose appeared to have seen its fair share of breaks. His skin matched his white jumpsuit from lack of exposure to sunlight.

"What do you want with me?" he asked, in a deep and emotionless voice.

Seth leaned close to the receiver Roxy held. "Cain, we need to know about the Blackwell murders in 2001."

Roxy shot Seth a look with a 'way to be subtle' expression. "Mr. Pierce, we're representing Cassandra Lovejoy, who is also on death row for the murders of her employers. The family lived at 206 Pear Tree Street in the Whitehead Estates addition located in Westlake. The Biggs family lived at 206 Peachtree Street until soon after the Blackwells were murdered, and then they moved. Do you know anything about this?"

She studied Cain as he appeared to mull over her words, and she allowed the silence to hang in the air. After an eternal few minutes, Cain answered, "I don't know what you're talking about."

Seth met her eyes with a nod, and she released the phone, leaning back so Seth could put the receiver to his ear.

"Cain, I studied the crime scene photos from both scenes, and I have to say they were the exact same except for Paul Blackwell. Here's our theory: someone hired you to settle the debt from Mr. Biggs, and you scaled the wall surrounding the neighborhood, wearing a black bandanna tied around your face. Next, you ran to what you believed was the Biggs home, slipped in the back door, were startled when Paul walked out of the family room, and in a millisecond of panic, you killed him. Not realizing you were at the wrong house altogether, you stepped over Mr. Blackwell, walked into the family room, and finished off Sarah and Faith before running out the same way you entered. How am I doing so far?"

Cain shook his head but didn't utter a syllable.

"Several months later, after the storm settled and Cassandra caught the murder charges, you finished your original task with the proper targets."

Crickets. Dead, earth-crushing silence.

Roxy took the phone back. "Mr. Pierce, Cassandra Lovejoy is an innocent woman a few months from her own execution date. Have mercy on her, and tell the truth. What else do you have to lose?" Her voice shook, and she knew he heard the fright in her tone.

He met her eyes. "Are you finished, yet?"

Roxy blinked, staring at him for any amount of emotion, whatsoever. "No, I have one more question: do you know Jesus, Cain?"

The smugness in his laugh made the hair on her arms prickle.

"Yeah, he's my cell mate." He slammed the phone down and yelled, "Guard."

Instantly feeling the defeat, Roxy pushed herself up and limped out of the visiting room before the guard came for the man she knew in her bones had committed the murders.

Seth sat unmoving in the chair, glaring at Cain. He recalled the rate of depression in inmates on death row. How grown men like Cain lose their minds in the quiet of solitary confinement. How many of them even refused the one hour a day they can escape their sixty-square-foot living quarters. Solitary makes the most stable man unbalanced and insane. We weren't created to be alone in small spaces, and the evidence of this could be found inside any prison. When Cain stood, turning around for the guard, he looked at Seth with a subdued countenance.

Seth rose to his feet and walked out of the room, wondering what he could've done differently. Cain had killed them, and he knew that, but he couldn't prove it, regardless how much he wanted to, needed to, for Cassie. Moments later, he picked Roxy up out of the chair and carried her out to his car, her crutches slung over his shoulder.

He didn't know what to say. He knew she was all too aware that they couldn't prove the innocence of their client again. How did he approach this with her in a productive and somehow positive manner? He could feel her heart shattering in the silence, and her fear of loss hung palpable in the car as he pulled out of the parking lot.

They rode in silence for almost an hour before Roxy spoke.

"What can we do now, Seth? All we have are hypotheticals and the nagging thorn in my side with Kenton." Her voice lowered to a whisper. "We're finished."

Seth shook his head, processing his opinions and desires to tell her everything would be all right when he knew it wouldn't be. A second failure would wreck her, his beautiful, courageous, strong, and intelligent woman, who was the love of his life.

Through the speakers he heard Natalie Grant's voice sing out in angelic sounds. "When did I forget that You've always been the King of the world? How could I make You so small when You're the One who holds it all?"

Seth smiled and thumbed the knob, increasing the volume and letting Christ answer this one for him. Allowing the lyrics to strike his heart with heavenly force, he prayed and remembered one of his pillar verses: "Every good and perfect gift comes down from the Father of heavenly lights." *Thank you, Lord. Give Roxy peace.*

As the words rang out, Roxy embraced the answer and laid her worries at God's feet. Understanding engrossed her soul, and she submitted, recognizing her first and utmost significant choice was trusting Christ with her entire life. No matter what happened, He had ordained everything from beginning to end. Even losing another case wouldn't sway her belief in the scriptures and the goodness of Jesus. As if God had opened the imaginary Bible in her mind, the Sermon on the Mount spilled into her thoughts.

> "Don't worry about your life, what you will eat or
> what you will drink; or about your body, what you
> will wear. Isn't life more than food and the body more

than clothing? Look at the birds of the sky: They don't sow or reap or gather into barns, yet your Heavenly Father feeds them. Aren't you worth more than they? Can you add a single cubit to his height by worrying? And why do you worry about your clothes? See how the flowers of the field grow. They do not labor or spin. Yet I tell you that not even Solomon in all his splendor was dressed like one of those. If that is how God clothes the grass of the field, which is here today and tomorrow is thrown in the fire, will He not much more clothe you—you of little faith. So, do not worry saying, "What shall we eat" or "What shall we drink" or "What shall we wear." For the pagans run after all these things and your Heavenly Father knows that you need them."

Closing her eyes and allowing the next words to flood her soul, she recited the truths her heart needed to rid the anxiety.

"But seek first the kingdom of God and His righteousness and all those will be provided for you. Therefore, don't worry about tomorrow, because tomorrow will worry about itself. Each day has enough troubles of its own."

CHAPTER 21

"I WANT TO PRESENT THE WHOLE THING to you and see if you think it's enough," Roxy said, to Sam the following evening. "Examining everything standing alone doesn't amount to much, but in its totality, I think we may be in good shape."

"All right. Let's hear it."

Seth walked down the hallway just as Roxy started her presentation, and she waved him in.

"Okay, let's put out of our mind what we're missing, and look at what we have in context."

Roxy laid out her blown up aerial photos of the neighborhood, zoomed in on the two streets.

Pointing at the various pictures, she said, "The sun set at roughly 6:07 that evening. We know the murders happened sometime between six thirty and seven, when Cassie returned from the store. Even the medical examiner used the same times, so this theory could work. There are only streetlights on the corners, here and here—" she pointed to the map "—which are quite a bit taller than the street signs. Hypothetically, if this was a mistake by Cain, he easily could've missed the whole sign, saw the 'P' at the beginning and went to the Blackwells' house. Mrs. Nichols had a visual of Cain coming out of the house, dropping his bandanna, running up the block, turning around briefly but deciding against it, and running down the block toward the wall. What we don't know is where he parked his car or if someone was waiting to pick him up. We have Jackie's affidavit about her lying to receive a plea deal and my testimony about Amanda, even though she won't sign anything. We have Mrs. Nichols' smoking gun that she gave Kenton a detailed statement about what she saw that night. At the very least, we have gross negligence, ineffective assistance of counsel, and more than one Brady violation. Doesn't that amount to reasonable doubt if we tried the case today?"

Sam rubbed the back of his neck, deep in thought for several moments.

"You know, it's not as solid as I'd like, but it's more than I thought we had. Since the levels of proof are diverse in my usual practice of law, I think this succeeds as unblemished and conclusive evidence for Cain, abundantly more than the state presented against Cassandra at trial. Now Judge Grey could argue that this amounts to contingent evidence and doesn't meet our tasked burden of proof, but I'm willing to give it a shot. The worst they can do is say no, right?"

Seth leaned back in his chair and interlocked his hands behind his head.

"You think we have a chance, or are you trying just to say you did?"

"Well, we have more than we had with Raleigh, but less than previous cases. Truthfully, it's a toss-up, but one I'm prepared to take for the sake of justice."

Roxy's eyes lit up, looking back and forth from Seth to Sam while she thought of the possibilities.

The phone rang, shaking all of them from their thoughts. Seth answered after realizing the receptionist was gone for the day. "Rollins and Carmichael."

Hearing only one side of the call, Roxy paid attention to Seth's facial expressions. "Yes, sir, he's sitting right here. Can you hold for a minute, please?"

Pressing the hold button, he turned toward Sam. "It's Butler Philsey."

Roxy looked at the clock. "Cain's execution probably just wrapped up. It's six thirty."

Taking the phone from Seth's hand, Sam hit the hold button. "Butler. This is a surprise. What can I do for you?"

After a few minutes, Sam said, "Yeah, sure. We can wait here. My team's already in the office. I'll unlock the front door, and we're in the last conference room on the right when you walk down the second hallway."

Sam put the phone in the cradle and turned. "The warden just alerted Butler that Cain's execution finished with no complications. He had to wait for that before delivering a document he and Cain put together during their visit earlier today. Cain gave specific instructions to deliver it to you, Roxy."

Roxy glanced at Seth before meeting Sam's gaze. "Did he say what's in said folder?"

"Nope, but he's on his way here, so we'll know soon."

Roxy's head churned with a million possibilities of what the document was. She'd never considered that Cain would spill his guts from the grave. She pulled her laptop toward her and navigated to the news stories from Cain's execution. She had to know what his final words were.

"He made no statement," she said.

"What?" Seth asked.

"Cain. He didn't say a word before his execution."

Butler appeared in the doorway, wearing dark slacks, a white dress shirt tucked in with suspenders, and a blue bowtie. He was a round, gray-haired man with small, black-rimmed glasses. Butler entered the room with confidence and offered his hand in greeting to the three of them before he sat next to Sam and across from Roxy.

He placed a manila folder in front of him. "Roxy, I took this affidavit from Cain during our visit earlier today. You were right, and hopefully this account will provide enough information to help your client."

Roxy's heart felt like a bass drum in her ears, and for a second, she thought she might pass out. Without a sound, she slid her hand across the table and took the folder from Butler. She opened it and took inventory of what the document was: a signed and notarized affidavit from Cain Pierce taken at eleven thirty a.m.

> "My name is Cain Pierce, and I am fifty-two years old. To the best of my knowledge, I swear that the following information is true. I'm making this statement of my own free will. I was not pressured into this by anyone, but my own conscience."

> "On February 9, 2001, I shot and killed Paul, Sarah, and Faith Blackwell."

Roxy sucked in a breath, and her hands trembled.

> "As a hired hitman, I murdered the wrong family that day. I originally received ten thousand dollars for killing the two people I'm currently sitting on death row for, Kay and Elizabeth Biggs. On February 9, 2001, I thought I was in the correct house, but I was off by one block. I did not intend to kill the man of the house, but as another mistake, Mister Blackwell startled me, and I reacted by shooting him. Cassandra Lovejoy was nowhere near the home, and I've never met her. She had nothing to do with killing the Blackwells, and I hope to set the record straight with this statement."

Roxy looked up, confidence and dread in her expression, to see Sam and Seth, who were staring at her with the eagerness of a kid given free-rein in a candy store.

"Sheriff Dale Kenton runs drugs stolen from busts his department makes. Off the books, I was his confidential informant, turned drug runner, and, finally, hitman. I did his bidding for about twenty years. I can provide detailed information, including names and locations to prove this."

Roxy reread that sentence as the dots connected. In her head, she screamed, *I knew it!*

"He has a drug complaint on his record, which also involved me. There's a cabin on the north end of Blue Rocker Lake, off the beaten path. I attached a hand drawn map to the cabin from memory. About one hundred feet back from the cabin, you'll find a shop, which will provide you with more than enough evidence against the sheriff. Todd Hutch is now his right-hand man. He won't admit anything without protection for his family. I also ask the same thing for my daughter, who is nineteen and lives with her mother in Houston. Please provide protection for them before you act against Kenton. Otherwise he'll kill her. Everything he withheld during the Blackwell investigation that implicated me is also in the shop."

Roxy lifted her head but couldn't manage to verbalize a sentence. She needed to process the information, but there was no time.

"Who knows about this, Butler?" Roxy asked, looking up at him.

"Nobody. Mister Pierce is still protected by attorney-client privilege, but I had permission to deliver this to you. What you do with the information is up to you. Am I needed for anything else?"

Roxy flipped through the three-page statement and eyed the included map. "Nope. We can take it from here. Thanks for bringing it by."

Butler let himself out and shut the door behind him. Roxy slid the file to Sam. "Will you read this out loud? I need to hear it again, and Seth is foaming at the mouth in anticipation."

Sam began, and within sixty seconds, his voice was shaking. Roxy had her eyes closed and built the scene in her mind. Everything fell into place, but how would they go about getting to the cabin and seizing the evidence?

Sam finished, set the papers down, and looked to Roxy in a daze of sorts. "How—what—we have to get to the cabin, but we can't alert the police."

The answer hit Roxy like a punch to the gut.

"I'll go to Clark first thing in the morning. You saw how he handled Raleigh's petition. He's on the side of truth. The sign behind his desk reads 'May justice be done even if the heavens fall,' and I can't believe I'm saying this, but I think he's one of the good guys."

Seth perked up. "Whoa. Someone get a recording device to document that Roxanne Hollis just admitted a prosecutor might be a good guy."

Sam chuckled but returned to being serious. "She's right. We can't go to the police; we certainly can't go ourselves, which leaves Clark as our last resort. The DA's office has investigators on staff, and if he takes the information to a judge, other than Grey, he may get a search warrant."

Roxy straightened her back. "That settles it, then. In the morning, I'll meet with Clark and see where his loyalty lays. I hope my instincts are right on this one."

Sam reached out his hands toward Roxy and Seth. "We should pray before we part ways."

CHAPTER 22

"ROXANNE, GOOD TO HEAR FROM YOU. How are you?"

Roxy called Clark's office at eight fifteen, hoping to catch him before court.

"I'm fine; thanks for taking my call. Sorry to drop this on you with such short notice, but I need to talk to you about something in person. Do you have time today?"

Roxy heard ruffling papers. "Well, I have court at ten. Can you get here soon? I need to head down to the courtroom around nine thirty."

Looking down at her pajamas, she said, "I'll be there in thirty minutes."

"I look forward to it."

Terminating the call, she met Seth's eyes. "I need to hurry. Can you grab my jeans, blue button-down, undershirt, and my black toms, please? I'll be in the bathroom."

"Of course," Seth said, jumping up. Going down the hall ahead of her, he said, "You sure you don't want me to go with you?"

"I need to handle this. They have an entrance with no stairs. Can you drop me off, though? I'm still not comfortable driving. I can call you when I'm done or take a cab to the office."

She heard his socked feet coming down the hall. "Here's your clothes. Are you presentable?"

She smiled and would never tire of his respect for her in moments like these. "I'm still dressed."

Without coming in the doorway, he stretched out his arm and dropped the clothes on the bathroom counter.

***

Roxy reached the elevator in the county courthouse, although she broke out in a sweat. She'd make up her missed physical therapy later. She crutched through the glass doors of the prosecutor's office and checked in with the secretary.

Sitting in the waiting room, she surveyed the bustling assistant district attorneys entering and leaving their offices. She pondered how many of them where on the up-and-up, honest, and truly fighting for justice, not their personal conviction rate.

"Miss Hollis, he'll see you now."

Roxy grabbed her briefcase, putting the strap over her head and situating the bag close to her side, before pushing herself upright on her good leg and donning her crutches. "Thank you," she said, walking by her desk to the open door of Clark's office. When she walked in, Clark's face registered concern at the sight of her.

"Do I still look that bad?" she asked, before landing in the chair with a thud.

Walking across his office to close the door and tell his secretary not to disturb him, he said, "No, not at all. I wasn't prepared. What happened?"

Roxy felt her face redden. "A car accident, pretty bad actually, but I'm on the mend now."

"Well, I'm glad to hear that. What's this all about?"

Clark took the chair next to Roxy, rather than the one behind his desk.

Roxy eyed the mural behind his desk and looked back at him. "Is that your motto or something?"

"When I graduated law school, that quote was one thing I carried with me. My favorite professor recited it, often. He said the difference between a good and a great attorney was the one who allowed justice to dictate their cases, not personal gain."

Roxy felt her prejudgment of Clark condemn her conscience but promised to allow those walls to fall and build trust with him. "Well, I'm about to test that theory. Cain Pierce's execution concluded yesterday, and after receiving confirmation of his death, his attorney delivered this to me."

She handed the folder to Clark, but before he could open it, she placed her hand over his. "Hang on, let me say something. This will be hard to believe, but I have further evidence to add once you're finished. Just promise me you'll consider what you're about to read with an open mind."

Clark nodded. "You have my word." He opened the folder, and faced the contents. Roxy watched his body language, trying to discern anything as he took in the information. She noticed his neck turning red when he flipped the second page. When he lifted his head, she detected apprehension.

"Wow. I don't know about this."

"I told you you'd have more questions than answers after reading it, but please, hear me out."

"You definitely have my attention." Clark said.

Without breaking eye contact, Roxy laid everything out for Clark to analyze. In her briefcase, she had Mrs. Nichols' and Jackie's affidavits, which she pulled out in step with the explanation of her investigation. She ended by showing him a photo of the handwritten threat in chalk on her driveway and the burnt remains of her home.

After she finished, she waited for Clark to speak. "What do you want me to do with all this?"

"We couldn't go to the police because Kenton's one of them, and we don't want to tip him off. We're counting on you to obtain a warrant and find this cabin, under the radar, of course."

Clark put his head down and studied the veracity of the information lying in his lap. She watched him, wondering if he felt the conviction to solve this as much as she did or if she'd misjudged him, after all. Time crept by, and Clark traveled from page to page, weighing the possible validity.

"I have some connections in Houston for Cain's family. Can you spare Mr. Carmichael for a few hours?

Wondering why he would ask that, she muttered, "Yes."

"Okay, I have a trusted investigator, but I'd like Seth to go with him. Do you think he'll come along?"

She fought immense jealously. "Of course he would, but why?"

"I think it keeps the scales balanced. Plus, Mr. Carmichael knows what we're looking for, and we don't have the time to get my guy up to speed. Will he be available late this afternoon? It's going to take me some time to think of which judge to go to with this because, as I'm sure you know, Judge Grey and Sheriff Kenton are old friends. We cannot afford to tip his hand."

Roxy nodded in agreement, swinging between rafters of thoughts in her mind. "What about Judge O'Malley? He seems pretty fair and more on the conservative side."

"Good point. He's in the pool of possibilities with Judge Watkins and Judge Snowden. I'll figure it out after I generate the warrant, but you have my word, this will be done today. Do you have Mr. Carmichael's number? The investigator I'm going to put on this is Daniel Harvey. He'll contact Mr. Carmichael once we have a signed warrant."

Roxy fingered through her purse and pulled out a standard business card from the firm.

"His cell phone number is on the back. I'll let him know he's on standby. I can't thank you enough for doing this."

Clark stood and looked down at Roxy, offering his hand to assist her in standing up. "Don't take this the wrong way, but this isn't for you. It's for Miss Lovejoy and the citizens of this county."

***

She settled herself in the office chair and told Sam and Seth everything. The expression on Seth's face when he heard that Clark had singled him out made her heart swell and her prior feelings of jealously melt away like candle wax.

"Now, we just wait for his call," she said.

"This is really happening," Seth said, almost singing the words.

"Good job, sweetheart," Sam said, putting his hand on her arm and squeezing.

"Well, we don't know if Cain's pulling our leg or not. We'll see if the proof is where he said it'd be. I'm not convinced of his integrity at this point."

Sam smiled. "We found a cabin in Kenton's late wife's name on Blue Rocker Lake. From the aerial map, we can see the shop, which I'd call more of a shed. Cain's right so far, but we'll see what's in the shed before we hang our bets on the information."

"Show me."

Sam grabbed Roxy's computer, keyed in the information, and flipped the screen back to her. Her eyes flew to the screen like a magnet, and she studied the map, zooming in on the shed. She saw the green-roofed, steel shed behind the cabin, which didn't appear well-kept or maintained at all. From the picture, she could see areas of the grass pushed down from tire tracks behind the cabin, leading straight to the shed door.

The hours crawled by, and the three busied themselves, waiting on the call from Daniel. Seth went home and changed to jeans and a t-shirt for the outing. She imagined arriving at the shed, breaking the lock, and opening the doors to find—what? Drugs, weapons, large amounts of cash, hidden evidence of past crimes, and secrets that would soon land the dear sheriff behind bars?

At four thirty, Seth's phone rang.

"Seth Carmichael."

Seth said, "Yes, Daniel, thanks for calling."

"Sure, we can do that. I have a BMW, so by the looks of the road, your truck sounds more appropriate."

After a few more seconds, Seth answered, "My office is six blocks west of the courthouse. You can pick me up here, if you want."

Half a minute passed, Seth nodded. "Sounds good, man, I'll be ready."

Turning to address the eager Sam and Roxy, Seth said, "With warrant in hand, he'll be here in fifteen minutes. Sounds like a nice guy."

"Are you going to take the video camera to film the search in the event we need it?" Sam asked.

"I think we should. I'll ask Daniel if he has a camera or if I need to bring ours when he gets here."

"You know what to look for, right?" Roxy asked.

"I have a pretty good idea of what we'll find if Cain's telling the truth. I promise to call if I see anything questionable, okay?"

She nodded. "All right."

Sensing that Roxy and Seth needed a minute, Sam said, "I'll be in my office" and left them alone.

Seth walked to Roxy and put his hands on her shoulders.

"Honey, I know what I'm doing. Would I prefer you go? Absolutely, but we work with what we have, and right now, this is it. I need you to trust me, and you have my word that I'll call you if I have doubts on anything, big or small."

"Oh, how I wish it was me; I won't lie. But I trust your abilities," she said. "I know you can handle this. I just have to submit to the situation and release control of the investigation, again."

Roxy heard the front door open, followed by footsteps echoing off the hardwood floor down the hall.

"Hello." Daniel spoke from the hallway.

"We're in here," Seth said.

Daniel came into the room, and Roxy looked at the linebacker-sized man with a bald head and bright blue eyes.

"Daniel Harvey," he said, offering his hand to Roxy and Seth in greeting.

After they exchanged pleasantries, Seth and Daniel discussed the game plan and equipment needed for the warrant.

"Miss Hollis, is there anything I need to know before we leave?" Daniel asked.

In her head, she processed through what to tell him but changed her mind. "Seth knows the case. He can tell you on the way."

Seth glanced at Roxy with new adoration in his eyes. She hoped he realized that had taken a great deal of strength for her to do. Taking the backseat on her case wasn't easy for her. Call it controlling or ambitious, but this role was temporary, and when she healed, she'd be back in the driver seat.

"Well, we better get going," Daniel said. "It was nice to meet you, Miss Hollis."

"Please, call me Roxanne. Good luck out there."

"I'll be out in a minute," Seth said, returning to his spot next to Roxy. "I love you so much. Thank you for what you just did; I know how difficult it was, and I appreciate it."

Roxy gazed into his eyes, feeling a conflicting combination of nerves, fear, and joy, admiring the man in front of her.

"I love you, too. Promise me you'll be careful."

He kissed her forehand, grabbed her hands, and prayed over his trip. Roxy watched him walk away, and her nose burned with impending tears.

Seth situated himself in the black Ford truck and buckled his seatbelt.

Once Daniel turned out of the parking lot, Seth said, "What did Clark tell you about the case and what we're looking for?"

Daniel kept his eyes on the road. "I read the affidavit from the convict, and he told me some background on the case. Do you actually believe him?"

Great, Seth thought, *so much for an unbiased counterpart to execute the search warrant with.*

Seth cleared his throat. "If you knew everything I knew, you'd have no trouble hanging credibility on Cain's statement."

"All right, please enlighten me, because at this point, I'm feeling like this is a massive waste of time. This guy is the sheriff, for crying out loud, not some two-bit criminal." He shook his head and looked at Seth. "We have about twenty-five minutes until we get to the cabin. I'm all ears."

Seth told Daniel everything about the case and his suspicions about Kenton. He left nothing out and figured they'd hit pay dirt in the shed, or he'd look like a fool, but at this point, he believed Cain.

After he talked nonstop for fifteen minutes, Daniel said, "You really think he tried to kill Roxanne?"

"Nothing else makes sense. Every time she made progress on the case, something happened to her. First her house burned down, which the fire investigator determined was arson, and then someone ran her off the road and left her for dead. I don't believe in coincidences."

Daniel shook his head.

"I don't either. That's one of the first things I learned as an investigator. Either Roxanne had terrible luck, or you're right. What's that old saying, if it walks and talks like a duck, it's probably a duck?" He chuckled. "We'll soon find out if your theory's true. I'm at least more curious now."

Seth let that hang in the air and decided against making small talk. He watched his surroundings through the window, the sun playing peekaboo through the trees, and prayed in earnest that Kenton was nowhere near his cabin.

The truck rocked as they turned onto a dirt road. Reading the map, Seth navigated Daniel's direction. Daniel stopped about a football field's distance from the cabin and took out a pair of high-caliber binoculars.

Seth watched Daniel zero in on the cabin. "We're clear. Let's roll," Daniel said, lowering the binoculars.

Seth saw the shed come into view and noticed the heavy-duty lock on the door. "Good thing we have lock cutters big enough to handle that," Seth said.

Picking up their pace, they put rubber gloves on, constantly looking around for anyone in the area. Seth looked up and calculated by the position of the sun that they'd soon run out of daylight. Pulling out the bolt cutters, Daniel strong-armed the tool and snapped the lock.

Seth tried the doorknob. "It's locked, too."

Daniel stood a foot away and said, "Watch out," before planting his massive foot on the door, busting it open. Seth began rolling the video when they crossed the threshold.

Panning his light around for better visibility, he saw a window covered by a blanket and watched Daniel pull it down to expose the inside. Dust and dirt littered the air. Seth coughed and closed his eyes for a few moments. Seth saw two file cabinets sitting in one corner, a makeshift desk with a chair, a heavy-duty lockable storage cabinet, and several cardboard boxes. Seth estimated the shed's size to be ten by twenty feet.

"We should start with the file cabinets; they are easiest to unlock. Come help me," Daniel said.

Seth walked across the shed and positioned the camera on the desk, facing toward the cabinets.

Daniel said, "Tilt the cabinet back from the front, and hold it there for a minute."

Seth complied and watched Daniel crouch down. Seconds later, Seth heard the clicking of metal-on-metal and Daniel stood up. "Okay, put it down."

Seth did and watched Daniel open the top drawer. "Works like a charm every time. Here, let's do the same thing with the other one, and we can each look through a cabinet."

The two performed the same routine, and Seth heard an identical click and opened the top drawer. Seth went through the first drawer and found nothing relevant. The second and third were the same. The last drawer, however, made Seth's pulse rise. He found a file marked "Blackwell." Inside the folder, he found Mrs. Nichols' interview notes, an outline of his investigation, and summaries on how to slant the evidence toward Cassandra. The last page took his breath—handwritten and earth tilting, it was a description of what Cain must've told Kenton about the murders.

"Bingo," Seth said, holding the piece of paper up.

"You might want to see this, too," Daniel said.

Seth walked over and looked at the file. Daniel said, "Educated guess here, but this looks like a detailed spreadsheet of how much drugs he took, on what date, from what case, and the street value."

Seth looked over to the locked storage container. "I'm betting we find the goodies in there. Can you open one of those, too?"

Daniel pulled a Gruber off his belt and chose a tool. "There's one way to find out."

Seth held his breath and watched Daniel attempt to pick the lock. A few moments later, Seth saw Daniel turn the handle and heard the click of victory. Daniel drew the door open and whistled.

Seth took several quick steps and saw what caused Daniel to take in a breath. Bundles of cash lined the top shelf, portioned bags of drugs on the second, and multiple guns on the bottom. Seth felt the blood drain from his face as he stared at the contents.

"Your guy was spot on," Daniel said.

Seth froze in place. *No wonder he was after Roxy the way he was. His career is over.*

They couldn't seize the evidence themselves, but they had Kenton lock, stock, and barrel. Daniel snapped several pictures and sent a text to Clark. Seth still had the Blackwell file in his hand when he heard the ground shifting under a vehicle's tires in the distance. The sun had set, and dusk was fading. Seth met Daniel's eyes as sweat beads formed over his brows. His palms dampened, and his vision blurred.

Daniel and Seth bolted from the shed, Seth cradling the camera under his left arm. They hid behind trees and shrubs as they darted toward Daniel's truck. Seth's stomach threatened to lurch out of his mouth when he saw a County Sheriff's SUV coming down the road. Seth fell on his face behind some tall greenery, sweat snaking down his back, and tried to quiet the loud thumping of his heart drumming in his ears. Daniel took the same posture about fifty yards ahead.

The SUV crept down the road at a snail's pace, passed their location and stopped at the truck. Seth grabbed his phone and sent a text to Roxy. "Call 911, give them the cabin address, and tell them it's urgent." He had no time to worry about the instant agony Roxy would feel reading his words. He turned his phone off and slid it back in his pocket.

***

Sam, Heather, and Roxy sat at the dinner table at Sam's house, playing air hockey with their food, nobody eating anything. Roxy heard her phone ding, put her fork down, and locked her hand around the device sitting beside her plate. The marrow in her bones turned to ice, and her hand flew to her mouth. Horror took over the second she read Seth's words.

"Sam, call 911." Roxy barely managed to get the words out, sliding her phone across the table.

Sam grabbed the phone, and his hands began to tremble as he jumped up from the table and put Roxy's phone to his ear.

"911, what's your emergency," a female voice said.

Sam's voice rattled. "Please send the police to 600 Greenwood Lane on the north side of Blue Rocker Lake."

"What's going on, sir?"

"I don't know," Sam yelled, before he could temper his emotions. "Just please send help to that location, and tell the responders it's urgent."

***

Seth heard the car door open and barely lifted his eyes from the ground to see Kenton stepping out of his SUV, simultaneously pulling his gun from the holster on his hip. Seth remained as still as possible, not making a sound. Seth heard leaves rustling and saw Daniel move up about fifty yards.

Seth heard two gunshots in quick succession.

Before Seth could complete that thought, he heard a third shot, followed by a gut-curdling scream, and saw Daniel's body landing on fallen leaves. Seth poked his head up and saw Daniel holding his leg, moaning. Sirens sounded in the distance. Seth crawled toward Daniel, but before he could reach him, another shot shattered the quiet around him. His shoulder flew backward with an explosion of what felt like a blazing torch coursing through his veins, and the pain pulled him to the ground.

***

The officers wouldn't tell Roxy anything and the idea of living without Seth was too much. Numbly going through the motions, Roxy focused on taking steps, refusing the wheelchair Sam suggested. She fought through the discomfort crawling up and down her leg, determined to walk this battle on her own two feet.

"Roxy," Clark yelled, coming through the emergency room doors. "They're all right. Both in surgery, but they'll be fine. Kenton shot them. Seth in the shoulder, and Daniel in the leg."

Roxy's feet became unsteady and Sam caught her before she fell. The waterfall of tears soaked her face and puddled on her shirt. She wrapped her arms around Sam and let the agonizing joy take over.

"Sh, sweetheart, he'll be fine. Seth will pull through. You heard what Clark said; it's probably a flesh wound," Sam said, rubbing her back.

"I know. My heart hasn't caught up with my brain. I just need to get it out," Roxy said.

Heather carried one crutch; Roxy used the other, with her arm over Sam's shoulder for added support. She welcomed the pale green cushioned chair in the waiting room and wiped her face with the palms of her hands.

Clark took the chair across from Roxy.

"What happened?" Roxy asked, holding a tissue to muffle any further tears.

"What I have so far is bits and pieces, but Kenton's in an interrogation room. When the police responded, he attempted to blame the whole thing on Seth and Daniel, explaining that they broke into his shed and he defended himself. What he didn't count on was the warrant falling out of Daniel's pocket, when the medical responders put him on the gurney. Once the lead detective saw the warrant, they cuffed Kenton and took him back to the station. From what I hear, the police are still at the shed. Oh, look at this," Clark said, handing his phone to Roxy, which displayed the picture Daniel had sent him of the loot.

"Oh, and here's this," he said, passing a manila folder to her. "The ambulance driver said Seth was adamant that you get this. I haven't even looked at it yet, figured it wasn't my place."

Roxy slowed her spinning head, feeling the smooth, paper file between her fingers. Her eyes zeroed in on the first piece of small white paper, and she instantly knew it was Mrs. Nichols' interview notes. Her heart quickened as she read the statement, which was nearly identical to the affidavit she obtained. The paper crinkled when she turned to the next page, a handwritten and detailed investigative outline of the murders, including what to "overlook" and "forget" in order to frame Cassie. She felt heat move up her neck. The last page sent a cold chill down her spine, as she read the words from Cain's statement and pictured the murder through his description.

Her eyes welled up when she handed the file to Sam. "We did it."

Sam took the file and went through the information, but much slower than Roxy. His head shook, and she noticed his fist clench when he arrived at the second page. A slight breeze hit her cheek from Sam closing the file. He met her eyes with vindication and anger masking his face. "We got him!"

Clark looked back and forth from Roxy to Sam. "Can I see the file now?"

Sam laughed. "Sorry. Here you go."

"Who's here for Seth Carmichael?" a male nurse asked. Roxy shot up too fast and moaned at the familiar pain that volleyed up her body.

"We are," Roxy said. She grabbed her crutches and made her way across the white-tiled floor.

"Right this way," the man said, motioning to follow him. Everyone, aside from Clark, took their place in the line behind the nurse. He stopped outside room seven. "Mr. Carmichael's waiting for you."

Roxy knocked, opened the door, and jokingly said, "Are you decent?"

"The voice I longed to hear," Seth responded.

Roxy moved the curtain and saw the man she now realized she never wanted to live without propped up in the bed, his face unharmed, and his right shoulder bandaged and in a sling. She hurried on her unsteady feet to his bed and fell on his chest, her body trembling with joyful tears.

"Now I know how you felt," she said, raising her head to face him. "I thought I might've lost you, and I couldn't bear it."

"I'm right here, babe, and Lord willing, I plan to grow old with you," he said, wiping her tears with his thumb.

She heard another knock and realized Heather and Sam hadn't followed her in but had allowed them to have a few moments alone.

"May we come in?" Sam's comforting voice connected with her ears.

"Please do," Seth said, and Roxy pushed herself up and sat in the chair next to the bed, grabbing his hand with both of hers.

"Boy, you two are a sight, both broken and injured and you're not even married yet," Sam said.

"I'll have her anyway I can, damaged and on the mend or unrepairable; I couldn't care less. Mine's just a flesh wound and did no real damage, although I'll have a nasty scar," Seth said.

Another knock startled everyone, and a female voice said, "Seth, honey."

Seth jerked his head toward the door. "Mom?"

Roxy felt her nerves kick in overdrive because she'd never met his mother. She glanced down at herself and realized her appearance was less than what she would've picked for the occasion. She smoothed back her ponytail and wiped at her cheeks before pasting a smile on her face.

"Honey, are you all right?" Mrs. Carmichael asked as she revealed herself. "Oh, I'm sorry, dear. You have quite the crowd here."

Roxy admired the woman's beauty with her groomed, gray hair, small amount of makeup, and her matching pink sweat suit.

"Mom, how'd you know I was here?" Seth asked, confused by her presence.

"I called her," Sam admitted. "I thought she should be here, and we didn't know how bad your condition was until after I spoke with her."

"Mom, you already know Sam and Heather, but this," he said, motioning to Roxy, "is Roxanne. Remember me telling you about her?"

"Well, it's about time I meet the woman who had my son smitten all these years." She blushed. "Oh dear, I hope you told her already, otherwise I just blew your cover."

The room exploded with laughter and Heather said, "I beat you to that already, ma'am."

Roxy stood to her feet and offered her hand. "It's nice to meet you, Mrs. Carmichael."

"Please, call me Caroline, and the pleasure's all mine. I can see why my boy chose you; you're beautiful."

Roxy lowered her head, hoping to hide the blush heating her cheeks.

"Thank you, but believe me—I'm the lucky one," Roxy said.

"Where's Dad?" Seth asked.

"He's out of town but is making his way back."

"You should tell him not to worry about it, Mom; I'm fine."

"I'll do that in a bit, dear."

Feeling uncomfortable and knowing that Seth and his mother needed some time alone, Roxy said, "Guys, should we go to the cafeteria? I'm getting hungry."

"Good idea, we did leave in the middle of dinner and could all stand to eat something," Sam agreed and walked over to help Roxy up and get her crutches in place.

"We'll be back in a little bit," Roxy said and kissed Seth's hand before releasing her grip.

After it was just the two of them, Caroline said, "Well, she's quite the girl, isn't she?"

"She's extraordinary, Mom." His cheeks spread with a big smile. "I'm proposing in a week or so. We just resolved a case, so I'll wait until our client's exonerated but not longer than I have to."

Caroline's eyes brimmed with tears. "Seth, I'm so happy for you. Can we be there?"

"Of course, Mom. It'll just be her and I for the big moment, but I want everyone to come afterward to help us celebrate."

"My, I bet she'll just be thrilled. How soon after will you get married?"

Seth smiled. "Very soon. People in our position don't have long engagements because of the whole sex thing."

Caroline chuckled. "I'm so proud of you, honey. I'll have the daughter I've always wanted."

CHAPTER 23

THE NEXT SEVERAL DAYS PASSED in a whirlwind of meetings with Clark, court appearances, and organizing press conferences. Clark supported the full exoneration of Cassie and Kenton's indictment on a laundry list of charges, which would easily put him in prison the rest of his life. The police found and arrested Todd Hutch, who was driving a black suburban with considerable damage to the passenger side, for similar crimes, including the attempted murder of Roxy. It would later surface that Todd, following orders from Kenton, had also burned Roxy's house down and written the message on her driveway.

Seth opened the glass door of the jewelry store and wiped perspiration off his forehead.

"Can I help you, sir?" A lanky man in a suit and tie asked from behind the cased selection of rings and necklaces.

"Yes, please. I'm supposed to pick up a custom engagement ring. Name's Seth Carmichael."

The man put his index finger up. "Give me a moment, sir," he said and disappeared behind a door in the back of the store. When the man reappeared, he held a silver box that would alter the rest of Seth's life.

"Here you are, sir. We'll look at the ring over here," he said, pointing to a chair.

Seth took his seat and waited as the man opened the lid with a click. Seth focused on the breathtaking diamond staring up at him.

"Here it is, and it's a beauty. This is the two-carat, pear-cut diamond, set in a cathedral tulip, on a thick, white-gold band. Down here is the inscription you requested."

After a few moments of silence, the man said, "Does the finished product meet your expectations, Mr. Carmichael?"

Seth gazed at the ring and pictured Roxy's face the moment her vision focused on it. He smudged tears with the sleeve of his shirt and nodded his head in approval. He couldn't wait to slip this on her finger and take her as his wife.

***

On Cassie's exoneration day, Sam, Seth, Roxy, and Patricia crammed into Sam's SUV for the two-hour drive. The glee in the vehicle was palpable, and the chatter never stopped. They discussed Patricia's health, rehashed the story of the final blow that had shattered the state's case, and Cassie's plan after her release. Patricia brought Cassie an outfit to reclaim her freedom in, which Roxy would take inside when they arrived.

Roxy showed her credentials at the gate and followed the guard escorting her. Cassie's face was red and her eyes puffy when Roxy stepped in the holding cell.

After they were alone, Roxy wrapped Cassie in a hug.

"Hey, you're supposed to be happy. You're getting out of this place today," Roxy said.

Cassie pulled back and put her head down, drying her face with the back of her hands.

"When you wrote me that letter, I told God I was mad at Him and didn't understand why this happened. I asked Him to vindicate me and—" Her voice broke. "He did. I'm going home today."

Roxy swallowed the lump approaching her throat and silently praised Jesus for this miracle. She often wondered what she'd done to deserve the front-seat view of life-changing phenomena such as this, but she never took the experiences for granted.

"I'm so proud of you, Cassie. The angels rejoice in your homecoming, both physically and spiritually. Here are your clothes; let's get you out of here."

Cassie combed her hair, put on fresh clothes, and relished the feeling of soft cotton on her arms and denim on her legs. She swallowed immense joy and walked out of the holding cell. At the discharge window, Cassie signed several forms, took the bag of her belongings, and with Roxy by her side, she walked out the door.

Roxy and Cassie sauntered the fifty feet of road between the door and the mechanical outer gate. Five feet from the gate, Cassie turned around, took a deep breath, allowed the smile on her face to extend, and left the prison in her past as she stepped toward her freedom.

"Cassie," Patricia shrieked, wrapping her arms around her the second she stepped outside the prison gates.

"I can't believe this is happening," Cassie said, her body quivering with emotion.

"Thank you, Jesus. Thank you for this," Patricia said.

Cassie leaned her head back enough to see Patricia's face. "God is good."

Patricia let out a scream and pulled her back in for a hug. She met Roxy's gaze and mouthed "Thank you," then closed her eyes to relish the moment. Roxy nodded and dried her face again.

After separating from Patricia, Cassie stood still, admiring a tree in the distance for several moments. She turned to Roxy, "You know, it's been almost sixteen years since I've seen a tree." She openly wept.

"It's the little things I missed the most." A gust of wind rushed Cassie's face, and she closed her eyes and smiled.

Roxy nodded and knew if she spoke, her composure would shatter. She held tightly to the memory of her client's first moments of freedom. Nothing compared to watching an innocent person reclaim their life. She fixed her eyes on Cassie as she took in her fresh perception of the outside world.

Cassie turned her head upward, observing the baby blue sky and marshmallow clouds. "Let's do this," she said, and stepped toward the media circus fighting to release the first glimpse of her independence.

"Cassandra, what are you feeling?" A female reporter asked.

"Liberated, vindicated, joyful, and thankful. I feel like the luckiest woman alive."

"What's the first thing you want to do?" Another anxious reporter asked.

"I want some real food, maybe ribs or a steak, then I just want to go home and put my life back together."

Without a prompting question, Cassie spoke. "I want to thank Roxanne Hollis and her team for their diligent work on my case. It's not every day a bulldog investigator and two talented attorneys devote countless hours on a case without receiving a penny for their hard work. I know now that God used Roxy to initiate the process of bringing me back to Him. I have no further comment; thank you for coming to cover this story."

Roxy heard a female reporter say. "Well, there you have it, ladies and gentlemen; the evangelist investigator wins again."

Roxy shook her head and smiled, linking hands with Seth and walking away.

The five of them climbed back into Sam's SUV and pulled away from the prison. Cassie watched out the back window as the facility shrank in the distance, wiping tears with the palms of her hands.

With Cassie settled at Patricia's, Seth geared up for the big event. His parents, Rebecca and Cliff, and Sam and Heather would join him and Roxy for what she believed was a celebratory dinner after the exoneration. Seth had also secretly contacted two of Roxy's closest friends from college, Camden Peacock and Kristen Maverick, to surprise her after the proposal.

Seth drove to the park, ran to the meadow, under the tree where their relationship had begun. He had picked this place knowing she'd pick up on the significance of the location. He spread the blanket out, plucked fresh rose petals, tossing them about on the blanket, hung white lights and plugged them in with an extension cord to the nearby pavilion, set out the candles, and notified Sam that he was finished.

Roxy clipped her hair up, put on her favorite stud earrings, finished her makeup, and reveled in how good she felt. She could finally walk unassisted, although slowly, and Cassie was at home where she belonged. Tonight, she'd celebrate with her loved ones. She stepped into her knee-length emerald dress and walked out of the bathroom.

Seth stood wearing a baby blue button-down with dark grey slacks. Roxy stopped and looked up at him, his eyes magnified by the blue in his shirt, and felt her insides twist up.

"You look absolutely stunning, Rox," Seth said.

Smiling, she lowered her face. "And blue suits you, my love."

He mentally commanded his palms to quit sweating to no avail.

"I'm so excited," Roxy said, buckling her seatbelt.

"Well, I have a surprise for you before dinner."

"Really? I love surprises."

"Will you humor me?" he asked.

"A blindfold—Seth Carmichael, what're you up to?" Roxy asked, taking the blindfold and putting it over her head.

Seth tested the blindfold, making funny faces and putting his hands close to her face. She didn't react. *All right, let's do this,* Seth thought.

Seth drove with shaky hands, navigating to their sacred point of origin. He felt his phone buzz but decided not to check the message, knowing Sam was alerting him that he had finished lighting the candles and setting up the video camera.

Seth helped Roxy from the car and guided her along the walking path. At first glimpse, Seth choked. *Okay, Lord. This is our moment; help me through this, please.*

Positioning her just the way he wanted, he knelt on one knee in front of her.

"Okay, you can take the blindfold off."

Roxy reached up, apprehensive to what she'd see, and pulled the fabric from her eyes. Looking up first, Roxy noticed the lights, and not Seth. Within seconds, her eyes met his and she knew. "Oh, Seth."

"Roxanne Hollis, you won my heart a decade ago, and I knew this moment would come, but I had no idea I could love you the way I do today. You're the most remarkable woman I've ever known; your confidence; your unwavering devotion to Christ, and your zeal for life are incredible. You introduced me to an existence that transformed me and made me into the man I am. I want to dance with you in the kitchen, run through the rainstorms, have children, and wake up next to you every morning for the rest of my life. Nothing could compare to a lifetime with you as my bride, and I can't wait to experience every day by your side. Rox, will you marry me?"

The tears streamed like tiny rivers down her cheeks, and all she could do was feverishly nod, her hand over her mouth. Seth rose to his feet, picked her up, spun her around, and kissed her. He placed her back on her feet, took the ring from the box with a shaky hand, and slid the band onto her finger. She studied the diamond, felt the inscription on the bottom of her finger, and removed it to view the message. She saw small letters, *'SoS 3:4.'* She knew the verse and why he had chosen it because of the last ten words. "I have found the one whom my soul loves."

Seth took Roxy's face in his hands, looked her in the eyes, took a breath, and kissed her.

When they parted, Seth said, "Now, everyone's waiting to celebrate our engagement. Are you ready to go eat?"

"Wait, that's what the dinner's about? I can't believe you did this," Roxy said, still looking down in awe of the ring, now a permanent fixture on her finger.

"Of course it is."

When they walked onto the patio of the restaurant, Sam and Heather were first to jump up and greet them.

"Congratulations, sweetheart," Sam said, hugging her.

"I cannot wait to start planning the wedding," Heather said, admiring her ring.

Before they reached the table, Roxy heard familiar screeches and saw her best friends from college, running toward her. She could no longer swallow back her tears.

"Girl, look at you! I'm so happy," Camden cried out.

"And that ring," Kristen said, grabbing her hand, "is absolutely beautiful. You have a keeper on your hands, girlfriend."

She was breathless with overwhelming happiness. "We have a lot to catch up on. How long are you in town?"

Kristen and Camden shared a secret glance, and Camden answered, "For the next few days."

Roxy felt another surge of excitement, "Really? Can we get together for breakfast in the morning; I have so much to tell you. I feel like it's been forever since we spoke last, and I'm sorry about that, but I had this case and—"

"Girl, please, you don't need to explain. We understand all you've been through, and yes, breakfast sounds wonderful, but how about this evening? Seth paid for a hotel room for the three of us! Girls night," Kristen said, pumping her fist in the air.

Roxy looked over at Seth, again in amazement. *He had thought of everything*, she pondered.

Roxy hugged Rebecca and Cliff, sharing in her excitement before greeting Seth's parents.

Donald, Seth's father, hugged her. "Roxanne, I've never seen my son so happy. Welcome to the family."

Roxy swallowed back the meteor-sized lump rising in her throat. "I love that man like I never knew I could love anyone under heaven. I'm thrilled to meet you, and I look forward to getting to know you much better!"

Caroline embraced Roxy. "I have the daughter I've always wanted."

Roxy turned back around to face Seth and marveled at the expression on his face. As if she had a new set of eyes, she saw him in an entirely different way. He was no longer her dearest friend, colleague, or boyfriend, but now her fiancé.

The conversation flowed easily as if everyone around the table meshed like an extended family, reconnecting after a lengthy separation. After a meal bursting with laughter, toasts, and full bellies, more cheers flowed followed by goodbyes.

Roxy walked out with Camden, Kristen, and Seth.

"Honey, I had Heather get your things together for the night," Seth said, pulling an overnight bag from his trunk. "Everything you need should be in here, but if you need anything else, just call me. Have fun tonight, and I'll see you tomorrow." He leaned over kissing her cheek. "I love you."

CHAPTER 24

ROXY, CAMDEN, AND KRISTEN SAT in a circle, wearing pajamas, with ponytails on their heads, and bowls of popcorn in their laps.

"Fill us in about Seth; I mean, last we knew, you were friends, working cases together. What on earth happened?" Kristen asked, her bright eyes shining.

"Well, this all transpired really fast, but Seth told me several months ago, that all these years he's had feelings for me."

Camden chimed in. "Why did he wait so long to move forward with all this?"

"He's not a virgin, and frankly, before he met me, he didn't have a relationship with the Lord. When he accepted Christ, he changed radically, but spent the last seven, eight, nine years rebuilding and restoring himself."

"Roxy, that's incredible. God chose a remarkable man for you, didn't He?" Kristen said, around a mouthful of popcorn, which caused the girls to giggle like children.

Stifling back her laughter, Roxy said, "You have no idea how wonderful he is, and I don't think remarkable describes him properly; I'd use something like extraordinary."

***

Roxy's eyes fluttered open, and she instantly felt tired but thrilled at the same time. They had stayed up until the wee hours of the morning, talking and reminiscing. She had never realized how much she missed having friends close to her.

"Are you up, yet?" Kristen asked, picking her head up off the pillow.

"Yep. Did you sleep okay?" Roxy replied through a long yawn.

"Yay. Girls, you're both up. I already have our day planned out," Camden said, skipping into the room from the bathroom.

Shaking her head, Roxy said, "Why does that not surprise me. What's on the agenda?"

Camden fired her response out so quickly, Roxy had to focus to catch everything.

"We can go get our nails, hair, and makeup done and then have a girl's night out. How fun will that be?"

"That's a bit much, don't you think?" Roxy asked.

"When was the last time you felt pampered," Kristen said.

Roxy thought for several moments. "Um, now that you mention it, I can't remember the last time. Okay, I'm in."

A familiar ringtone sounded from Roxy's phone, and she smiled, lifting the phone to her ear.

"Good morning, my bride. What're you girls up to today?" Seth asked.

"Good morning, fiancé," Roxy said, with emphasis. "We're going for makeovers."

"But you don't need one," Seth offered.

"It's fun to indulge sometimes," Kristen yelled.

"Well, I can't argue with that. Call me later. Have fun. Love you," Seth said, ending the call.

After their manicures and pedicures, Roxy closed her eyes as the hairspray hung around her. She faced her reflection with awe. The stylist had pinned her hair up beautifully.

"I could never get my hair to do this on my own," Roxy said eyeing the stylist in the mirror.

Roxy smoothed out light pink lipstick and waited for her friends to finish.

"All right, let's go." Camden said, coming into the waiting room arm-in-arm with Kristen.

In the car, Kristen said, "Okay, Roxy we have a surprise for you. Will you trust us?"

Roxy whirled her head to the backseat, "Wait, what? What do you mean a surprise? I've had enough of those the last twenty-four hours."

"Just trust us," Camden said, facing her before turning her attention back to the road.

"Okay. I trust you," Roxy said, submitting to whatever her friends had in store.

"Put this on," Kristen said, handing her a black blindfold.

"Another one? I'm having deja vu. I wore this last night."

"I know. We borrowed it from Seth." Camden giggled. "Just do it."

Roxy gave in, slipped the elastic band behind her head, and secured the front fabric to her eyes.

"How many fingers am I holding up?" Camden asked.

"Oh, stop it; you know I can't see anything."

Roxy accepted defeat after attempting to guess where they were going with the direction of the car. Feeling the vehicle stop and hearing the gearshift move, she put her hand up to remove the blindfold but felt a hand grab her arm, "Not yet," Camden said.

Roxy relaxed, while her friends guided her into a building and followed their lead through several twists and turns. A door closed, and once Kristen let go of her shoulders, she said, "Okay. Now you can take it off."

Roxy reached up and pulled the blindfold off. She blinked, adjusting to the light, and turned around several times. When the realization hit her, she froze.

She stood in a large, modern room with windows lining one side, pearl-white walls, silver tables adorned with fruit platters and flowers, vanity tables along the wall opposite the windows, and a large, white sectional with bright red throw pillows in the middle of the room.

Her eyes landed on three dresses, one angelic white gown, and two long, lavender dresses.

Roxy put her hands over her mouth. "Is this a dream?"

Camden dried her face. "Roxy, you're getting married today. Seth orchestrated the entire thing, I mean, we helped some, but he did most of the work."

A knock on the door made Roxy jump. "Can I come in?" Sam's unmistakable voice rang out.

Roxy's face lit up. "Sam."

Camden and Kristen excused themselves, and Sam took Roxy's hand, walking her over to the couch.

"So, what do you think, honey?"

She shook her head. "Did you know about this?"

"I'm afraid so. Seth asked my opinion on doing the ceremony this way and wondered if you'd rather plan the whole thing yourself. I went with my gut that you'd be fine either way. Hope I was right."

"I think I'm in shock. This is crazy. You look so nice, by the way," Roxy said, admiring his tuxedo

"Thanks. Heather helped, and so did your friends. Even Rebecca took care of a few things."

"Where's Seth?"

"He's wearing the carpet down, pacing in his dressing room, worried that you'll be upset. He wanted me to ask you if you'd meet him in the corridor, so he can pray with you."

"He isn't supposed to see me yet."

"Don't worry. There's a corner where, if you stand with your back to the wall and he does the same, you can hold hands and pray."

Roxy followed Sam to the corner he described and waited, her heart thudding in her ears, and sweat trickling down her back. She felt footsteps permeate the plush carpet before her hand met Seth's.

"Are you okay?" Seth asked, his voice breaking.

A quiet sob and a squeeze of his hand. "Yes, I can't believe you did this for me."

"For my bride, I'd do anything. Let's pray."

Roxy bowed her head and cried as Seth prayed over their union and their future with such passion it made her knees tremble. He lifted her hand to his mouth and kissed it. "I'll meet you at the altar, my love," he said and let go of her hand.

Back in the bridal suite, Roxy stepped into her beautifully made wedding gown and admired the detail of the stitching. The dress, simple and elegant, was made of chiffon fabric; it was sleeveless on her left and went over her right shoulder, not revealing too much skin. She inwardly thanked Seth for paying such close attention to her conviction of modesty. Surely, he didn't pick the dress out, but whoever did took his advice on her style.

Feeling the zipper ride up her spine, she sucked in a breath as she turned around and saw her reflection in the mirror.

"Roxy, you look like a queen," Kristen said.

"See how good it feels to get dolled up," Camden added.

Roxy didn't answer but continued observing her reflection. Her mind stilled. Her stomach settled. Her heart soared. Today, she'd become Mrs. Roxanne Carmichael.

"Are you ready for this, sweetheart?" Sam asked, sticking out his elbow for her to lock arms with him.

"I wish we could run," Roxy responded, laughing, and kissed him on the cheek. "Thank you for being here for me today. I don't know what I'd do without you."

The lump in Sam's throat took over, and he relented to the emotions, allowing the tears to fall.

"You're the daughter I never had. I wouldn't be anywhere else in the world at this moment."

The French doors opened at the first note of the wedding march, and Sam and Roxy faced forward. Roxy locked eyes with Seth, handsomely dressed in a tailored tuxedo, and sucked in a breath.

Seth gasped at his first glimpse of Roxy walking toward him. His smile stretched, and tears spilled from his eyes. *She's the most beautiful thing I've ever seen.* He rocked back and forth on his feet.

Roxy scanned the faces of the people in the white chairs and noticed each one of her previous clients and their families: Natalie and Martin; Rebecca and Cliff; members of her church; Heather; and even Clark and Daniel. She took in the elegant decorations of white roses and large ribbons tied in perfect bows on the back of every chair.

Sam looked up at Seth as his foot made contact on his last stop before giving Roxy away. "Take care of her," Sam said.

The men hugged, and Sam took his place next to Seth's father.

While the pastor spoke, Seth gazed into Roxy's eyes and took in her beauty. He was always captivated by her inner magnificence more that her outer appearance. She was breathtakingly gorgeous in the flesh, but the real radiance was her heart.

Roxy's hand quivered while she slid the wedding band onto Seth's finger. "You may now kiss your bride," the pastor said, before Seth wrapped his arms around her, picked her up off her feet, and kissed her with feverish desire.

At the reception, Seth and Roxy danced the night away. Slow dances, funny songs, and crazy moves kept everyone on their feet. Laughter bellowed, and camera flashes never stopped. Roxy smashed cake in Seth's face, and he did the same.

At the end of the night, everyone sent Roxy and Seth on their way with rose peddles and bubbles as they ran through the center of the mob. Once in the limo, Roxy asked, "So, where are we going?"

Seth slid across the seat. "First thing in the morning, we're headed to the beaches of Bora Bora for seven glorious days."

CHAPTER 25

ROXY STEPPED OFF THE PLANE onto American soil, feeling like a new woman. The last seven days were indescribable, and she had never known she could feel so connected to another person. They snorkeled, went scuba diving, parasailed, enjoyed a candlelight cruise and couple's massages, and stayed in the most remarkable honeymoon suite, discovering every consecrated inch of one another.

"How do we go back to regular life after a week like that?" Roxy asked.

Throwing his arm over her shoulder, Seth said, "We don't. We start our new life, and believe me—regular isn't the category I'd place our future in."

Mulling that thought over in the car, she pulled her cell phone out and powered it on. "Only three messages."

She went through the prompts, pressing the required buttons, and passcode.

"Roxanne, this is Clark. I know you're gone, but when you return, please call me. I have something I'd like to discuss with you."

"Hello, Mrs. Carmichael! We hope you enjoyed your honeymoon, and we love you. Call us so we can have brunch," Sam said in the next message.

"Roxy! We cleaned up Seth's, well, now your home and put all your gifts on the kitchen table. We love you! See you next time," Camden sang over the line.

"Anything noteworthy?" Seth asked, turning out of the airport parking lot.

"Clark wants me to call him about something, Sam and Heather want us over for brunch, and the girls cleaned up for us. I completely forgot about the wedding gifts. How fun!"

"I wonder what Clark wants?"

"Well, there's one way to find out," Roxy said, thumbing through her contacts to find Clark's number.

"Hi, Clark, it's Roxy. We just got back. What's up?"

"Hey, Roxy. I didn't mean for you to call so soon. Can you come to my office in the next few days?"

"Um, sure. Is everything all right?"

"Everything's fine. I have a proposition for you."

"Really? Okay. How about Monday. We need the rest of the weekend to unpack and take care of some personal things."

"Sounds great. I don't have court that day, so come whenever you want, and I'll make the time. Thanks, Roxy, and congratulations again to you and Seth."

Roxy looked at Seth. "Well, that was weird. He has a proposition for me. I wonder what it could be."

"You think he wants you to work for him or something?" Seth asked.

Laughing, Roxy said, "Fat chance of that happening. I oppose the state. I can't imagine jumping tracks and working for the prosecution. I'll admit Clark changed my perception on DAs, but not enough to leave what I'm doing and join their team."

"You never know, Rox. The sky's the limit with your abilities. Don't rule out the possibility until you hear the man out."

Roxy stepped out of the elevator and guffawed when Seth picked her up, unlocked the door, and carried her across the threshold. "Welcome home, my bride," he said, kissing her before setting her down.

"You know, we could rebuild on my lot and live there," Roxy said.

"We can do anything. I like the sound of that, and I'm sure I'd have no problem selling this place."

Setting eyes on the mountain of wedding gifts in the kitchen, they sat on the floor and acted like kids on Christmas morning, tearing through wrapping paper and oohing over gifts. Roxy giggled opening some gifts and sighed in awe over others.

CHAPTER 26

"OH SWEETHEART, YOU'RE GLOWING," Sam said, meeting her and Seth at the gate to his backyard for brunch after church the following day.

"We had a really, really good time," Roxy said, squeezing Sam in a hug.

"Look at you," Heather screamed, running toward them.

"Hi, Heather! It's good to be back."

"So, how was it, Roxy?" Heather asked.

"I'm not sure how to answer that," Roxy said, feeling her face redden. "It was an amazing experience. I'll leave it at that."

"We acted like high school kids newly in love with the world at our fingertips," Seth added, winking at Roxy.

"Well, it looks like you had a great time," Sam said.

"That's an understatement," Roxy said. "So, changing the subject, Clark wants me to come to his office tomorrow to talk about some sort of opportunity."

"That'll throw a wrench in your work," Sam said.

"Yeah, no kidding. I could never see myself working for the other side, so I'm not too worried about what he has to say. I respect him, and all, but I go after the state when they mess up, and I can't see myself changing that passion."

"I'm curious to see what he'll say," Seth said.

"So, what's the big deal," Heather said. "I guess I'm missing the point."

"I fight against the government when I have an innocent client. The lies, hidden evidence, bias, slanted scales of justice abused by the state, and tunnel vision developed by detectives and prosecutors. Now, I'll give credit where it's due, and Clark is proving he's different."

"That makes sense," Heather said.

"Once you're committed to one side, it's hard to abandon ship and cross over. People grow and change, but I don't foresee my professional passion switching that much. I don't know, we'll see," Roxy said.

***

"Thanks for coming, Roxy. I want you to hear me out before you answer. I know enough to realize you would want nothing to do with working for me, but perhaps this arrangement could work out." Clark said, the next afternoon. Roxy sat in the white chair in front of Clark's desk, her interest peaking.

"I came to listen, and you have my word that I won't jump to answer whatever you're about to ask of me, without at least praying about it and talking to Seth first."

Clark sat up straighter and put his elbows on his desk.

"I want to create a prosecution oversight committee. For the most part, you and I are the members, unless we need to bring others aboard. I want to fight wrongful convictions before they happen, and I think, with my ideas, we can do that."

Roxy had a hard time digesting what Clark said. She knew several jurisdictions had conviction integrity units within the district attorney's office, but they were unheard of on the front end of a case because that's precisely what the police were supposed to do.

"Okay. You have my attention."

"I thought you might have an interest in this. I won't ask you to do every case, only the questionable ones. We'll meet, go over the evidence, and you can determine whether you believe the case has merit with the current suspect or if you'd like to do your own investigation. I'll pay your hourly rate. If you decide to consider the case, it'll be between you and me. I want your actions in this committee to stay under wraps, if we can manage that. I'll be honest and say I don't know what this looks like because I've never done it before, but I vow that I'm on your side. May justice be done even if the heavens fall." Clark ended there, his tone questioning.

"Three questions: what if I'm working another case when one of yours comes up, why now, and you do know this is specifically what the police and your office are supposed to do, right?"

"We'll wing it. Honestly, with the cases I ask you to look at, we won't have much time because of trial dates and discovery rules. I can't see you working on these longer than a few weeks, tops, but I really can't say definitively because this is innovative for me, too. As you know, I'm newly elected here, and knowing whether I can trust my detectives and investigators is pivotal. I can't stomach another loss like Raleigh's on my watch."

"Okay, give me twenty-four hours to mull this over and talk to Seth. I won't keep secrets from my husband, but he poses no threat. I'll call you tomorrow. I feel honored that you'd approach me with this. Truly, thank you."

Standing up, Clark walked around the desk. "I've never met an investigator with your level of passion and hunger for what's right. Whether it's your gift or God's hand on you, I'm not sure, but I'm keen enough to not allow your wisdom or instincts go to waste. I'll wait for your call." He offered his hand.

Roxy shook his hand and left the office. Her thoughts were like a tennis ball in an active game, going back and forth on the pros and cons of taking an opportunity like this. The unknown aspect of this made her crazy; taking an endeavor that was foreign to her and Clark was scary, to say the least. How could she hide her involvement when she'd have to interview witnesses, view the evidence, and investigate the crime entirely? The complexity of the task made her uneasy, but she also enjoyed the challenge.

***

"Wait, he wants you to investigate cases before they even go to trial?" Seth asked over dinner.

"Pretty much. He said he'd hand pick the cases that are problematic to him and present them to me, but beyond that, it's my choice."

"I never saw that coming. Where's your head at?"

"I spent the afternoon in the scriptures and in prayer, but I'm still not sure. I think it's a remarkable idea, but is it something I want to be involved in?"

"You'd essentially be sparing someone the many unjust years in prison, and taxpayers the money a trial would cost. This could be huge, Rox. I mean really, think about how much this endeavor could change the fabric of wrongful convictions."

"I know, and I thought about all our previous clients and what their lives might be had someone like me caught the inaccuracies before their cases graced the ears of a jury."

"How long do you have?" Seth asked, putting the plates in the sink.

"I told him I'd call him tomorrow."

Seth reached his hand out to pull Roxy to her feet. "Well, let's go read and pray some more."

Roxy looked up at her husband. "I love you."

After hours of reading and praying with Seth, she laid her head on her pillow, completely at peace wrapped in his arms, and drifted into a deep sleep.

***

Roxy's eyes sprang open the next morning with wonder and excitement at the direction of her life. After her devotional time and breakfast, she picked up the phone and stared at it for a few minutes before dialing.

"Clark, it's Roxy. I'm in."

EPILOGUE

Nine months later

CASSIE STOOD BACK, ADMIRING the metal sign that hung on the front of the recently opened Immanuel's House, in awe of God's faithfulness. The 25,000 square-foot light brick facility was accented with dark wood pillars, lining the wraparound porch. Her vision for the architects had stayed the same, an inviting environment where everyone, no matter where they came from, felt like they belonged. After the state of Texas settled her lawsuit out of court, she had built this facility on the outskirts of town. She had enough land to house horses for her tenants to enjoy and an outdoor chapel, complete with an oversized wooden cross at the front and large treated trees dug into the ground for seating.

IH, as she called it, would serve the exonerated from any state, assisting them with housing, rehabilitation back into society, job searches, interview preparations, counseling, and, of course, Bible studies and church services. When she walked out of prison, to say she felt lost would be inaccurate; an alien in her own skin was more accurate. Everything had changed in the sixteen years she'd spent incarcerated, from technology to the pace of life. Without the help of everyone around her, she'd still be misplaced in her environment. This opened her eyes to a profound need that others like her would experience after trading in their shackles and handcuffs for freedom. Although her focus area changed after her exoneration, this center had always been a dream of hers, and perhaps her misfortune with the court system propelled her into the area God predestined long ago. Everything had happened for a reason, and although she wouldn't go through that again if someone paid her, she could now see the goodness God promises.

Patricia passed away three months after Cassie's release. Cassie moved in with Rebecca and Cliff until IH opened. She expected her first resident in the morning, a woman exonerated from Georgia. Nothing could articulate her feelings of anticipation and the excitement for her part in leading people to Jesus. She had God and Roxanne Hollis to thank for her future.

Printed in Great Britain
by Amazon

49279754R00144